SHIPWRECKED WITH THE CAPTAIN

Diane Gaston

MILLS & BOON

First Published in Great Britain 2019
by Mills & Boon, an imprint of HarperCollins*Publishers*
1 London Bridge Street, London, SE1 9GF

© 2019 Diane Perkins

ISBN: 978-0-263-26892-8

MIX
Paper from
responsible sources
FSC C007454

This book is produced from independently certified FSC™ paper
to ensure responsible forest management.
For more information visit www.harpercollins.co.uk/green.

Printed and bound in Spain
by CPI, Barcelona

To Jane Austen,
who briefly lived in Bath and in whose footsteps
I was honoured to walk.

Chapter One

June 1816

Lucien Roper stood at the rail of the packet ship, watching the Dublin harbour recede into the distance. He inhaled the salty breeze and felt the bracing wind on his face. Voices of the sailors tending to their tasks rang in his ears.

Only a few more days, then, with luck, he'd be back on the deck of a ship of his own, with his old crew, and back to the life from which he'd received so much. A fortune in prize money. Recognition and respect. A place he belonged.

A woman's laugh sounded over his shoulder, its sound so joyous, so unlike his restless mood that he turned, startled. She wore a grey cloak, shrouding her face.

What pleased her so? he wondered.

This was the sacrifice the navy life demanded of him. He was not free to court a young woman with a joyous laugh. Not for him to marry a woman and leave her for his mistress, the sea. He'd seen what happened when a navy man married and he and his wife spent most of their days apart.

As his own parents had done.

It had been a long time since he'd suffered the effects of having an absent naval father. Lucien himself had been at sea for more than twenty years now, since the age of twelve. This was his life and before it, a mere memory.

He was eager to get back to it. His beloved *Foxfire* had been sold for breaking up, no longer needed now the war was over, and the Admiralty had promised him a new ship. Of course, there were dozens of captains like him, clamouring for a ship, but he'd earned a spot near the top of the list. At least with the wind this brisk they could count on making it to Holyhead by the next afternoon and he'd be in London a few days later.

He studied the sky and frowned. This crossing would be rough. Maybe too rough. Likely their departure should have been delayed a day, but the sooner he reached England, the better.

Still...

He sauntered over to where the packet captain stood.

'We're in for a patch of bad weather,' Lucien remarked.

The Captain knew who Lucien was—a decorated navy captain, a hero of the Adriatic Sea and Mediterranean.

'What?' The Captain looked surprised Lucien had spoken to him. 'Oh. Bad weather. Yes. Must sail through it.'

Lucien had made it through many a storm. He'd make it through this one. He'd prefer, though, that the Captain seem less preoccupied and better able to attend to the weather and what was happening on his deck.

Like noticing the young grey-cloaked woman back away from sea spray and stumble a little.

'Would it not be a good idea to order passengers to stay below?' Lucien asked him in a tone more demanding than questioning.

'Hmm?' This Captain was as sharp as a slop bucket.

Pay attention, man.

'The passengers,' Lucien snapped, gesturing to the young woman, 'should stay below.'

'Oh?' The Captain's brows rose. 'Of course. Was about to make that order.' He called one of his men over. 'Tell the passengers to remain below.'

Lucien shook his head in dismay and strode away. He traversed the deck and, out of habit, took notice of the seamen preparing for the storm. He scanned the sails and the ropes. All seemed well enough. Shipshape. He glanced back at the Captain who held a hand to his chest and seemed to be studying his coat buttons.

Lucien expelled a frustrated breath. He'd better get below himself before he began barking orders.

He walked to the companionway and opened the hatch. At the bottom of the stairs stood two women, both in grey cloaks. Which was the woman with the captivating laugh? He could not see the face of one, but the other was a beauty. An expensively dressed beauty. He might have spoken to them and hoped to finally see who had uttered such a lovely laugh, but it was clear he'd intruded on them. They stepped aside.

He nodded and passed them, but turned back. 'You ladies should stay in your cabins. The sea is rough. Do not fear. A seaman will bring your meal to you.'

At least he hoped such an arrangement would be made—if the Captain thought to order it.

Lucien continued to his cabin.

Claire Tilson had quickly averted her face when the tall, dark-haired, broad-shouldered gentleman opened the hatch and descended the stairs. Her heart was already beating fast; this encounter—this lady—had been disturbance enough, but she'd glimpsed the man on deck and he was every bit as handsome as she'd suspected, with thick brows and eyes as light brown and as alert as a fox's.

What was wrong with her? Taking notice of any man. She'd just fled from the country house where she'd been governess to three lovely little girls, because their father had tried to seduce her—practically under the nose of his sweet wife. He'd sworn his undying love. As if she could trust a man who so ill-used his wife.

Claire shook herself. She need not be distracted. She needed, instead, to address this lady standing next to her, this lady she'd met a moment ago.

This lady who looked exactly like her.

Same brown hair. Same hazel eyes. Same face.

What do you say to a stranger who looked like your twin?

Lady Rebecca Pierce was her name, she'd said.

Claire waited until the handsome gentleman disappeared into one of the cabins near the end of the corridor, but she debated whether it was her place to ask for explanations.

'We should do as he says, I suppose,' she said instead. She went to a nearby door and opened it. 'My cabin is here.'

What she wanted to say was, *Wait. Talk to me. Why do you look like me? Where are you from? Are you a relation?*

Claire would love to have some family relation to claim her.

She ought not to push herself on a lady, though. She took a step across the threshold.

Lady Rebecca called her back. 'I would like to speak with you more. I am quite alone. My maid suffers the *mal de mer* and remains in her cabin.'

Claire glanced down. 'The sea has never bothered me. I suppose I have a strong constitution that way.'

'Will you talk with me?' Lady Rebecca asked. 'Maybe there is some sense to make of this.' Her hand gestured between them.

Claire gazed into her cabin, perfect for a poor governess, but unsuitable for a lady. 'You are welcome to come in, but there is very little room.'

'Come to my cabin, then,' the lady said. 'We may be comfortable there.'

Claire followed Lady Rebecca to her cabin, which included a berth larger than the one in her cabin and a table and chairs that provided a view of the sea through a porthole. As the gentleman had said, the sea was rough, with choppy waves and white foam.

Lady Rebecca waved towards a chair, inviting her to sit. When they were both settled across from each other at the table, Lady Rebecca asked, 'Where are you bound, Miss Tilson?'

Claire would have thought she'd ask the obvious question, the one that burned inside her—*why do we look alike?*

'To a family in the Lake District,' she responded. 'Not a family, precisely. Two little girls whose parents were killed in an accident. They are in the care of their uncle now, the new Viscount Brookmore.' And with any luck at all, the Viscount wouldn't often be in residence.

'How sad.' The lady frowned sympathetically.

Yes. The little girls were alone in the world. Claire knew how that felt.

But she did not wish to dwell on gloomy feelings, not when her life might improve. 'And you, Lady Rebecca? Where are you bound?'

'To London,' she replied.

'London!' Claire smiled. A city of shops, palaces, theatres and town houses in picturesque squares. The Tower. Westminster Abbey. Hyde Park. 'How exciting. I was there once. It was so... vital.'

'Vital, indeed.' Lady Rebecca, looking like Claire herself, appeared scornful.

Claire peered at her. 'You sound as if you do not wish to go.'

The lady met her gaze. 'I do not. I travel there to be married.'

Claire's brows rose. 'Married?'

Lady Rebecca waved a hand. 'It is an arranged marriage. My brother's idea.'

There were worse things than an arranged marriage. 'And you do not wish to marry this man?'

'Not at all.' Lady Rebecca straightened in her chair. 'May I change the subject?'

Claire blinked. She'd forgotten herself and had spoken out of turn, as if they were equals. 'Forgive me. I did not mean to pry.'

Lady Rebecca shrugged. 'Perhaps I will tell you the whole story later.' She leaned forward.

'For now I am bursting with questions. Why do we look alike? How can this be? Are we related somehow?'

The same questions Claire longed to ask.

They discussed possible family connections, but came up with none that connected them.

It would have been more of a surprise if they had been relations. Lady Rebecca was the daughter of an English earl whose estate was in Ireland and Claire was the daughter of an English vicar who'd rarely travelled out of his county.

They had both grown up in English boarding schools, however, although Lady Rebecca's was a rather progressive school in Reading and Claire's Bristol school had catered to girls like her, who would eventually have to make their own way in the world. It was through her boarding school that Claire had procured the governess position in Ireland.

Lady Rebecca blew out an exasperated breath. 'We are no closer to understanding this. We are not related—'

'But we look alike,' Claire finished for her. 'An unexpected coincidence?'

Lady Rebecca stood and pulled Claire towards a mirror affixed to the wall.

'We are not identical.' Claire was almost relieved to find some differences. 'Look.'

Claire's two front teeth were not quite as prominent and her eyebrows did not have Lady Rebecca's lovely arch, and Claire's eyes were closer together. Still, the differences were so minor as to be easily overlooked.

'No one would notice unless we were standing next to each other,' she admitted.

'Our clothes set us apart. That is for certain.' Lady Rebecca turned from the mirror and faced Claire. 'If you wore my clothes, I'd wager anyone would take you for me.'

Claire admired the travelling dress Lady Rebecca wore, a vigonia-wool confection with ribbon trim at the hem. She'd also admired Lady Rebecca's cloak, grey, like hers, but of a much finer wool. 'I cannot imagine wearing fine clothes like yours.' She sighed.

'You must wear them, then.' Lady Rebecca's eyes—so like Claire's eyes in colour and shape—brightened. 'Let us change clothes and impersonate each other for the voyage. It will be a great lark. We will see if anyone notices.'

Claire was horrified. 'Your clothes are too fine for you to give up. Mine are plain.'

'Precisely.' Lady Rebecca crossed her arms. 'But I believe people pay more attention to dress than to other aspects of one's appearance. Perhaps even more than one's character. In any event, I think there is nothing undesirable about wearing a simple dress.'

Claire's dress was certainly simple. A plain brown poplin.

She touched the fine wool of Rebecca's travelling dress. 'I confess, I would love to wear a gown like this.'

'Then you shall!' Rebecca turned her back to her. 'Unbutton me.'

They undressed down to their shifts and swapped dresses, acting as each other's maids.

'Fix my hair like yours,' Lady Rebecca said.

Claire pulled Lady Rebecca's hair in a simple knot at the back of her head, feeling inexplicably sad to make Lady Rebecca as plain as she.

'Let me do yours now.' Lady Rebecca removed Claire's hairpins and her hair fell on to her shoulders. She brushed Claire's hair high on her head and, with a little pomade, twisted curling tendrils around her face.

Claire and her likeness gazed in the mirror again and laughed. They had indeed traded images.

There was a rap at the door.

'Answer the door as me.' Lady Rebecca grinned.

Impersonate a lady? 'I could not.'

Lady Rebecca gave her a little push towards the door. 'Of course you can!'

Claire straightened her spine as Lady Rebecca sat back down at the table.

Taking a deep breath, Claire opened the door.

It was a seaman deftly balancing a tray as the boat continued to pitch. 'Some refreshment, m'lady.' He took her to be Lady Rebecca!

The lovely clothes made Claire feel like a lady. 'Thank you.'

Would he also assume Lady Rebecca was the governess? Claire gestured to her. 'Miss Tilson passes the time with me. Will you bring her food here for her?'

'That I will, miss.' The crewman stepped into the cabin and placed the tray on the table right in front of Lady Rebecca. He returned a moment later with two more trays. 'Your maid, miss?'

Claire looked to Lady Rebecca for guidance, but the lady turned away.

Claire finally answered, 'My—my maid is resting. Perhaps you might leave her tray here, as well? We will tend to her.'

The seaman bowed. 'Very good, miss.' He placed both trays on the table.

When he left, Claire put her hand on her chest to still her rapidly beating heart.

'I was afraid he would notice we look alike,' Lady Rebecca said. 'He must have glimpsed me when he left the trays.'

The crewman had taken no more notice of Lady Rebecca dressed as Claire than the handsome gentleman had done in the companionway.

Claire knew why. 'A governess is not important enough to notice, my lady.'

She joined Lady Rebecca at the table and they continued to talk as they partook of the bread, cheese and ale the crewman had brought. Claire relaxed in this woman's company. She forgot their difference in status and felt as comfortable as if they were sisters.

Rebecca was apparently feeling a similar kinship. 'I believe we should call each other by our given names,' she said. 'It seems silly to be formal to one's mirror image.'

Claire was flattered. 'If you desire it… Rebecca. Then I am Claire to you.'

'Claire!' She grinned.

Claire felt emboldened. 'Might you tell me now why you do not wish to be married?' Marriage was what every woman wanted, was it not? 'Now that we are no longer formal?'

Lady Rebecca—Rebecca, she meant—turned solemn. 'A woman gives up everything by marrying. Any wealth or property she might have. Any right to decide for herself what she wishes to do.' Her chin set. 'If I am to give up everything, it should be to a man who loves me and respects me and will not confine me.'

Those were lofty sentiments. But life rarely fulfilled one's deepest wishes. 'And this man?' Claire asked.

Rebecca grimaced. 'I met him only once. He merely wished to assure himself I could produce an heir.'

'But, of course he would want an heir,' Claire responded. 'Especially if he has a title and property.' Gentlemen, especially peers, needed an heir.

'He does.' Rebecca tapped her pewter tankard with her fingernail.

'Is the gentleman wealthy enough to provide for you?' Claire asked.

'He is said to be prosperous,' Rebecca replied. 'He must be, because he is willing to marry me with a mere pittance for a dowry.'

She certainly did not look as if she had a mere pittance for a dowry.

'Will you tell me who he is?' Claire asked.

Rebecca shrugged. 'Lord Stonecroft.'

This was not a name Claire knew, but, then, why would she?

'Baron Stonecroft of Gillford.' Rebecca said the name as if biting into rancid meat.

'Ah.' Now Claire understood. 'You were hoping for a higher title than baron. I mean, you said you are the daughter of an earl.'

Rebecca sniffed. 'I care nothing for that.'

Then, what? 'Did he seem like a cruel man, then? Is that your objection?'

Rebecca sighed. 'I do not believe there is precisely anything to object to in him. I simply do not wish to marry him.'

'Refuse, then.' Surely this lady had choices.

Rebecca rolled her eyes. 'My brother—my half-brother—says I am too much of a burden for him to wait for me to find a husband I would like. I've refused every offer he's arranged for me. This time he made certain. I will be turned out without a penny if I do not marry Lord Stonecroft.' Her face turned red. 'I've no doubt he means what he says.'

Claire knew how it felt to have no choices. Her heart wrenched in sympathy. 'How sad. One would hope a brother would understand. Family should understand, should they not?'

Rebecca gave her a curious look. 'Do you have any brothers or sisters? Any family at all?'

Claire's throat tightened with emotion. 'I am alone in the world. Any relations are too distant to be concerned with me.'

'My parents are gone,' Rebecca responded in a like tone. 'And my brother might as well be dead. He said he never wishes to see me again. Ever. Even if he visits England. He made that very clear.'

Another way they were alike. Both alone. Both without parents. Lady Rebecca went on to say her father died two years before, her mother, a decade ago.

At least she'd known her mother. Claire's mother had died giving birth to her; her father, over five years ago.

But Rebecca had one choice Claire would probably never have. The chance to make a good marriage. 'I think you are fortunate to marry, Lady Rebecca—Rebecca,' she finally said. 'You have little money or property, correct? You can only gain by marrying. You'll gain a home of your own to manage. Children of your own. Comfort and security. Even status and a respectable position in society.'

It sounded like a wonderful choice to Claire. She yearned to have a man to love her—that is, the right man, one she was free to love in return. She suspected she would even enjoy the pleasures of the marital bed, because sometimes when seeing a handsome man—like the man who'd spoken to them in the hallway—she'd wonder how it would be for him to kiss her or hold her.

Could men sense such impulses in her? It often seemed the wrong men paid her attention.

How much easier it would be to simply be married. To have such security.

She opened her mouth to speak of this to Lady Rebecca, but the lady's expression had turned desolate.

Claire wanted only to comfort her now. 'Perhaps it will not be so onerous to be Lady Stonecroft.'

Rebecca gave a polite smile. 'Perhaps not.'

Claire changed the subject, to save Rebecca more discomfort. They talked about their interests. What books they'd read. What plays they'd seen. Their favourite pieces of music. From time to time, Rebecca convinced Claire to impersonate her and check up on her maid, Nolan. The woman accepted her as Rebecca, each time.

* * *

They talked until night turned the angry sea dark. It felt lovely to Claire. She'd not had such a friend in a long time.

But Rebecca's eyes, so like Claire's, grew heavy and, as they talked, she tried to stifle yawns.

Claire, feeling guilty for claiming her company for so long, stood. 'I should return to my cabin so you might get some sleep. I'll help you out of your dress, if you help me out of this lovely gown.'

Rebecca rose and turned her back so Claire could untie the laces at the back of the plain dress she had owned for years. It had been such a pleasure to wear something a bit decadent, if one could call wool decadent. Ladies who frequently purchased new dresses did not realise how it felt to wear the same drab garments, day after day.

As Claire loosened the laces of the dress, Rebecca turned to her. 'Let us see how far we can carry this masquerade. You be me tonight. Sleep in my nightclothes, in this bed. And I will continue being you.'

Claire blanched. 'I cannot allow you to be closeted in that tiny berth they gave me!'

'Why not?' Rebecca looked defiant. 'It will be an adventure for me. And you will have the comfort of this cabin as a treat. When Nolan enters in the morning, we shall discover if she still believes you are me.'

She pulled out her nightdress, made of the softest of muslin. 'Here.'

Claire fingered the fine cloth of the nightdress. 'Perhaps. If you desire this.'

'I do desire it,' her likeness insisted. She helped Claire out of her dress. 'I desire it very much.'

By morning, though, the weather had worsened and the boat pitched and rose even more fiercely than the night before. Claire was awoken by Rebecca knocking on the door of her own cabin. She rose and had difficulty crossing the room to answer the door to admit her new friend. They looked even more alike, both in their nightclothes, their hair loose about their shoulders.

'I checked on Nolan,' Rebecca said. 'She is even more ill today. I also saw the seaman who brings our food. He said we must stay below.' She lifted her arm. 'I brought your bag.'

Claire had packed a clean shift, her brush and comb, and a small bar of soap for the boat trip. The small trunk that held the rest of her clothing was stowed away. The dress she'd wear again today was draped over one of the chairs.

'We can help each other dress,' Rebecca said.

Dressing was a challenge, though. They had difficulty staying on their feet and the pitcher of water for washing had mostly spilled on to the floor. They managed to get into their shifts and corsets, and Claire reached for her dress.

Rebecca stopped her. 'Oh, do let us continue our masquerade. It was such a lark.'

Claire did not need much convincing. She'd relish wearing Rebecca's lovely dress again and having her hair in curls.

As the day crept on, though, their impersonation of each other was forgotten. It was clear the ship was in very rough waters. A seaman did attend them, bringing food and drink, but his face seemed pinched in worry.

'A bad storm brewing,' he told them.

Lucien had spent most of the day on deck, though he had no control over the lack of decision by the Captain. Curse naval discipline! It was clear to him that the ship could founder at any moment. The time was past to do anything to prevent it.

He ran over to the Captain. 'Give the order to abandon ship! Get these passengers into the boats while there is still time.' They were near the coast. The boats might make it to shore.

'Yes, yes.' The man's face was ashen. He suddenly clutched his arm and his face contorted in pain. He collapsed on the deck.

'Blast,' Lucien cried. He grabbed one of the men to attend to the Captain and another to see that the order to abandon ship was given. He ran to the cabins to get the passengers to safety.

Suddenly there was a loud crack and Lucien

watched lightning travel down the main mast. It split in two and crashed on to the deck.

Time was running out. He dashed back to the cabins and burst into the next one.

He found the lady and her companion. He'd learned the lady was Lady Rebecca Pierce, sister to the Earl of Keneagle. Certainly that had been a surprise. The other woman was a governess. But he had no time to lose.

'Come above,' he commanded. 'We must abandon ship. Bring nothing.'

Lady Rebecca jumped to her feet, but the governess defied his order and pulled a reticule from her satchel. He'd still not seen her face.

'Come on!' he ordered.

When they reached the stairs, the governess shoved the reticule into the lady's hands. 'Here. Take this,' she said. 'I'll be right behind you. I'm going to get Nolan.'

'Miss!' Lucien yelled to her. 'We must leave now.'

'I will be right behind you,' she called over her shoulder.

'Blast!' He pushed the lady up the stairs and seized her arm when they climbed on deck.

The deck was in shambles. Ropes and sails and smashed wood everywhere. The main mast lay like a fallen soldier in the midst of it all.

'To the boats!' he ordered, still gripping her arm.

He pulled her over the debris to the railing, but

as they reached it, the ship dipped. A huge wave, as tall as a mountain rose above them.

God help them. Lucien wrapped his arms around her.

The wave engulfed them and swept them into the swirling sea.

Chapter Two

Lucien held on to her as the roiling water pushed them into its depths along with pieces of the broken mast, barrels and other rubble.

Nearly twenty years at sea in all kinds of weather, all kinds of battle, he'd be damned if he'd perish from crossing the Irish Sea in a packet boat.

A large piece of wood smashed into them, hitting her on the head. She went limp, but Lucien hung on to her. He let the sea do its will, pulling them deeper and deeper. With luck it would release them. His lungs ached, but he forced himself to wait. He hoped she was not breathing in too much water.

After an eternity, the sea let go. He kicked them to the surface. When his face broke through, he gulped in air. Lady Rebecca remained limp.

Was he too late?

Lucien resisted panic. Their lives depended upon him remaining calm.

Part of the mast floated nearby. Still keeping hold of her, he swam to it and laid her over it. He blew into her mouth, a trick an old sailor taught him years ago. She coughed and spewed water and mumbled something unintelligible.

He expelled a relieved breath. She was alive.

It was fortunate the debris that had hit them had knocked her unconscious. She might have struggled otherwise. He might not have been able to keep hold of her.

A piece of rope floated nearby. Lucien grabbed it and tied her to the mast, doing his best to keep her face above the water.

A bolt of lightning lit the sky and he could see the ship a distance away heading towards the rocky shore. The sea pulled them further from it, but into calmer waters. He looked around him for anything that might be useful. A small floating barrel. A large piece of canvas sail. More rope. A hatch door appeared, a piece large enough to hold them both. He took a chance she'd be secure enough on the mast and swam to the door, pulling it back to her. He strained to place her on the door. He gathered the other items he'd collected before climbing on to the door himself.

The storm had cleared, but the shoreline narrowed into no more than a thin line against the sky. He wrapped them both in the canvas sail and held her against his body to keep her as warm as possible. They'd be on the water all night, he guessed.

Lucien doubted anyone would search for them, but perhaps some vessel would sail near enough to find them.

He gazed down at her, still unconscious, but breathing. She had a lovely, refined face.

How ironic that, of all people, he should have saved the granddaughter of the Earl of Keneagle, the Earl who'd cheated his mother's family of their fortune, impoverishing them and changing the course of their lives. His mother's life.

But what of the governess? Had she survived?

Lucien hoped so.

Morning dawned to clear skies. Lucien's arms ached from holding Lady Rebecca the whole night. She'd struggled against him, but never gained full consciousness. The night had been dangerously cold, but soon the sun would warm them.

Before it, too, became an enemy.

At least he had the piece of sail to shade her.

She seemed to be merely sleeping now. She'd been lovely enough in her travelling finery when he'd encountered her in the companionway, but she looked more appealing to him now, with curls gone and her expression vulnerable. Was she the lady with the lovely laugh? It could have been the woman with her, the governess. He hoped her running back to find someone else had saved her. He could not have held on to them both.

He glanced away. He'd never been tempted by aristocratic ladies, those few he'd encountered. They seemed shallow and silly, too eager for pleasure and too ignorant of how the rest of the world lived. He'd seen privation and could never forget how wretched life could be. As a boy, he'd heard the story over and over, how the Earl of Keneagle had impoverished his mother's family. How his mother had lost the chance to marry a title. How she'd had to settle instead for his father, a mere captain in the navy, like Lucien was now. Even though his father had risen in rank and had provided well enough for her, his mother preferred the company of the local Viscount when his father was away at sea—which he'd been for months, even years, at a time.

Lucien had grown up feeling a responsibility to his Irish relatives. They had been the reason he'd sailed to Ireland, to provide financial help to his uncles, who struggled to make ends meet. Lucien could afford to help them. He'd squirrelled away almost all of his prize money over the last twenty years. Thank God it was safe in Coutts Bank in London and not at the bottom of the Irish Sea.

Like he and Lady Rebecca might be if the sea claimed them.

His lids grew heavy and the rocking of their makeshift raft lulled him.

'No!' Lady Rebecca pushed against him. 'No!'

Fully awake now, he tightened his grip on her. 'Be still,' he ordered. 'Do not move.'

Her lovely eyes flew open. 'What? Where am I?'

'You are safe, my lady.' She would panic, certainly. He kept her restrained. 'But we are on the open sea.'

'On the sea?' Her voice rose in confusion and she struggled. 'No! Let me go!'

'I cannot. Not until you are still.' He forced his voice to sound calm. 'You are safe if you remain still.'

The waves bobbed them up and down and slapped water on to the raft. The canvas covering them fell away and Lucien blinked against the blazing sun.

Her head swivelled around and her voice became more alarmed. 'No! Why am I here?'

'Do you remember?' he asked. 'We were on the packet from Dublin to Holyhead. There was a storm—'

She raised a hand to her head. 'I was on a packet ship? Where is it now?'

He didn't want to tell her it had probably crashed into the rocks and that some people would not have survived. 'We were swept away from it.'

'But someone will find us, won't they?' she asked. 'Someone will be looking for us?'

More likely they'd think they'd perished. 'Many

ships cross the Irish Sea. Chances are good we'll be rescued.' Chances were at least as good as finding a needle in a haystack.

She scanned the horizon again as if a ship might magically appear.

'I don't remember being on a ship,' she finally said accusingly.

Perhaps that was a godsend. 'Best not to remember.'

She looked at him with hysteria in her eyes. 'You do not understand. I don't remember the ship. I don't remember anything.'

'You suffered a blow to the head. It happens sometimes to have difficulty remembering.' Or perhaps it was the trauma itself, of the storm, of being swept into the sea. He'd heard stories of soldiers in battle forgetting where they were. No one had suffered a similar affliction on his ship, though, and they'd been through plenty of trauma. 'Try not to worry over it, my lady,' he reassured.

She peered at him. 'Why do you keep calling me "my lady"?'

He gaped at her. 'I was told you are Lady Rebecca Pierce. Was I misinformed?'

'Lady Rebecca Pierce,' she repeated in a whisper. Her voice rose. 'Is that who I am?'

He searched her face. Her distress seemed genuine. 'You do not remember your name?'

'I do not remember anything!' she cried. 'My

name. Why I am here. Why I was on a ship. Why you are here.'

None of that mattered at the moment. They were in a battle with the elements. If the wind stirred the sea again, they might be tossed off this makeshift raft. If they could not shield themselves, the sun could burn their skin. And if they survived today, would they survive another cold night? They had no food, no water. How long could they last without water?

But he did not tell her any of that. He held her closer. 'Try not to fret. It will not help. It is important to stay as calm as you can.'

She leaned against him and turned quiet again. He knew she must be cold so held her closely.

After a time she spoke. 'Do I know you?'

'We met briefly on the ship. I am Captain Lucien Roper. No reason for you to know me.' Except that her family had ruined his mother's family, but what use was it to tell her that? 'I am bound for London.' Or will be if they survive.

She stirred a little. 'I wonder where I am bound.'

Claire pressed her cheek against his warm chest. She was cold and her head ached and her situation terrified her. She was adrift on the sea with a stranger, a man who stirred some unsettled emotion inside her, an emotion she could not name.

Was she to die in the arms of a man she did not know, without even knowing her own name? Her past?

Was she Lady Rebecca Pierce, as he'd said? The name meant nothing to her, but then, her mind was a blank when she tried to think of something, anything, about herself.

There was only this man. His chest was firm and warm and his manner confident and able. He'd covered their heads with the canvas again, but she could glimpse the sea from beneath it. The vast empty sea.

The sun's reflection on the water hurt her eyes, but when she closed them the rocking of their raft seemed even more pronounced.

Would they die here? she wanted to ask him. But that was one question the answer of which she feared the most.

Had other people died? Had there been someone on the ship she knew? Someone dear to her? She tried to conjure up a feeling of attachment to someone, anyone, but there was only this man. Only he seemed real.

Maybe he knew. 'Was I with anyone on this ship?'

He hesitated before answering. 'I saw you with another woman. She was in the cabin with you.'

'Who was she?' A mother? A sister? Did she belong to anyone? If so, had they survived?

'I did not learn her name.' He sounded regret-ful about that.

'Was she related to me?' She wanted to belong somewhere, to someone.

'I do not think so,' he replied. 'She was dressed plainly and I was told she was a governess. I never saw more than a glimpse of her.'

A governess? Was she connected to this gov-erness in some way?

Was there anyone who cared for her? Who would search for her? All she could conjure up was a feeling of being alone. She lifted her arms, wanting to press her fingers against her temples. On one of her arms dangled a lovely but sodden red-velvet reticule.

She stared at it. 'Is this mine?'

'I remember now,' he said. 'The woman with you handed it to you as we left the ship.'

Who had she been? Why would she hand her a reticule?

Claire strained to remember, but nothing came. She shook her head. 'What happened to her?'

'I do not know,' he replied. 'She hurried off to find someone else and we never saw her after that. We climbed up on deck.' He paused. 'Then the wave came.'

The wave that swept them into the sea? How could one forget such an event? How could she not know who'd sailed with her?

How could she not remember her own name?

She shivered and stared at the water. How easy it would be to slip beneath its surface and join the void, so like the void in her mind.

Lucien Roper tightened his arms around her again, stilling her trembling, reminding her that she *was* someone, even if she could not remember who.

And, no matter what, she wanted to live.

'Do you know anything about me?' she asked him.

He paused before answering. 'Very little. That you sailed from Dublin. Your name. That you are sister to the Earl of Keneagle.' His voice stiffened.

She did belong to someone! 'Do you know the Earl of Keneagle?'

He shifted his body a little. 'He is an Irish earl, that is all I know.'

'Then someone will look for me.' She relaxed against him again.

'These waters are well travelled,' he said.

He did not sound convincing.

The waves beneath them rocked them like a bumpy carriage ride and the air smelled of brine. Her skin itched from the salt. They'd lapsed into silence. Only the slapping of the water against their raft made a sound.

The emptiness was driving her mad. She needed memories, any memories.

Even his would do. 'Will you tell me about you, Lucien Roper?'

He stirred a little. 'I am in the navy.'

'The navy?' Keep talking, she wanted to beg. He was her only reality at the moment. He and some brother she could not remember. A governess who'd been her companion.

And probable death. 'What do you do in the navy?'

He shrugged. 'I am a captain.'

'Do you have a ship?' Captains had ships, she somehow knew.

His ship, his home, was likely scrap by now. 'Not at the moment. I'm bound for the Admiralty to be given a new ship.'

How could she know what the navy was and nothing about herself?

Maybe if he kept talking...

'Are—are you on half pay?' she asked.

Half pay, Lucien thought. She obviously knew what half pay was.

He nodded. 'Until I'm given a new ship.'

'You had a ship? What happened to it?' she asked.

'The war is over. The navy does not need so many ships. It was sold.' He could not bear to tell her the *Foxfire* would be broken up. The ship had more life in her.

'How sad for you.' Her voice sounded genuinely sympathetic. 'What was the name of your ship?'

'The *Foxfire*.'

'A lovely name,' she remarked. 'What kind of ship was it?'

'She was a Banterer-class post ship with twenty-two guns.'

'How impressive sounding,' she said. 'I know nothing of ships—at least nothing I can remember—but I know of the war somehow. I know it is over. Is that not strange?'

Strange that she remembered some things and not others? 'I suppose it is.'

'I—I cannot remember anything to do with me.' She said this quietly, but he heard the pain of it in her words. She moved enough to look him in the face. 'Would you tell me more about you? About being in the navy, perhaps? I need to know that there is more than us drifting on this water. I need to know someone has memories.'

His heart resonated with her pain. The fact that they were drifting on these boards in the middle of the sea would be terrifying enough without amnesia on top of it. She might be a spoiled aristocratic lady, but at the moment she did not know even this. And, although he would not say it to her, she must realise they faced probable death.

If talking about himself would ease her anguish, he would talk about himself.

'My father is an admiral,' Lucien said. 'My grandfather was an admiral. I was always meant for the navy, as well. It is in my blood. And I've done well in it.'

'How long have you been in the navy?' she asked.

'Twenty-one years. Since age twelve. At fifteen I was in the Battle of the Nile. At twenty-two I was at Trafalgar and, since then, countless encounters with French, American and Danish ships. Mostly in the Adriatic Sea and the Mediterranean.'

'You did well in the war, then.' Her sympathy seemed genuine.

He gazed out to the horizon. 'I also sent good men to their deaths.' He closed his eyes and saw the carnage of battle. He saw his quartermaster blown apart. His midshipman, a mere youth, set afire. Why had these memories come and not the glory of capturing enemy vessels?

'Did you earn prize money.'

There it was. He should have known she would ask about his money. A man's monetary worth was of prime importance to aristocrats.

'I did well enough.' Good enough for him to retire, if he chose to—if they ever made it to shore again. Good enough for him to pay his uncles' debts and set them up more securely. They should have no financial worries now.

'And you will be given a new ship?'

'So I have been told.'

If they survived, that was.

As the day wore on, the sun warmed them as he'd expected. It dried the canvas and most of their clothes. Lucien scanned the horizon for ships, to no avail. Lady Rebecca remained calm, eerily calm, as if detached from the danger they were in and the suffering they would endure if rescue did not come soon. She must be as hungry and as powerfully thirsty as he was, but, unexpectedly, she did not complain. Instead, she asked more questions about his life and Lucien found himself telling her things he'd never shared with anyone.

Like being left to his own devices as a young boy in a village outside Liverpool. How his mother, in her loneliness when his father was at sea—which was most of the time—sought amusement elsewhere by pursuing the local Viscount, who took his pleasure from her when the fancy took him. His mother was always too preoccupied by this love affair to bother much with a little boy or to make certain his nurses attended him. Lucien told her about how he'd been left to his own devices, sometimes to cope with situations he was too young to understand. His mother seemed happy when he was sent to sea.

He told her how his life changed after that. He'd loved the structure of rank and the discipline the navy required. Every man had his place and his duty and together they conquered the enemy and the sea itself. The sea, which so often was beautiful. A beautiful, if often treacherous, mistress.

Lucien shared with this woman what he'd never spoken of with anyone else. How he loved the sea.

He didn't tell her that he'd be happy to die at sea and be sent to his rest beneath its depths.

Not yet, though. He wanted to live. He wanted her to live.

The sky darkened as the sun dipped closer to the horizon. Lucien continued talking, recounting his experiences at sea and his ship's victories. He left off the close calls of horrific storms and the carnage of battle.

She listened and asked questions that showed some knowledge of naval matters, not entirely without memory of facts, at least.

He'd thought about telling her of the connection between their families, of how her grandfather had cheated his grandfather out of his property and fortune, but what good would that do? She had enough agony without him adding to it.

Her predicament almost made him forget his thirst, his hunger and the dire consequence of spending another night floating to nowhere.

He kept his eye on the horizon as he talked. His years at sea had given him sharp vision for which he was grateful.

Suddenly he saw a shape form in the distance. It sailed closer, but still too far to notice them, a mere speck in the vastness. He watched it, saying nothing to Lady Rebecca. Why spark an expectation that likely would never come to fruition?

He eventually could tell it was a two-masted

ketch, a fishing boat, likely. And it looked as though it was sailing straight for them.

Lucien waited as the ketch sailed closer. Odds were still greatest that it would pass them by, but his heart beat faster.

He quickly tied the rope to the latch on the door that was their raft. 'Hold on to this,' he told her. 'And be still. There is a ship. I'm going to stand and try to signal it.'

'A ship?' Her voice rose.

In hope, he supposed. 'With luck they will see us.'

When she'd secured herself he carefully rose to his feet and waved the piece of sail that had sheltered them. He waved the canvas until his arms ached with the effort. From time to time the waves threatened to knock him off balance.

The ship came closer and closer. It still could miss them, though. Lucien knew how easily their small raft could be a mere speck, but he continued to wave the canvas.

When he could faintly hear voices from the ship, he shouted to them, 'Ahoy! Ahoy!'

Lady Rebecca added her voice to his.

Finally a voice from the ketch returned their call. 'Ahoy! Ahoy! We are coming.'

Lucien sat down and again put his arms around Lady Rebecca. 'They see us, my lady. We are rescued.'

Chapter Three

It took another hour for the ship to approach and lower a boat to row out to them, but Claire did not mind the wait. They were rescued.

Soon enough they were safe on board the ketch and greeted by a man who introduced himself as Captain Molloy.

Lucien immediately told the Captain, 'The lady needs water and food.'

Claire had not realised the strength of her thirst until Lucien mentioned it.

Lucien.

She could not think of him in more formal terms than his given name. He'd saved her life and he was the only person she had in her memory.

He kept an arm around her, though she thought she could walk on her own.

'We'll get you both below.' The Captain ushered them towards a hatch. 'What vessel are you from?'

'The *Dun Aengus*,' Lucien replied. 'Packet from Dublin to Holyhead.'

Captain Molloy walked them to his cabin, a tiny space, but one with a table, four chairs and a berth. Anything else in the room must have been stored behind the cabinet doors which lined the walls.

One of the men brought water. Claire nearly pulled the tin cup from the man's hands.

'Take small sips,' Lucien warned her. 'You'll want to keep it down.'

She nodded.

He watched her drink before taking any water himself.

'Can we find the lady some dry clothes?' Lucien asked the Captain.

Captain Molloy signalled to his man, who nodded and left. 'We've been out only a few days, so there should be enough clean clothes to be found.' He nodded to Lucien. 'For you as well?'

'I would be grateful.' He took another small sip of water. 'You are fishermen?'

'That we are,' the Captain said. 'We're after cod and haddock.'

Claire saw concern flash on to Lucien's face.

'I am afraid you will be with us for a bit.' The captain looked apologetic. 'We'll be at sea for three weeks at least.'

'Three weeks?' She gasped. It seemed so long a time.

But why was she concerned? She knew of no other place she must go, no other place she belonged. She might as well be at sea.

'My lady, you will have the use of my cabin.' Captain Molloy glanced over at Lucien. 'We'll find a place for you, as well.' He looked away and muttered, 'Although I cannot imagine where.'

Claire spoke up. 'I do not wish to trouble you so. Is there not room for Lucien here with me?'

She was not entirely selfless. She dreaded being alone with the emptiness in her mind. He was her one link to her previous life, the life she could not remember.

'I cannot stay here,' Lucien protested. 'Your reputation—'

'My reputation cannot matter here.' She turned to Captain Molloy. 'Can it, Captain? No one will speak of this, will they?'

The Captain answered eagerly. 'I'll see they don't.'

A muscle in Lucien's cheek tensed. 'As you wish.'

'Well, that is settled.' The Captain clapped his hands together. 'I need to return to my duties. Food and clothing will be brought to you shortly.'

'Thank you, Captain,' Claire said.

He bowed to her, a gesture of respect that seemed foreign to her.

After he left, she lifted her cup to sip more

water, holding back from gulping the whole contents at once.

Lucien frowned. 'Are you certain about sharing the cabin, my lady?'

'They saved us, Lucien.' Was it not the least they could do in return? 'I cannot repay them by causing more discomfort.'

He nodded. Grudgingly, she thought.

The reticule still hung from her wrist. She untwisted its strings and slipped it off.

'Look inside,' he said. 'Its contents might tell you more about yourself. Spark a memory, perhaps.'

It looked as alien to her as this fishing boat cabin, but she loosened its strings and reached inside to pull out the contents.

A small purse filled with coin. A tortoiseshell comb. A white enamel etui painted with exquisite flowers and containing a tiny scissors, needles, pins and hairpins. A linen handkerchief with an embroidered edge and a monogram—R.P. Rebecca Pierce. The name that didn't seem like her name. The items that didn't seem like her possessions.

'Nothing looks like mine.' She trembled. 'It is as though I have never seen these things before.'

He moved closer.

If only he would hold her. She'd become accustomed to his arms around her.

Instead he crossed his arms over his chest. 'Too

much has happened. Your memory will return in time.'

At the moment, he was her memory.

A few minutes later, one of the fishermen brought two tankards of ale and bread and cheese, which she ate slowly, as Lucien directed. When another man brought clothes, Claire looked down at herself. The lovely travelling dress she wore seemed as unfamiliar as the fishing boat. It had laces at the back.

She glanced over at Lucien. 'I fear I must ask for your help.' She turned her back to him.

He stood. 'You could not have undone this by yourself. Might you have been travelling with a maid?'

She turned her head to look at him over her shoulder. Her insides twisted in pain. 'Do you suppose I was?' She turned back. 'Did she die?'

Did someone who tended to her needs die and she did not even remember them?

His hand flattened against her shoulder and his voice softened. 'We survived. Others would have, too.'

'I cannot remember.' She also could not remember if another man had ever touched her so—so gently.

He loosened her laces and stepped back. 'You'll want me to leave. Give you some privacy.'

'No!' she cried, then felt guilty for it, but she

had a dread of being alone. 'Just—just turn your back.'

He did as she asked and she slipped off the dress. But there were her stays. They tied in front, but she could not undo the knot.

'Lucien, I need more help.' She drew a ragged breath. 'My stays. The knot is too tight.'

He turned again and stepped towards her. His gaze was downcast as he worked the knot, his gentle hands touching her even more intimately.

His touch was more quenching than the cup of water.

Her breath quickened and her breasts rose and fell. He was only inches from her.

He made quick work of her stays, though, and stepped back once more. 'I'll turn around again.'

She slipped out of her stays and removed the rest of her underclothes, aware she stood naked in the presence of a man.

Lucien clenched a fist, letting his fingers press into his flesh. Being so close to her in her un-dressed state had stirred him. The sounds of her removing her underclothes aroused his senses even more. He was only too aware of the vision she must present in her nakedness.

And of how it felt to touch her.

In the past twenty-four hours he'd rarely not been touching her, but his fingers brushing against her skin stirred him as a man, not a rescuer. It had been a long time since he'd been with a woman, true, but this situation certainly did not warrant such a response.

And she was the last sort of woman he needed to be aroused by—the aristocratic daughter of the family he'd been raised to despise. Besides, she was much too vulnerable for a gentleman to take advantage.

'I am dressed,' she said. 'You may turn around now.'

He turned. She'd donned the loose shirt and breeches the fishermen wore and held the rough knitted stockings that covered their legs and feet.

'I must remove my half-boots, but I'm well covered now.' She sat in one of the chairs.

For the first time he noticed her half-boots. Something about them… They looked worn, not at all what he would have expected her to wear.

She removed one and held it up. 'I have no memory of these.' She shrugged and set the shoe aside. 'You must change now, as well. I promise not to look.'

He smiled. 'Will you help me if I cannot undo my buttons?'

She coloured. The flush on her cheeks only made her more lovely.

Lowering her gaze, she said, 'Of course I will, if you need me.'

He coughed. 'It was a jest, my lady.'

She turned her chair away from him and

quickly donned the stockings. He continued to watch as she then busied herself taking pins from her hair, most of which had already fallen to her shoulders in tangles. It was remarkable that any pins remained. She took the comb from her reticule and started working on her hair, one strand at a time.

Lucien forced his eyes away and changed into the clothes the fishermen provided.

He hung their old clothing and her reticule on pegs on the wall and joined her at the table.

She looked over at him and smiled. 'These clothes are remarkably comfortable, although I feel a bit as if I am in my nightdress.' Her face fell. 'How is it I remember how a nightdress feels and I do not remember owning one?'

He had no answers for her. 'When we are back on land you can consult a physician.'

Her eyes widened. 'I would fear he'd send me to Bedlam.'

Such a worry was not unfounded, but surely her family would not allow such a thing. *He'd* not allow it.

'We are likely to be on this boat for three weeks,' she said after a time. 'Is that not what the Captain said?'

'It is,' he responded. 'We must make the best of it.'

Her expression turned determined. 'I am glad

of it. I am certain I can manage such a small world.'

'And, who knows?' he added. 'Perhaps your memory will return by then.'

She detangled her hair strand by strand and it calmed Lucien to watch her. When done, she put her hair in a plait.

She held the end of her plait in her fingers. 'I suppose it will only come loose again without a ribbon.'

Lucien rose and picked up the neckcloth he'd taken off. He cut the edge with the knife they'd used to slice the cheese and ripped a long strip.

He handed it to her. 'This should work.'

'But you've ruined your neckcloth.' She reached for it.

He laughed. 'I'd say the sea ruined it already.'

She wound it around the end of her plait and tied the ends with a bow.

They finished the rest of the bread and cheese and soon Lady Rebecca's eyelids closed and her chin dipped on to her chest.

She jolted awake.

'You must go to bed.' Lucien rose and helped her to the Captain's berth.

She curled up beneath the blanket, her eyes blinking in an effort to stay awake.

'Sleep now,' he murmured.

She seized his hand. 'Where will you sleep, Lucien? There is only one berth.'

He tried again. 'I should not sleep in this cabin with you, my lady. It is not proper.'

'I do not care.' She gripped harder. 'To tell the truth, I am a little afraid to be alone.'

She looked very afraid.

'Very well,' he said. 'I'll make a bed for myself on the floor.'

Lucien waited until she was sound asleep before gathering their dishes and slipping out the door. He found the galley and the Captain, who again said how pleased he was that he did not have to squeeze his men any more than merely finding another berth for himself. The fishermen managed to give Lucien another blanket and he returned to the Captain's cabin.

She still slept.

Dead tired himself, Lucien formed a hammock of sorts with the blanket. As soon as he was settled in it, he, too, fell asleep.

He was awoken by Lady Rebecca's cries. The room was pitch black.

'No! No! Stay away! Stay away!' She thrashed around in the berth.

He made his way to her in the darkness and held her arms to still her. 'Wake up. You are having a dream.'

Her thrashing stopped and she threw her arms around his neck. 'Lucien! I was being chased and then I was in the water and you were too far away to reach me.'

He unwrapped her arms from around his neck. 'Only a dream.'

She kept hold of his hand. 'Yes. A dream. I am awake now.'

'Who chased you?' Someone from her past? This was hardly the sort of memory he wished returned to her.

'I do not know. It was as if the blackness pursued me.' She trembled. 'I am quite recovered now.'

He remained at her side. 'Are you certain?'

'Oh, yes,' she said, but her hand trembled.

The nightmare was still with her then. 'I'll sit beside you for a while,' he told her.

Her hand seemed small and vulnerable in his larger one.

In the darkness he heard her murmur, 'Everything was black, then all I could see was you.'

He sat with her until her hand relaxed and her breathing came soft and rhythmic.

When Claire woke the next morning, Lucien was gone. She sat up quickly, her heart pounding.

She was alone!

But she remembered where she was—on a fishing boat—and she remembered Lucien.

She remembered, too, that he'd woken her from that terrible nightmare and remained beside her in the narrow berth. She also remembered how she'd thrown her arms around him.

Her cheeks burned.

Although she could not remember who she was or anything about her past, she knew with certainty that it was shameful of her to embrace a man like that. Even if he had been a perfect gentleman.

Perhaps she was wanton. Could that be? Could it be she'd already compromised herself and that was why she'd felt no hesitation to insist he share the room with her? She might be a lady, but was it possible she was anything but ladylike?

She glanced down at herself and realised the fisherman's clothes she wore had come loose of her makeshift belt. Standing, she straightened her clothing, but the breeches seemed ready to fall down at any moment. She remembered the etui from the reticule—she could not think of it as *her* etui or *her* reticule. She found it hanging from a peg. She took the pins from the etui and used them to fit the breeches to her body.

The door opened.

It was Lucien. 'I have brought you some breakfast.'

He'd brought a steaming bowl of porridge and a mug of warm cider. How kind of him.

'Thank you, Lucien.'

Her appetite was hardy. Was she always a big eater? Scenting the porridge, she remembered how it tasted—but she could not remember a time she ate porridge.

She felt Lucien's gaze upon her as she ate.

She swallowed a spoonful and looked up at him. 'I am sorry I woke you last night.'

He paused before speaking. 'How do you fare this morning?'

She laughed lightly. 'I wish I could say I feel quite myself this morning, but I do not know who myself is. I do feel rested, though.'

He nodded.

'And you, Lucien,' she asked. 'Are you well?'

He waved off her question. 'Very well.' He leaned forward. 'Rest today, if you need to, but I want to assist the fishermen. There are only five of them, including Captain Molloy. I am certain they can make use of me.'

She had not expected him to help catch fish, not a captain in the navy. How good of him. Did he always consider others, perhaps even over himself? How could she be selfish enough to insist he stay with her?

Just because she was afraid to be alone.

'I do understand.' She took a nervous breath. 'I will amuse myself somehow.' She managed a smile.

His eyes pierced into hers. 'I will check on you, my lady. Or make certain someone else does.'

She lifted her chin and nodded, hoping she looked braver than she felt.

* * *

Lucien had expected her to complain and demand he remain with her. It was clear that she did not want to be alone. But she had not. And why had she insisted he stay in the cabin with her? If it became known, it would certainly ruin her in her aristocratic circles. Was it her memory loss? Did she not remember how important reputation was for an earl's daughter?

Spending the night in the same room posed a different problem for Lucien. The intimacy of sleeping near her fuelled fantasies of sharing her bed, of tasting her lips, of feeling her naked skin next to his. He would never seduce her, though, would he? It would be taking advantage of her in the most reprehensible way.

Over the years he'd met many high-born men who'd boasted about conquests, usually leaving the lives of lower-born, but respectable, young women in tatters. Even Lucien's mother had been an easy conquest for Viscount Waverland.

Not that she'd been anything less than willing.

In any event, Lucien had no patience for aristocrats who called themselves gentlemen and behaved like rutting animals around any woman dazzled by their status.

And he refused to sink to their level.

He watched her finish her porridge. He could at least keep her company that long.

'Do you know about fishing, Lucien?' she asked between spoonsful.

He gave a dry laugh. 'Very little. But there must be something I can do.'

She blinked up at him. Her eyes were a remarkable mix of brown circled by green. 'You could captain the ship, could you not?'

'I could, but this boat has a captain.' Although if he had taken over from the Captain of the *Dun Aengus*, perhaps the ship would not have foundered.

There was no reason to doubt the Captain of this vessel, though. He and his crew depended upon the sea for their livelihood.

'I know nothing of fishing,' Lady Rebecca said. 'They use nets, do they not?'

He smiled. 'Yes, they do, so you do know something of fishing.'

She lowered her gaze to her bowl and carefully scooped out another spoonful. She lifted it to her mouth.

Lucien looked away. Her lips had become a distraction, one he could not resist for long. He glanced back.

Her expression sobered. 'I cannot understand why I know so many things, but I do not know anything about me.'

'Take heart in that,' Lucien replied. 'If you remember those things, then surely your memory of yourself will return.'

She took another spoonful of porridge. He looked away again.

'I am becoming accustomed to not knowing.' She averted her head for a moment before turning and looking directly into his eyes. 'It is as if my life started on the raft when I woke.'

He reached over and put his hand on hers. 'I believe you will recover your memory.'

She merely continued to stare into his face.

He withdrew his hand and stood. 'I should go on deck.'

A look of panic flitted across her face, but she quickly forced a smile. 'Yes. I believe I will see if our old clothing needs mending. I think I remember how to use a needle and thread.'

Lucien was surprised that her first idea was to do something so useful. 'I will come back to check on you, as I said.'

He turned to leave, but Lady Rebecca stopped him. 'Wait a moment, Lucien.'

Just when he thought she would not become demanding.

She gave him a determined look. 'I—I wish you would not call me "my lady" or "Lady Rebecca." It simply does not feel right to me.'

He stood at the door. 'That is who you are.'

'What I mean is, I am not formal with you. I call you Lucien. I realise I never asked if I could call you Lucien. Is it offensive to you? Should I call you Captain Roper?'

Her use of his given name could be meant as condescending, but, if truth be told, he rather liked the sound of his name on her lips.

'Call me what you wish,' he responded.

'Then will you call me something less formal as well?'

His brow furrowed. 'I think not.'

Her head turned as if she were flinching from a blow. 'I see.'

'Lady Rebecca.' The name did not rest easy on his tongue. 'It is better if I preserve the formalities.' It helped him keep his distance. And keep his hands off her.

She seemed to force another smile. 'Of course. If that is what you want.'

Chapter Four

That first day Lucien did indeed check on her when he could and he was surprised that she worked so diligently at mending their clothes. She even found a brush and tried to brush away the salt and seaweed that clung to the cloth.

When finished she held up her dress and his coat to show him. 'They still look like they've been in a shipwreck.' She sighed.

'At least they can be worn,' he responded.

She'd done an excellent job.

On the second day Lucien felt badly about leaving her with nothing to do.

'I will find something,' she assured him.

At mid-morning he looked up from his toil to see she'd ventured on to the deck.

She sought out Captain Molloy. 'What might I do to help?' she asked him.

'You wish to help, m'lady?' The Captain laughed. 'We will find you something.'

He soon had her carrying water to the men and serving food in the galley.

But at the end of the day when she had swabbed the deck, cleaning off the fish parts that littered the boards, Lucien approached her. 'You are not required to work.' He frowned. What lady swabbed up fish guts? 'Especially tasks like this one.'

She stopped mopping and faced him. 'I like helping. I like being a part of it all.'

And she quickly became a part of it all, as if she were another crew member, not a lady. The others began to depend on her. Seeing her on deck became familiar. At night they both slept soundly, fatigued from the labour of the day.

Claire relished the days at work. The ship became her world, a world that remained in her memory as did the men's faces and names. It was as if her world—and her mind—was complete.

At the centre was always Lucien. It was his presence that made her secure, like an anchor secured a boat. As the days wore on, his face became shadowed with a beard making him look as swarthy as a pirate. The Captain and the other men wore beards as well, though none as dark and dashing as Lucien's.

She watched him help haul in the nets and load the fish into the hold. She silently prayed for his safety when he climbed the tall mast to untangle the rigging.

At night the blackness of the cabin reminded her, though, that most of her life she could not remember. It helped that Lucien was near. He stirred within her a yearning she did not quite understand, a desire to feel the strength of his arms around her, the warmth of his breath, the beating of his heart, as she had on the raft.

Some of her dreams were of him, of his bare skin against her bare skin and his lips against hers. What did it mean that she dreamt so? It made her blush to think of it.

Of being so intimate with him.

Other dreams were no more than jumbled images that slipped from her mind by morning. She much preferred the days of toil and people she recalled from day to day.

By the third week, the boat's hold was filled with fish and the Captain set sail to Ireland, a place she knew about, but of which she had no memory. The wind would carry them to port this very day.

She donned her mended dress with Lucien's help and folded the clothes the fishermen had lent her. 'I will miss these,' she said to Lucien. 'They are ever so much more comfortable than wearing this dress and stays.'

He smiled. 'I'm glad to be out of mine.'

His were soiled and smelled of fish and sweat.

She took his borrowed clothes from his hand and folded them with the others. No doubt some fisherman's wife would be laundering them soon.

She tied the ribbon around her plait and remembered how he'd torn it from his neckcloth for her. How nice it was to have memories.

She felt tears sting her eyes. 'I will miss this boat.' She blinked them away. 'I suppose because it is so familiar now. I do not know what happens next.'

He gazed at her, sympathy in his eyes. 'You've endured a shipwreck and three weeks on a fishing boat; you will be up to whatever comes next.'

She was not so certain. 'You are right. I must buck up, mustn't I?'

She would not tell him what she feared even more than the unknown was losing him, but she'd been enough of a burden to him already. He had a life to pursue, a new ship, plans he'd talked about with her, this next phase in his life.

From above them they heard a voice cry, 'Land, ho!'

His face appeared strained. 'We should go up on deck.'

She nodded and picked up the reticule that seemed to be her only possession.

They made their way to the deck and stood at the railing. A narrow line on the horizon slowly formed into land.

'Where will we sail into?' Claire's heart beat faster. Would she remember anything once they landed?

'Bray,' he responded.

'A fishing village, is it not?'

'You know it?' His brows rose.

She gazed at the land, now rising green. 'I know of it, but I do not know why.'

She had asked him many things about his life over the last three weeks, because, of course, she knew nothing of her own life, but she'd never asked him what would happen when they reached shore. That was as black to her as the night, as black as her past. As long as they were on the boat she'd been content to avoid the topic.

'You will travel to London, I expect. For your new ship.' She watched the shore coming ever closer, not daring to look at him for fear she'd crumble. 'Will you catch another packet from Dublin?'

He would leave her and be as distant and unattainable as her past.

He paused before answering. 'I will see you safe to your brother, first.'

She swallowed. 'No, Lucien. I have troubled you enough. I am certain I can manage.' Somehow.

* * *

'I will see you safe to your brother,' Lucien repeated. 'I'll not leave you on your own.'

Lucien had no desire to meet the present Earl of Keneagle, but he could not simply leave Lady Rebecca to fend for herself. True, she could mail her own letter to her brother and arrange her own transportation to his estate, but how difficult would it be for her to not even know if a man standing before her was her brother or someone else?

'We will travel together to Dublin and contact your brother from there,' he said to her. 'I will be able to draw funds from the bank there as well.' He'd dealt with a Dublin bank to transfer funds to his uncles. 'We should be able to purchase whatever we need, as well.'

She lifted her reticule. 'I have some money. Perhaps I have other funds to repay you.'

He shook his head. 'I am well able to afford whatever we need.' What else did he need his money for?

He leaned his arms on the railing.

'We are getting closer to land,' she said in a shaky voice.

Soon enough the ketch was moored at a dock and they were saying goodbye to Captain Molloy and his men. To Lucien's surprise, Lady Rebecca hugged each man who, after three weeks, like him, was rather reeking of sweat and fish.

Captain Molloy pointed. 'Walk to the top of that street and you'll find the inn. My cousin runs the place, Niall Molloy, so give him my name and he will see to your needs.'

Lucien shook the Captain's hand. 'We owe you a great debt of gratitude.'

The man looked abashed. 'Aw, 'twas nothing. You more than earned your keep. The lady, too, poor *bhean*.'

Still, Captain Molloy and his men would each receive a generous gift from Lucien as soon as it could be arranged.

He climbed off the boat and on to the dock, turning back to help Rebecca disembark. She jumped the gap and landed in his arms. She felt too good in his arms.

She found her footing and turned back to say a final goodbye.

He offered his arm. 'Your legs may take time to get used to land.'

'I will miss the crew.' She allowed him to steady her as they walked away from the dock up the street.

On the small boat, they were rarely not in someone's company.

'At least you will have a room of your own in the inn,' Lucien reassured her.

She sighed. 'It will seem strange after the fishing boat.'

They found the inn and entered its public rooms, seeking out the innkeeper who was serving ale to several men seated at tables.

'Niall Molloy?' Lucien asked.

'That I am,' he answered.

'We are off your cousin's boat,' Lucien told him. 'Rescued at sea from the wreck of the *Dun Aengus*.'

The man's bushy red eyebrows rose. 'From the *Dun Aengus*? We heard news of it. Finn picked you up? Is that not a jest? My cousin. Imagine. How long before Finn rescued you?'

'The second day,' Lucien replied.

'I imagine that was time enough.' He wiped his hands.

Lady Rebecca broke in. 'Can you tell us about the shipwreck. Did—did many die?'

The innkeeper lowered his head. 'All but a handful, reports say. Maybe a dozen survived, as I recall it.' He smiled. 'A dozen plus the two of you.'

Her face pinched in pain.

'Well, sad it is, but the sea giveth and the sea taketh away.' He clapped his hands together. 'You need a room? What else may I do for you?'

'Two rooms,' Lucien said. 'But, for now, a good meal.'

The man laughed. 'Finn's food not the best, eh? I guarantee we will show him up.'

He gestured for them to sit at a table separate

from the other diners and quickly served them large tankards of ale and mutton stew.

The other men seated there did not hide their curious glances.

'Am I not presentable?' Rebecca asked. 'They keep looking at me.'

Lucien turned and glared at the other patrons and they quickly averted their gazes. 'Presentable enough. They probably are not accustomed to seeing a lady here.'

She looked up, her eyes questioning. 'Should I not be here, then? If I do not belong here?'

He must remember that much would be new to her. 'You can certainly be here.'

'Good,' she said. 'Because I am happy to be eating so well.'

So well? Compared to the last three weeks, perhaps, but surely this food was as beneath her as the simple fare on the fishing boat.

She dipped her spoon into her stew and lowered her eyes. 'They are staring again.'

He shrugged. 'More likely, then, it is your beauty that attracts them.'

Her eyes flew up and were filled with anxiety. 'My beauty?'

'You are a beauty,' he said. 'Did you not know that?'

She blushed. 'I—I have not seen a mirror since—since the shipwreck. I do not know what I look like.' She dropped her spoon and lifted her hands to her face.

The innkeeper entered the room. 'Stop acting the maggot, fellas. Leave the lady alone.'

'No harm in lookin',' one of the men grumbled.

'Yeah?' the innkeeper said. 'I'll give ye a knuckle supper if ye do not stop.'

Rebecca lowered her gaze again. 'I am causing commotion.'

Her distress disarmed him. 'It is mere banter. Do not pay it any mind.'

Lucien tore off a piece of bread and dipped it in the stew. She took careful spoonfuls, as if made self-conscious for being an object of attention.

It had never occurred to him that she would not know what she looked like. Was it possible she had no memory of her appearance?

She placed her spoon on the table and folded her hands in her lap.

He put down his piece of bread. 'Would you like to see your room now?'

She'd want to be away from the staring eyes. Or where she could look in a mirror.

She set her chin determinedly. 'Yes.'

He called the innkeeper over.

'My wife will take you to the rooms,' the innkeeper said.

A kindly faced woman with hair as red as her husband's met them in the hall. 'I am Mrs Molloy, I am. My husband told me you were in a shipwreck and Finn saved you. Finn is a good man.'

'A very good man, ma'am,' Lucien agreed.

She took them up a flight of stairs to two

rooms side by side. She opened the doors to both of them and gave them the keys.

Claire noticed right away there was a mirror above a bureau.

'Shall I come and help you undress when the time comes?' Mrs Molloy asked.

Claire forced her gaze away from the mirror. 'That would be very kind.'

'Anything else we can do for you?' the woman asked.

Claire responded. 'I can think of nothing—'

Lucien interrupted her. 'Baths? May we arrange baths?'

Mrs Molloy smiled. 'To be sure you'll be wanting baths after what you've been through. Would you want your clothes laundered, as well?'

'I am not certain they are salvageable,' Lucien said.

'We'll just have to find you something else to wear, won't we?' She patted his arm and left.

Claire could not take her eyes off the mirror, but she hesitated.

Lucien took her by the arm. 'Delay never helps.' He walked her over to the mirror and stood her directly in front of it.

His grip gave her courage. She lifted her head and looked in the mirror.

'What do you see?' he asked.

She laughed in relief. 'I see me! I feared I

would see a stranger, but I look like me. Same brown hair, same eyes, same nose that is unfashionable, same lips. I look like me.'

Was she a beauty? If so, she disliked the stares of men.

Except for Lucien. That he thought her beautiful made her feel warm all over.

His reflection was behind hers, his expression unreadable. He was so very handsome. Tall, broad-shouldered, hair and beard dark as the night, eyes as brown and alert as a fox's.

Alert as a fox's. Where had that thought come from? She inhaled a quick breath. Had she remembered him?

She opened her mouth to tell him she might have had a memory, but shut it again. How could she explain it was all about him?

Instead she turned to face him. 'Brilliant of you to ask for baths, Lucien. A bath will seem like heaven.'

She remembered how pleasant it was to lie in a warm bath, to rub soap against her skin and to feel clean again.

She just could not remember a time or place before this when she'd taken a bath.

The bath was in a room close to the kitchen, so the hauling of water would not be too onerous for the maids and the water would remain hot. Lucien allowed Lady Rebecca to go first and he went in search of Mr Molloy, mostly to distract himself from thinking of her naked in the tub, stroking her skin with soap.

'Molloy,' he said, finding him back in the public rooms. 'I need your assistance. We have nothing. Where can I purchase necessities?' He had some coins that had remained in his pockets, sufficient to buy what they needed.

'You'll be wanting Brady's store.' The innkeeper directed him to the place.

He purchased a razor and comb for himself, toothbrushes for them both, a hairbrush and hairpins for Rebecca. And ribbons.

Mrs Molloy made good her promise to find them clothes.

By the time the sun had set, the last vestiges of the sea were washed away and clean clothes replaced ones ruined by salt water.

'It feels wonderful,' Rebecca said. 'I wonder if I have ever had a bath that felt as glorious or clothes that felt as good against my skin.'

He could agree. He was glad to be rid of his beard and the only clothes that would feel more right to him would be his uniform.

They returned to the public rooms to dine. The rooms were more crowded than before, with both men and women sharing food and drink, but the people were warm and welcoming. Their story of surviving the shipwreck had spread and they spent the meal answering questions about the event.

Lady Rebecca, so at ease among these simple villagers, surprised him at every turn. When had he known any aristocratic lady like her? Even his mother, who merely aspired to the aristocracy, looked down her nose at those she perceived as inferior. Of course, Lady Rebecca did not remember being of high birth. That must explain it.

They were treated to endless tankards of ale and the inn's brew was particularly hoppy and refreshing. All the voices in the room grew louder as the night wore on, but Lucien could hear Rebecca's laugh above the din.

A lovely sound, one he remembered from the packet. So she had been the lady with the captivating laugh. She swayed and caught herself by leaning against a table.

Lucien came to her side. 'It is time to retire, my lady.'

She nodded with a grateful look and coloured with the hum of approval that followed in their wake.

'I feel so unsteady,' she said as they entered the hall and started up the stairs.

'It is the ale.' He kept a firm hold on her.

'It was quite delicious ale, was it not?' She reached for the banister. 'I wonder if I liked ale before, because I quite like it now.'

'I noticed, my lady.'

She stopped on the stairs. 'It feels so odd for you to call me "my lady."'

'Because you do not remember,' he said.

'I do not like it.' She leaned against him and tipped her head up to look him in the face. 'It makes me different from everyone else.'

'That is not so bad a thing,' he reassured.

'I suppose I am different.' She kept staring into his eyes. 'I have no memory.'

'Even so, you have done well in every situation you've encountered,' he told her.

'Have I?' She smiled and swayed closer to him, tantalisingly close.

He took a bracing breath and eased her away. 'It is time you were abed.'

Her eyes widened and her lips parted.

God help him.

He clasped her arm. 'Come.'

After a few steps, she leaned against him again, but he managed to walk her to her room without taking her in his arms and pressing his lips against hers.

He took her key and opened the door. 'I'll send Mrs Molloy to assist you.'

She put her arms around him and pulled him inside the room. 'You could assist me, Lucien. Like before.'

His head dipped down and she reached up and brushed her lips against his.

God help him.

Before he lost all control, he gripped her upper arms and eased her away. 'No.'

She put her hands to her temples. 'Did I just kiss you? Forgive me, Lucien. I cannot imagine why I acted that way. I am not so scandalous, I would hope.'

'You merely had too much ale.' That did not explain his desire, though.

'Perhaps I *am* scandalous.' She sat on the bed. 'Then it would do no harm for me to kiss you again, would it?' She half-reclined on the bed, resting on her elbows.

Was she trifling with him now? He'd once been propositioned by a countess looking for a new plaything. He'd easily turned down that woman. It was proving more difficult to resist Lady Rebecca.

'Perhaps you are virtuous,' he countered, 'and need to preserve your reputation.'

She sat up. 'You are correct, of course.' Her enticing hazel eyes looked up at him, shining like exotic jewels.

He turned and walked to the doorway. 'I will send for Mrs Molloy.'

'Goodnight, Lucien.' Her voice was low and soft, stirring him even more.

He managed only a nod before closing the door. He needed a barrier between them this night.

Chapter Five

When Claire woke the next day her head ached and she wished there was one memory she could banish from her mind. She'd acted like a brazen trollop with Lucien. Goodness! She'd wanted him to kiss her and hold her and spend the whole night in her bed. She still could feel his breath against her lips and the warmth of his touch.

Surely that was brazen? Was she truly such a woman?

She tried again to remember something about herself that could answer that question.

There was nothing.

Lucien hired a carriage to take them to Dublin. Claire felt almost as grief-stricken saying goodbye to the Molloys as she'd felt leaving the fishermen. Captain Molloy, his cousin, Mrs Molloy, the fishermen and the others at the inn were the people in her life, the only ones, except for Lucien. Now she was headed to a city she did not remember to eventually reunite with a brother who was a complete stranger to her.

After the buildings of Bray receded into the distance and she'd wrestled her emotions into some sort of order, she became aware of how close Lucien was seated next to her and of how comfortable it was for her to be beside him. She did not want to face saying goodbye to him, but that would come soon enough.

Lucien was everything to her. She, on the other hand, was merely an obstacle to his returning to London and back to the life at sea he so loved.

She must take care and never let it slip that she wanted him to stay with her longer.

She looked out the window at the countryside rolling past. Had she seen it before?

She did not know.

Their journey would take half the day and so far Lucien had said little to her. Of course, she, as well, only spoke to him when absolutely necessary. What could she say? That she regretted trying to seduce him? Or that she regretted not succeeding? Perhaps she should say she was sorry to be such a burden.

After changing horses one last time and taking some refreshment at the coaching inn, they finally reached the bustling streets of Dublin.

'I wonder if I will remember anything here,' she murmured, more to herself than to him.

'Perhaps something will spark a memory,' he responded.

She studied the scenes passing by her window. 'Nothing I see is a surprise.' Not the wagons or carriages or riders or people walking. 'I simply cannot remember another time I saw such things.'

His eyes looked sympathetic and she felt a pang of guilt.

'I do not mean to sound as if I am complaining,' she explained. 'What is important is that I am alive. I owe that to you.'

He averted his gaze. 'And the fishing boat.'

'And the fishing boat,' she agreed.

The carriage pulled up to a large red-brick town house.

'We are here,' Lucien said.

A footman emerged from the building and opened the carriage door. Lucien climbed out and turned to help her disembark, then he reached in and picked up the two small parcels that contained their meagre belongings.

They wore the clothes that the Molloys had found for them. The clothes they wore in the shipwreck were gone. The footman looked them up and down with haughty contempt, no doubt due to those plain clothes of a simple fishing villager.

'Your luggage?' the footman said with a sneer.

'We have none.' Lucien turned to the coachman and paid him out of some coins he took from his pocket.

The man grinned. 'I thank you, sir!'

Lucien then straightened and glared at the footman with an expression that would make any man quake. 'We require two rooms and I am well able to pay.'

The footman nodded curtly. 'Follow me.'

They entered a large hall with marble floors covered in part with a brightly hued floral carpet that looked like it came from the looms at Axminster.

Axminster? Somehow she knew such carpets were made at Axminster. That was not a memory, though. It was knowledge.

Along the walls were pale green sofas and tables with brass embellishments. It was all quite opulent and Claire had the sense she'd never seen anything go grand.

But that was not a memory, was it? More like an absence of memory.

There also was an impressive mahogany desk and a finely dressed man rising from its chair.

Lucien strode over to him. 'Mr Castle.'

The man peered at him for a moment before gasping. 'Captain Roper? You are returned.' He continued to look puzzled.

'Unexpectedly,' Lucien replied. 'Forgive our simple clothing.' He turned to Claire. 'Lady Rebecca, let me present Mr Castle, the hotel owner. I stayed here when previously in Dublin.'

Before the shipwreck, he meant.

'Mr Castle.' Claire curtsied.

Lucien turned back to Mr Castle. 'This is Lady Rebecca Pierce, the Earl of Keneagle's sister. We will need two rooms, Mr Castle. And a great deal more.'

Mr Castle's gaze darted between them. 'Your luggage?'

Lucien was quick to reply. 'We have none. Our ship to England foundered. We survived, but lost everything.'

'Foundered?' Mr Castle turned to her, an expression of sympathy on his face. 'Oh, my. Were you on the *Dun Aengus*? We heard it wrecked. What a terrible ordeal. The hotel will assist you in any way we are able.'

'We are most in need of clothing.' Lucien gestured to the plain brown, ill-fitting coat he wore.

'I will make enquiries as to how we might attire you quickly.' Mr Castle took keys from a drawer in his desk.

'That would be so kind of you,' Claire said.

Mr Castle smiled and signalled to the footman to escort them to their rooms on the second floor.

Their rooms were again next to each other. Lucien would not be so far away.

He stood in her doorway. 'I will leave you here to rest. There is time for me to visit the bank.'

Her stomach fluttered.

How silly to have nerves simply because he

was leaving her alone. This was not some wilderness—or the open sea—but a respectable hotel.

She could try to do something useful. 'Perhaps I should write to my brother. There is bound to be pen and ink somewhere.' She began opening drawers until finding the one with paper, pen and ink. 'What should I say? I don't have his direction.' She gave a dry laugh. 'Or his given name. He will think me odd to call him Lord Keneagle.'

He remained in the doorway.

She turned to him and made herself smile. 'But you must go.'

He hesitated longer before finally speaking. 'I will write to your brother, if you like.'

'Would you?' Her muscles relaxed. And she hadn't realised she'd been tense. She caught herself, though. 'I cannot ask you to do so much for me.'

'I offered.' He shrugged. 'I will write it before I go to the bank and have it sent by messenger.'

Lucien returned to his room and opened the desk there, removing a pen, ink and paper.

It made sense for him to write the letter, even if it was to the descendent of the man who'd created the genesis of his mother's unhappiness.

Perhaps his own, as well.

Neither he nor Lady Rebecca had anything to do with that event, however. They'd not even been born. It was his mother who'd kept the angry fires burning all these years.

He uncapped the ink and dipped the quill into it. As concisely as he could, he described the shipwreck, Lady Rebecca's amnesia and their whereabouts in the weeks since.

The Earl would send for her, Lucien was certain. Would he send someone to accompany her? Without a memory it would be hard for her to travel alone. Perhaps Lucien would be compelled to go with her and see the estate that had reaped the benefits of his family's financial demise.

He finished the letter and wrote its direction on the envelope.

Leaving his room, he made his way back to Mr Castle's desk. 'There is something you can do for me, Mr Castle.'

'I am at your service.' The man smiled.

He handed Castle the letter. 'Send this by messenger. To the Earl of Keneagle. Make certain it reaches his hands.'

Mr Castle took the letter. 'It will be done.'

Lucien left the hotel and walked the two miles to Number Two College Green, the Bank of Ireland.

The clerk he had dealt with before greeted him with the same level of surprise Mr Castle had shown. 'Captain Roper? I thought you were already in England.'

Lucien repeated the story of the shipwreck, explaining his duty to see the Earl of Keneagle's sister back safely to her family. He did not mention her amnesia.

'I need access to funds,' Lucien explained. 'All was lost in the shipwreck.'

As well as seeking funds for his own use, he arranged for generous rewards to be sent to Captain Molloy and his fishermen. And to Molloy's cousin and his wife as well. When everything was settled, he returned to the hotel.

When he entered the hall, Mr Castle called him over.

'I hired a messenger for you. He has started the journey.' He handed Lucien a piece of paper. 'And I procured the name and direction of a second-hand shop that sells clothing that should meet your standards. I can arrange a hackney coach to take you there today, if you like.'

They desperately needed clothes. What Lady Rebecca wore now was serviceable, but certainly inappropriate for an earl's daughter.

'I am very grateful, Mr Castle,' Lucien responded. 'I will ask the lady what she wishes and have your answer directly.'

He hurried up the stairs and knocked on her door.

She opened it. 'Lucien. You are back.'

Had she expected he would leave her alone all day? 'Mr Castle has found a shop where we might purchase clothing second-hand. We can go there right now, if you desire it.'

* * *

Claire did not mind the clothing she wore. The dress fit her well enough, even though it was nothing like the dress she had worn during the shipwreck. That dress must have once been very elegant. It would be expected of her to wear fine clothing, she suspected.

'I will get my hat.'

Claire donned the bonnet Mrs Molloy had given her and returned to the hall with Lucien.

'I sent a messenger with the letter to your brother,' he told her as they waited for the hackney coach. 'He should receive it tomorrow.'

That gave her a whirlwind of nerves and no pleasure. Meeting her brother and losing Lucien.

'I do appreciate that, Lucien.' Although she felt disingenuous saying so.

'And I have arranged ample funds,' he added. 'We can purchase whatever we need.'

She lowered her gaze. 'You must let me repay you.'

He shook his head. 'I said before. No need.'

But there must be some way to repay him.

When they entered the shop, a male clerk greeted Lucien by name. 'Captain Roper? Mr Castle said to expect you today or tomorrow. What may we show you?' Obviously Mr Castle had provided his name when he arranged the visit.

'We need everything,' Lucien said.

A female clerk took Claire in hand, while Lucien went with the man.

'You were in a shipwreck, we were told, my lady,' the woman said. 'How very frightening for you.'

Perhaps she was lucky not to remember it. 'Yes. But we were saved.'

'Well.' The clerk pressed her hands together. 'We shall have to find you a new wardrobe. You will see, of course, that all our garments are clean and mended.'

The items were, indeed, almost like new, but Claire had no idea what to select. She feared the cost as well. These appeared to have been very expensive dresses.

The clerk suggested she at least purchase two of everything. Two shifts. Petticoats. Stays. Stockings. Another pair of walking boots and two pairs of slippers. Another nightdress to add to the one Mrs Molloy had given her. A robe to wear over it. A shawl. A cloak. The list seemed staggering.

After nearly an hour she'd selected the other necessities, but still had not settled on dresses or hats. She loved the finest dresses, much like the one she'd been wearing when she woke up on the raft, but her eye kept being drawn to more sensible, simple, nondescript designs.

She chose one to try on and stood before a mirror.

Her image looked as she expected. It also made her sad, but why she could not say. There was nothing wrong with the dress. It was very... serviceable.

'My lady, are you certain you want such a dress? It is so drab.' The clerk pointed to two other gowns draped over a chair. 'There are so many other prettier ones.'

'I am trying to be practical.' But the other dresses were lovely.

'I will ask your gentleman what he thinks.' The clerk left the room before Claire could stop her and explain that Lucien was not *her gentleman*.

Claire turned to the mirror again and frowned. The dress *was* drab.

Lucien entered through the curtain behind her. 'You need me?'

He was attired in a tolerably well-fitting deep blue coat with a matching waistcoat, grey trousers that hugged his thighs and brown leather Hessian boots that covered his calves. His neckcloth was as bright white as the shirt beneath.

He took away her breath.

She swallowed and finally could speak. 'I am uncertain what to choose.'

His gaze swept over her. 'Not that one, certainly.'

She felt her cheeks flush.

The clerk stepped forward. 'I would suggest these.'

She showed him the dresses draped over the chair and brought out some others.

Claire tried on dress after dress, watching the admiration in Lucien's eyes when she donned the prettiest ones. His opinion as to what she was to select was the most important criteria. All the dresses were beautiful to her.

She twirled around in an evening dress of pink silk with an overdress of white gauze trimmed in lace.

'This seems too extravagant, Lucien,' she said, although she yearned to wear such a lovely gown.

'We do not know how much of your wardrobe was on the ship,' he responded. 'You need clothes. Enough to cover any situation.'

But so many at once? It would cost a fortune!

In the end he bought her two day dresses—one a gossamer white muslin with embroidery on the bodice and hem, the other a sprigged muslin with a matching green spencer—two travelling dresses—one dark blue silk with gold stripes, the other, a patterned dark green silk—and the beautiful evening dress. In addition to the essentials she'd already selected, he added slippers to match the dresses, hats, gloves, even reticules.

The clothing needed only minor alterations. 'I will send the seamstress to you at the hotel tomorrow,' the clerk said. 'Every dress will be perfect.'

Claire had entered the shop dressed as a tavern maid. To leave, she wore the dark blue travelling dress and the new half-boots, with a lovely bonnet and gloves to match. While Lucien made the final arrangements to have the clothing packed in portmanteaux and delivered to the hotel, Claire took a final glance at her image in the mirror.

This dress and the others were probably out of fashion, having made it to the second-hand shop, but she thought every piece was exquisite.

Had she once worn such elegant clothes? If so, why did she feel so strange in them? Was it because of all the weeks dressed so comfortably as a fisherman, then as a tavern maid?

She loved the feel of the fine fabric against her skin and she'd felt beautiful when Lucien looked at her approvingly.

She could not remember feeling beautiful before.

Lucien glanced at her, looking at herself in the mirror, so pleased with these clothes that were some wealthy aristocrat's cast-offs. Surely she'd once been accustomed to the latest fashion in finery.

Her face was flushed with colour and her eyes sparkled. She even carried herself differently. More regally. She was exceptionally lovely, even more so than when he'd glimpsed her on the packet ship, when her complexion had not been brightened by the sun and when she had been so carefully coifed. And confident. Now she was unconscious of her allure. And of her status. Little did she know a woman of her station would scorn purchasing clothes at a second-hand shop rather than delight in the experience.

Her pleasure was disarming, though. As was her concern about being too extravagant. His prize money was more than he could imagine ever spending. It caused him no sacrifice to enable her to look presentable as she re-entered her former life.

Perhaps such clothing would help her remember who she was.

And that she belonged in a world that valued a title over character, where one married to improve one's status, a higher title, more lofty connections. He disdained such shallow pretensions. He would shun such a world even if its door opened to him.

Lucien completed the transactions and approached her. 'The shop will send someone to deliver the purchases.

Her eyes shone. 'Thank you, Lucien. I assume I wore pretty clothes before, but I do not remember them. Surely they could not have been as pretty. I love all you purchased for me. I am very grateful.'

'You look well in them.'

The colour heightened in her cheeks, making her look even more beautiful.

She thanked the clerks and took Lucien's arm, walking with him to the door of the shop and a waiting hackney coach.

When they reached the hotel, the same footman who had met them with such disdain earlier in the day now showed them every respect.

'He does not look at us with contempt this time,' he murmured to Rebecca. 'Because now we are dressed the part.'

'I suppose one is always judged by appearances,' she responded. 'I would like to think I would not judge so precipitously, but I suppose I am like everyone else.'

Except she wasn't like everyone else, at least not everyone else in her class. She'd accepted the fishermen, the innkeepers and the villagers just as they were.

Because she could not remember to disdain them?

They ate dinner in the hotel dining room, the first formal meal they'd eaten together. Lucien noticed that men at other tables stole admiring glances at her, perhaps a bit more subtly than the men in Molloy's inn had done. She seemed oblivious of the fact this time.

They chatted throughout the meal about the day's events and their unusual adventures.

'I wonder how our fishermen are doing,' she said, taking a sip of wine. 'I miss them all. I hope they received good money for the fish.'

They'd soon receive good money from Lucien. 'I hope so.'

She glanced away. 'Think what would have happened if they had not found us.'

The sea would have claimed them.

He did not want her to dwell on that. 'Luck was with us.'

She lifted her wine glass. 'To luck—and fishermen.'

He lifted his glass as well.

When dinner was over they walked back to their rooms.

'There will be a maid coming in to tend to you,' he told her.

She smiled. 'I promise I will not ask you to do it this time.'

The memory of that night flooded back. 'We did what we had to do. But it is over now and life should feel more like it should.'

She sighed. 'If I knew what it should feel like.'

They reached her door and she handed him the key. He unlocked the door and opened it. Better he escape to his own room. Resist temptation.

She stepped across the threshold, but turned back to him. 'Do you mind if I do something?'

He had no idea what she had in mind.

She did not wait for an answer, but stepped back to him. Her arms encircled his neck and he bent down to her.

'Thank you, Lucien,' she murmured. 'My rescuer. My modiste.'

She placed her lips on his.

* * *

Lucien's body flared into arousal. How easy it would be to lift her in his arms, carry her to her bed and make love to her.

Was that her wish? It was hardly the behaviour of a proper lady. Had she forgotten what was expected of a lady of her status?

She broke off the kiss and stepped away. 'I—I am so grateful to you. That is all. That is why—' She blinked. 'That is why I kissed you.'

He nodded slowly. It had not felt like a kiss of gratitude, but was that his fault? Was that because it aroused him?

'Will I see you in the morning?' Her tone was uncertain.

'For breakfast?' he asked. 'I rise early.'

She smiled. 'It would be nice to share breakfast, unless you have more errands.'

He ought to put more distance between them, but, at the moment, he was fighting to keep his hands off her.

'No errands,' he responded. 'Breakfast, then.'

Lucien left her, but did not go to his own room. He walked back downstairs to ask the footman attending the hall to have a bottle of brandy sent up to his room.

* * *

Claire leaned against the closed door, covering her face with her hands.

She'd done it again. Kissed him.

She'd meant the kiss as one of gratitude, just

as she'd told him, but touching him, feeling his lips on hers, had enflamed her senses. She did not wish to feel this way towards Lucien. She esteemed him too greatly.

He'd been everything to her.

Was this the sort of woman she was? It must be, because it seemed so natural to her, much more natural than donning pretty dresses.

But she must have always worn pretty dresses.

A knock at the door made her jump. Had Lucien come back? Her heart beat faster.

She opened the door to a young woman. The maid.

'You asked for a maid, my lady?' the young woman said.

'Yes. Yes. Come in.' Claire stepped aside, trying not to show her disappointment.

She'd wanted it to be Lucien.

Chapter Six

The next morning when Lucien knocked on Lady Rebecca's door, a maid answered. From behind the maid, the lady said, 'I am ready, Lucien.' She addressed the maid. 'Thank you, Ella.'

'M'lady.' The maid curtsied and stepped past Lucien out of the room.

Lady Rebecca wore another of her new dresses, a white one with dots of green all over it. Her hair was not pinned into a knot at the nape of her neck. Instead it had been piled atop her head with curling tendrils escaping and framing her face.

For a moment her expression turned sad, but she quickly seemed to school her features into the very picture of an aristocratic young lady— a beautiful one.

It was his turn to feel sad. He missed the girl in the fisherman's clothes.

Not that he would tell her. 'You look very nice today.'

She turned back to the mirror. 'Do I? The dress is pretty, but my hair looks wrong. Too fancy.'

'It looks as it should,' he responded, not much of a compliment, but she glanced away as if not even hearing him.

They ate breakfast in the dining room, where a sideboard had been set up, much as was done in aristocratic houses. Not that he'd been in many.

She continued to look preoccupied during their meal.

'Are you feeling unwell?' he asked.

'Unwell?' She glanced up in surprise. 'No. I am very well.' She smiled wanly. 'Troubled by what is ahead of me, perhaps.'

How he wished he could fix it. Bring back her memories, even though he'd lose this version of Lady Rebecca.

'It looks to be fine day,' he said. 'Would you like to take a walk? Explore Dublin a little?'

Her smile turned more genuine. 'I would love that.'

Lucien knew from his previous stay at the Castle Hotel that this part of Dublin catered to the titled and wealthy. If Lady Rebecca had ever visited Dublin—it would be odd if she had not—she likely would have walked these same streets. Perhaps something would jog her memory.

She gave no signs of recognising anything, though. Just the opposite—she reacted as if everything was new.

They stopped to look in the window of a print shop, showing cartoons, one of the Prince Regent, before and after he became Regent, another of several people trying to board a ship.

Lady Rebecca pointed to the one of the Prince Regent. 'I know that is the Regent and I understand the cartoon. It is so odd I cannot actually recall another time I saw a caricature.'

He did not call attention to the one about a ship. It made him think of the shipwreck. She had enough to cause her distress.

There were more prints of Dr. Syntax, that popular fictional character who appeared in cartoons satirising British life.

She frowned at the one of Dr Syntax trying to romance a dairy maid. 'I know of Dr Syntax, as well.'

'Perhaps that is encouraging.' He believed her memory would return. She'd eventually remember she was an earl's daughter, a privileged lady.

She shivered. 'It is cold for summer, is it not?'

It was August.

'The whole summer has been unusually cold,' he agreed.

His uncles had worried about failed crops and rising prices. At least the money he'd given them would keep them in food and supplies until better weather returned.

They continued walking and he resisted putting his arm around her to warm her.

One of the shops showed a window display of paisley shawls and other ladies' accessories. He pulled her to the doorway. 'You need a shawl.'

She resisted. 'Lucien! You have bought me enough! You purchased one shawl.'

'You need another.' What woman did not want more than one shawl? Even his mother had loved the exotic shawls and other gifts his father had sent from faraway lands.

Almost as much as she'd valued the trinkets Viscount Waverland had purchased for her.

There were colourful shawls displayed on pegs all around the shop. She blinked at them, looking overwhelmed.

'Do you see any you like?' he asked.

Before she could answer, a female clerk approached. 'M'lady, welcome back to my shop. How may I assist you?'

Lady Rebecca blinked as if in confusion.

The clerk recognised her. Did she not realise that?

Lucien quickly spoke for her. 'The lady is looking for a shawl, something to complement this dress.' He turned to her. 'Is that not so, my lady?'

'Yes. Yes.' She cleared her throat. 'To complement this dress.'

'I have several that would look lovely with that dress.' The clerk pulled five shawls, all with designs that favoured her green spencer and the green dots on her dress.

She made a quick decision. 'This one will do.'

Its background colour was green, but the rest was embroidered with a melee of colourful flowers in pinks and purples and vivid aquas and oranges.

'An excellent choice,' the clerk said. 'This shawl is from Kashmir and is one of our finest. I believe you purchased one very like it the last time you visited. Different colours, of course.'

Lucien saw the confusion return to Lady Rebecca's eyes.

'We will take that one,' he told the clerk.

'Shall I wrap it?' the clerk asked. 'Or have it delivered?'

'She will wear it.' Lucien pulled his purse from his jacket pocket.

The clerk turned to Lady Rebecca as she waited for Lucien to pay her. 'And how did you find London, m'lady?'

'London?' Her voice rose. 'Oh...very pleasant indeed. London is very pleasant.'

Lucien handed the clerk the money.

'It was a short trip, then, was it not?' the clerk added.

'Very short,' Lucien replied for Lady Rebecca.

He wrapped the shawl over her shoulders and they walked out of the door.

'Lucien!' She stopped him a few steps from

the shop. 'She recognised me. I was in that shop before. I purchased something before.'

'Was the shop familiar? Was anything familiar?'

Her expression looked anguished. 'No. Nothing. As though I'd never seen it before.'

Over the next three days, they walked as many streets of Dublin as they could and visited any sights she might have visited before.

Nothing seemed familiar to Claire. The closest she came was when they happened upon a coaching inn. She knew at a glimpse that it catered to public stagecoaches and the mail coaches, but how she should know that, they could not fathom.

'It is not the sort of inn you would visit,' Lucien told her.

'Is it not?' she asked. 'Why is it not the sort I would visit?'

'It is for more common folk.'

So perhaps she'd merely guessed that it was that sort of inn. She didn't remember it, but neither did she remember not being common folk.

Their efforts to discover something she remembered had been to no avail that day, but Claire relished the time they spent together. She was glad he did not purchase anything else for her. Goodness! The Kashmir shawl was extravagant enough.

Had he meant the shawl as a gift or had he

merely felt obligated to outfit her as the lady she was supposed to be? Perhaps she would never know which, but she was certain she would treasure the shawl the rest of her days.

They explored yet one more street of shops.

This time he stopped in front of a jewellery shop. 'That is what we forgot,' he said. 'You should have jewellery.'

'No, Lucien.' She tried to pull him past the shop. He'd spent enough on her.

He resisted. 'It will look odd if you have no jewellery at all. It does not need to be extravagant.'

'Please, Lucien,' she said. 'You cannot spend so much on me.'

'I can make one more purchase.' He took her inside.

Glittering necklaces, bracelets and rings were arrayed on black velvet in glass-covered display cases.

She must have looked awed, because Lucien murmured to her, 'Surely as the daughter of an earl you wore such jewels.'

'I feel as if I wouldn't dare wear such expensive things,' she responded.

'We will select something modest, then.' He picked out a simple pearl pendant and matching earrings. They were quite the loveliest things.

Before they left the shop, he fastened the pendant around her neck, his fingers against her skin sending a thrill down her spine.

The thought of him touching her ears to help her with the earrings made her feel giddy. And she'd been so careful over the last few days to keep from overstepping her bounds with him.

'I—I think I should carry the earrings safely in my reticule,' she said.

She fingered the pearl pendant that she would treasure for ever. The pearls, gifts from the sea, would remind her of him for ever.

It was mid-afternoon when they returned to the Castle Hotel. Mr Castle was seated at his desk, but he rose when he saw them.

'Captain. M'lady.' He called them over. 'There is a gentleman waiting for you in the drawing room.'

Lucien halted. 'Who?'

'Lord Keneagle,' Mr Castle replied.

Claire's heart pounded. This was the moment she'd dreaded. This brother she did not remember had probably come to take her away to a home she could not recall. Worse than that, this meant saying goodbye to Lucien, her anchor.

Lucien walked with her to the drawing-room door, but stopped her before they entered. 'Are you ready for this?'

She drew in a long breath and nodded, although she thought she could never be ready.

A thin, russet-haired, impeccably dressed gentleman rose from a sofa.

'Lord Keneagle?' Lucien asked.

The man gave him no heed, instead strode up to Claire. 'What are you about this time, Rebecca?' he sneered.

'Sir!' Lucien's voice broke in like a hard blow.

Her brother looked stricken for a moment, but collected himself quickly. 'And you are Roper, I presume?'

'*Captain* Roper.' Lucien straightened. 'If you received my letter, you know what happened to your sister.'

'My half-sister,' Keneagle corrected.

Claire stared at this man—she was nearly his height—but she was staring at a stranger. She'd feared meeting a brother—*half*-brother—she didn't know, but she'd also yearned to know she belonged to somebody. She never expected he'd not be pleased to see her. What sort of man would not welcome his sister—even his half-sister—presumed lost at sea?

'Explain yourself, Rebecca,' he demanded.

She faced him. 'You know I cannot explain myself. I am certain Captain Roper wrote about my loss of memory in his letter. It has been a nightmare. It does have some benefits, I am newly discovering.' She looked him directly in the eye. 'I do not remember you.'

Her insult seemed to escape him. 'Do not give me that nonsense about losing your memory—'

Lucien stepped closer and Keneagle shot him

a wary glance, turning back to her with a slightly more moderate tone. 'You can see how I would think it your latest ploy, can you not? To escape doing what I've obliged you to do?'

'What you've obliged me to do?' she repeated.

He shook his head. 'You pretend not to know what I speak of?'

'As I explained to you in my letter, sir, her loss of memory is genuine,' Lucien stated icily.

Keneagle swung back to him with a sneer. 'I thought you were a captain, not a *physician*.'

Lucien glared directly into his eyes. 'Captain of the HMS *Foxfire*.'

Keneagle stepped back in apparent surprise. 'The renowned *Foxfire*? From the war?'

'The same.'

Claire wished she could have remembered reading of Lucien's ship. She'd had no idea he was renowned.

Her brother recovered his nasty tone. 'Precisely what is your connection to this woman?'

Claire responded this time. 'He saved me. I would have drowned otherwise!'

Keneagle scoffed. 'I was informed you had drowned. It was vastly more convenient that way.'

Lucien made a dangerous sound. Like a growl.

Keneagle's rant continued. 'For all I know this shipwreck story is to cover up cohabiting with this man—'

'Good God, man,' Lucien broke in. 'How dare

you make such an accusation? I have accompanied Lady Rebecca to see her safely to you.'

Keneagle lifted his hands in submission. 'I meant only that if her reputation is ruined, Stonecroft will never marry her.'

'Stonecroft?' Claire cried. 'Who is Stonecroft?'

She was expected to marry this Stonecroft? How could she? She remembered nothing of this. Of that man.

Her half-brother laughed drily. 'Very well. I will play your game. Baron Stonecroft of Gillford. He was awaiting you in London. I was compelled to inform him of your death. You will be very lucky if he has not married someone else.'

None of this made any sense to her. None of it. 'I agreed to marry Baron Stonecroft?'

Surely she would remember a man she had agreed to marry. Would that not be the most important decision a woman could make in her life?

Keneagle peered at her, his expression turning shrewd. 'Of course you agreed to marry Stonecroft. Why otherwise would you have been on the packet to England?' He darted Lucien a scathing look. 'If this man has ruined you, tell me now. Otherwise, I will post a letter to Stonecroft this very day and inform him you are alive. We can only hope he will still accept you after this debacle.'

How dare this man accuse Lucien when Lucien had been completely responsible for saving her life?

Her temperature rose. 'I assure you Captain Roper has been honourable. My virtue is intact.' She was the one who'd lacked propriety.

Lucien's eyes blazed at Keneagle. 'Stop these accusations. Now.'

Keneagle shrugged. 'What I believe is of no consequence. You had better hope Stonecroft believes your story.'

Lucien broke in, his voice firm. 'Enough. So you will write to Stonecroft. Will you wait in Dublin or in the country?'

Keneagle's brows rose. 'I am not waiting.' He reached into a pocket and pulled out a purse, shoving it towards Claire. 'This should pay the way to London for you and the maid.'

The maid? 'What maid?' she asked.

He rolled his eyes. 'Oh, yes. You would have *forgotten* her, as you say.' He shoved the purse at her.

She froze. 'Did—did she accompany me?' Her heart pounded again. 'What happened to her?'

Her half-brother huffed. 'Well, we never heard from her.'

'She drowned,' Claire whispered, her insides twisting in pain.

She'd had a maid who likely drowned in the packet ship and she could not even remember her.

Keneagle pulled the purse back. 'You won't need all that money, then.'

Lucien reached out and took the purse from his hand. 'She will need all of this money and more. Everything she'd packed was lost.'

Keneagle opened his mouth as if to protest, but Lucien's expression brooked no argument.

'Oh, very well,' her brother said. 'I will arrange for a money draft in her name.'

'See that you do.' Lucien glared at the man. 'What of her dowry?'

'Dowry?' she cried. She had a dowry?

She'd never thought about it, but certainly, as the daughter of an earl, she'd have a dowry.

Keneagle finally spoke. 'I will write to the solicitors. Stonecroft will expect a dowry. I'll see he gets it. Assuming you do marry him.' He glanced around the room. 'Customarily I stay at Castle Hotel when in Dublin. Much easier than opening the town house, but this time I prefer the house.'

Her family had a Dublin town house? Had they walked past it in the last couple of days?

Her brother ran a hand through his hair and turned to a table containing his hat and gloves. He picked them up.

He was leaving?

After this meeting, if she never saw him again, she'd be glad of it.

Keneagle pointed to the purse. 'You make this work with Stonecroft, because the draft I send you and this purse are all the funds you will receive from me.' He made a mocking bow to her and a more respectful one to Lucien. 'Good day.'

Claire's emotions swirled inside her. Anger at her brother's ill treatment of her and of Lucien. Shock that he so easily washed his hands of her. Anxiety at the prospect of marrying a man she could not remember.

And, worst of all, grief for the maid who had probably died in the shipwreck. The poor maid who, if it had not been for the need to accompany her to London, would never have been on that ship.

It all was too painful to think about.

Lucien stared at the door through which her brother had departed. 'What a cursed cur.'

He tried to quiet his rage at Keneagle. The damned man showed no caring of his sister, no compassion for her situation. The man had no honour. No honour at all. He was precisely like the stories Lucien's mother told of his grandfather.

The Earls of Keneagle must be bred to be miscreants, caring for no one but themselves. Was that Lady Rebecca's true character, equally as self-centred? He descended into gloom, as if such a transformation had already come to pass.

No matter. She'd already endured much tribulation and now, thanks to her brother, her situation had become even more difficult.

'Am I to travel to London. To be married?' She said this more to herself than to him.

Still, the words *to be married* echoed in his mind.

A marriage of an Irish earl's daughter to an English baron was probably not the best match in the eyes of society. Why this man? Why not one of the highest rank?

She sighed. 'At least I will not have to share a house with the Earl of Keneagle.'

Lucien seethed at the mere thought of the man. 'He came a hair's breadth from being challenged to a duel.'

'I almost wish you had,' she murmured. She seemed to gird herself. 'So I must travel to London to this Lord Stonecroft, this man I am supposed to marry.'

At least it was an aristocratic marriage. That was as it should be for her. When she recovered her memory, an aristocratic marriage would be the sort she would desire. Among the aristocrats, love and true regard were less necessary than status and dowries and what other aristocrats thought.

'Well, I suppose I must make arrangements.' She lifted up the purse, heavy with coin. 'At least I have funds. Perhaps even enough to repay you.'

'Keep your money,' he said too sharply.

She turned her head away.

He'd not meant to snap. God knew he needed to calm down.

He quieted his voice. 'You might need it.'

She kept her gaze averted.

Suddenly he felt her pain. She'd thought she would be taken back to a place where she belonged, one she might some day remember. Now she was facing more unknowns. Quite alone.

His heart ached for her. 'I will escort you to London. If you desire it, that is.'

She turned back to him, her eyes glistening. 'Are you certain, Lucien? I have been such a burden to you.'

He was caught for a moment in those hazel eyes. They'd turned green against her green spencer and the Kashmir shawl. And they glistened with tears. He admired her for trying to put on a brave front.

'I must travel to London anyway,' he responded. Although in that moment he would have done anything for her. 'So it is no burden to escort you. Mr Castle will take care of all the arrangements.'

She lowered her gaze. 'Lucien, you are too good to me.'

They walked out to the hall and Mr Castle called them over. 'There is someone else to see you.' He indicated a man dressed more as a merchant than a gentleman.

The man approached. 'Lady Rebecca, Captain Roper, I am from the *Dublin Journal*. Might I have a few moments of your time to interview you about your ordeal?'

Lucien frowned. What next? 'How did you hear of us?'

The man turned stoic. 'I cannot say who told me of you. He asked not to be revealed.'

Someone from the hotel? Or the second-hand shop. Or the bank. His bet was on the hotel's footman, the man who'd scorned them on their arrival because of their clothing.

Lucien turned to Lady Rebecca. 'Do you wish to speak to a reporter?'

'I already have the story,' the man told them. 'I know you were both passengers on the *Dun Aengus* and when the ship sank, you were reported lost at sea. Instead a fishing boat picked you up and you were forced to wait until the fishing was over before coming to Dublin.' He looked sly. 'The story needs embellishment. It might as well be with the truth.'

Lucien took Lady Rebecca by the arm and led her a short distance away. 'I will send him packing if you desire it.'

She shook her head. 'He will only invent something to write. The truth is better.'

Lucien walked back to the reporter. 'We will speak with you.'

They returned to the drawing room where the man pulled out a notebook and pencil. 'Tell me how you survived the shipwreck,' he began.

Lucien related the tale, ending with their arrival in Dublin.

The reporter turned to Lady Rebecca. 'How was it for a lady such as yourself, to endure such hardships?'

'I was so grateful to be alive.' She spoke fondly of the fishermen and everyone who helped them. 'I would not be alive if not for Captain Roper. You know who he is, of course. The Captain of the famous *Foxfire*.'

Lucien wished she had not mentioned that. It would only bring more attention to the story.

The reporter asked for more details about their stay on the fishing boat and they both obliged him with a more respectable version of their stay than the truth.

'And you are still together?' the reporter asked, clearly wanting more details.

'Lady Rebecca is a lady alone,' Lucien replied. 'As a gentleman I must see her to where she belongs.'

'So you will take her back to Keneagle House?' the man asked.

'To London,' Lucien responded. 'We were both headed to London before the shipwreck.'

That was enough for the reporter to know.

He didn't need to know about Lady Rebecca's amnesia. Or how despicably her half-brother had just behaved towards her. Or how close Lucien had come to doing precisely what her brother had accused him of.

Chapter Seven

Mr Castle had booked them passage on a packet ship that was leaving in two days. He'd also arranged for Ella, the maid who'd attended her at the hotel, to attend her on the trip.

How nice it was to have the services of a maid, but each time Ella untied her laces, Claire remembered when Lucien had done so.

How tender he had been. In everything.

So opposite to the thoughtlessness and cruelty of her brother.

Her brother's letter to Stonecroft would probably arrive a day or two before they reached London. Stonecroft would know she was alive and he would be told she'd show up on his doorstep. Would she be welcome?

How would it be to see this man without remembering him from before? Had she loved him? Was that the reason she'd agreed to marry him? If so, would she still love him even though she couldn't remember him?

How could she forget a man she loved?

How could she marry a man she could not remember?

What was the use of agonising over this? What other choice did she have? She must marry him.

Unless he refused her, that was.

What would she do if Stonecroft, like her half-brother, believed her ruined merely because Lucien rescued her? What if it became known she and Lucien had shared a cabin on the fishing boat?

Her head ached with these thoughts that had swirled around her mind throughout the two days until the carriage picked them up at the hotel to take them to the packet boat.

The carriage left them off at the dock which was a jumble of sailors, passengers and wagons filled with boxes and barrels and chests.

The maid had gone ahead in another carriage and would meet them at the packet ship with their luggage.

Claire took Lucien's arm to navigate the commotion at the docks. The rough seamen they passed reminded her of the fishermen. How she wished they were both back on the fishing boat with them. She'd been happy on the fishing boat.

She gazed at the bustle on the dock to the ship they were to board. She must have been here once before, but she could not remember it.

Ella, the maid, waited at the gangplank, a young man at her side.

The young man removed his hat.

Ella curtsied.

Ella and the young man were together, Claire realised, and the exact opposite in looks. Ella was fair with almost white-blonde hair and light blue eyes. The young man was black-haired, dark-eyed and swarthy.

Ella spoke. 'M'lady, sir, your luggage is on board.' She glanced nervously at the young man. 'This is Cullen. Rory Cullen. My—my friend. We have something to ask of you. I pray you'll hear him out.'

'Cullen.' Lucien nodded kindly. 'What do you have to ask us?'

The young man straightened. 'I wish to go with Ella.' He spoke with determination. 'I offer my services as your valet, sir, for the time of the trip or as long as you will have me. I ask only for passage over and I will repay that as soon as I am able.'

'We want to stay in England,' Ella added. 'There are good jobs there and Cullen is a hard worker. He will do well.'

Claire heard the yearning in the voices of the young couple. They wished to be together, not separated by the Irish Sea. She turned to Lucien, ready to plead their case, ready to pay for the young man herself, if necessary.

'You may very well meet my needs, Cullen,' said Lucien. 'I have no valet.'

Both the maid and her young man broke into smiles.

'I have already ascertained that there is a berth for me, the cheapest, as well,' Cullen said.

'Only one thing—' Lucien said.

The young couple's smiles dropped.

'If you do work for me, then I must pay you.'

Their smiles returned.

Ella gave Cullen a worshipful look. 'It was Cullen who saw to your luggage. He knows exactly what to do in everything.'

'Then we are already indebted.' Lucien gestured with his arm. 'Shall we board?'

Claire smiled as well, infected by their happiness.

They boarded the ship and made their way to their cabins. Claire's cabin was near Lucien's. Ella and Cullen said theirs were not far.

Ella followed her into her cabin. 'Shall I unpack anything, m'lady?'

Claire shook her head. 'Not for one night.'

Her portmanteau was already in the cabin. Thanks to Lucien, she also had a small trunk with her other clothing stowed in the hold.

'I really do not need you now,' she said. 'Not until bedtime. Please do as you wish.'

Ella's eyes widened. 'Are you certain, m'lady?'

Claire stifled a smile. 'Yes. Do as you wish. I am going on deck. I like to watch the ship leave the harbour.' She felt a chill rush up her spine.

How did she know she liked to watch the ship leave the harbour? Had she remembered it?

She hurried up on deck.

Lucien stood at the railing near the stern of the ship.

She rushed over to him. 'I think I had a memory.'

He turned his entire attention on her. 'A memory? Of what?'

'Nothing of consequence.' It was a very small thing. 'I remembered that I like to watch the ship leave the dock.'

He smiled, but his eyes remained serious. 'Perhaps this is a start.'

'Yes.' But she suddenly did not feel any enthusiasm. She leaned against the railing and watched Dublin recede. 'But I do not precisely remember ever watching a ship leaving the dock.'

He gazed back at the dock, as well. It was still as busy as when they had been there.

'I remember you watching the ship sail. On the *Dun Aengus*,' he said. 'You stood at the railing, much like this. You jumped away when the sea sprayed you with water.'

She had no memory of this.

'You wore a grey cloak with a hood covering your head,' he went on. 'And I did not see your face until I met you again in the companionway.'

It warmed her that he had noticed her then.

She sighed. 'So it was almost a memory. I must

have been on deck because I like to watch the ship leave the dock.'

'It very well could be,' he agreed.

Ella and Cullen emerged from the hatch and walked to the bow of the ship.

How ironic that they'd aim their sights on where the ship was headed, while she watched where it had been. They were filled with optimism for their future, whereas she could only look upon her future with dread. And she had no past at all.

Until she woke up in Lucien's arms on a raft in this very sea.

She scanned the sky. 'It looks like a clear day.'

Had the sky been clear when she'd stood on the deck of the *Dun Aengus*? she wondered. She closed her eyes and tried to remember. When had the storm started? Had she been frightened? Had all the passengers been frightened, even all those poor passengers who'd drowned?

'No storm clouds,' she added.

'This should be an easy crossing,' Lucien assured her. He had already examined the skies and the rigging and the ship's Captain and crew. He was taking no chances with this voyage.

She closed her eyes and they fell silent for a time.

She opened them again. 'I just tried to recall the other crossing. Or the storm. Or being swept overboard. I can't remember.' She shuddered. 'I only remember waking up on the water.'

That was terror enough, Lucien thought.

She turned and glanced at her maid and his new valet.

'Look at how happy they are!' She turned back to him. 'Thank you so much for agreeing to hire him.'

He shrugged. 'I had no desire to crush their hopes.'

'You saw what I saw, then?' she said. 'That they belonged to each other?'

'It was clear as a windless sea.' He even envied them a bit. A lot.

'I hope life will be kind to them,' she said wistfully.

Life had already been kind to them. They'd found each other and they had the foresight to know it would not do to be separated. 'They'll have the strength of being together.'

'But life could still be cruel to them,' she said.

'Having each other will make up for much.'

She gave him a quizzical look. 'I did not realise you possessed such romantic notions.'

He'd talked of this on the raft.

He frowned. 'I told you about my father and mother's loveless marriage and how his absence made her turn to the local lord.'

She nodded. 'I recall you telling me of your parents.'

He gestured towards Ella and Cullen. 'They are the antithesis of my parents. My father was wrong to marry my mother. He was gone most of the time and they were always like strangers. Absence is not good in a marriage.'

Her brows knitted. 'Surely navy men marry all the time.'

'I do not think they should,' he said emphatically. 'I will not marry, not as long as I have a ship to sail in.'

She spoke soberly. 'Perhaps your parents' marriage met their needs at the time. Your father wanted a son. Your mother needed security.'

'I have no doubt those needs were met.' But there was so much more to life than security and heirs. 'But they abandoned happiness.' And they abandoned him. He again directed his gaze at the maid and valet. 'Those two might achieve happiness.'

She turned quiet while she gazed back towards the shore, growing more and more distant.

It seemed a long time before she said anything. 'Different people have different needs, Lucien,' she finally said. 'You, at least, have a choice, a way to support yourself well. Most women, like your mother, do not have choices. Perhaps she did the best she could.'

He felt his cheeks heat. What choice did Lady Rebecca have, besides going to this marriage she could not remember wanting?

She stared out at the sea. 'My choices are not good ones.' She straightened, pushing away from the railing. 'I must make the best of what fate has handed me, though. I must believe that I wanted to marry this man, so I must make the best of it.'

'You cannot love him.' He spoke his thoughts aloud.

'You would think I would remember a man I loved, do you not?' She turned to him and looked straight into his eyes. 'You are lucky, Lucien. You can choose the navy life. The sea. And I hope you never compromise on what you most desire.'

At that moment he wished he could give her what she most desired, as well—her memory.

He could easily give her a choice about her future. He could offer to marry her, like his father married his mother. He could give her a life of comfort and security. And she would not have to be bothered by him much, except the brief times he was on shore.

No. One thing he could never give her was her rightful place in society. Any regard she had for him would certainly perish when she must live on the outskirts of the aristocracy.

Besides, theirs was an attachment created out of necessity and gratitude. Not love.

One thing Lucien knew for certain. If his parents had loved each other—and him—things would have been very different.

They remained at the railing until Dublin and Ireland disappeared and the sun dropped lower in the sky. Claire's mind calmed some from the rhythms of the sea and the ship. She let go of her worries for the moment and simply enjoyed Lucien's companionship.

Ella and Cullen approached them.

'Sir?' Cullen took a respectful tone. 'They have informed us that dinner will be served soon. I will bring the food to you. In your cabins?'

Claire frowned. She'd rather not eat than eat alone in her cabin where her unhappy thoughts would certainly return.

Lucien shot her a look. 'There is a table in my cabin, if you would wish to share the meal with me.'

How did he always know what would make her most comfortable?

She released a breath. 'I would love to share a meal with you.' She turned to Ella. 'There is also a table in my cabin and you and Cullen are welcome to eat there.'

There would not be tables in their cabins.

Ella's eyes lit up. 'Truly, m'lady?'

'Yes. Truly,' she responded. 'If I dine with Captain Roper, I will not need that table. You might as well use it.'

Ella and Cullen brought them their meal and quickly fled to be private together.

Should she have made it so easy for the young maid and her young man to be private together? Perhaps she should have been more protective.

On the other hand, Cullen clearly adored Ella and Claire could not bear to separate them any more than she wished to be separated from Lucien, her anchor.

Claire sat across from Lucien. She lifted her spoon, but stopped mid-air.

How had she known there would not be a table in the servants' cabins? She'd not seen them. 'Lucien, I think I had another memory, as if I'd seen what the servants' cabins would be like. I knew they would not have tables.'

He looked up from his plate. 'Another small piece. Your memory may come back like that. A little at a time.'

She took a bite of the stew. 'I wonder. I am used to what I remember from the raft onwards. Will everything change again when my old memories return?'

'You will be who you were, then.' His tone seemed solemn. 'You will know what you want, what you think, what your hopes are.'

Yes, but she had new hopes. Impossible ones, but she didn't know if those hopes came from fear or desire.

She wished she could stay with Lucien.

But she could not tell him that. Any obligation he felt towards her could not go that far, not so far as for him to give up the sea. Or to marry without love.

'Will I be different, I wonder,' she said instead, 'when my old memories return?'

He stared down at his food. 'Different than you are now, certainly.'

Her throat tightened. Was she to lose this fledgling sense of herself, born of all the frightening and wonderful experiences she'd had with Lucien?

He went on. 'We will dock tomorrow at Holyhead and I will engage a carriage to take us to London.'

A frisson of anxiety ran up her back. 'Very well. It should take days, should it not?'

'About four days.'

Four more days with him. Four more days to get used to having to say goodbye.

When she got her memory back, it *would* change her, Lucien knew. How could it not? She had a lifetime of memories as the daughter of an earl. A few weeks of new memories would count for little.

But did he hope her memories returned soon? No. He wished to spend these last few days with the lady he knew, not the one he feared she would become.

For the rest of the meal he tried to return to their former ease with each other. It was becoming more and more difficult. He, too, missed those days on the fishing boat. When they'd been close. When they'd touched. When he'd slept near her.

Dinner included a bottle of wine and she poured herself glass after glass.

'Tell me about the shipwreck,' she asked. 'You never spoke much about it and, I confess, I did not feel ready to hear it. Tell me what happened. There were storms?'

He'd not spoken of the shipwreck, not in any detail. He'd not wanted to cause her more distress than she'd already experienced.

On the other hand, she'd nearly remembered two things about the ship. Would talking more of it spark still more memories?

Even if remembering changed her back into a selfish, thoughtless aristocrat, how could he refuse?

So he spoke. 'We never should have sailed that day. The sky filled with storm clouds even before we left port. We should have delayed a day, but the Captain...' He paused, picturing the Captain and recalling his concerns about the man. 'Something was wrong with the Captain. He was ill. He must have been ill. At the time I thought he was merely preoccupied, but I was concerned enough to walk the deck and check on the ship and crew. All seemed well.'

'He was ill?'

Lucien nodded. 'I think he was unable to command.' His chest constricted. 'I went below—that is when I encountered you and the other woman in the companionway—I stayed below even when the storm began, but I should have remained on deck. I could have taken command. I could have sailed us out of danger.'

'Would that have been possible?' she asked.

'To sail us out of danger?' He knew he could have done so. 'Yes.'

'No,' she said. 'I meant, was it even possible for you to take over for the Captain? Are there not rules for that?'

'You are right,' he admitted. 'The Navy drove it into us. The Captain is in command. I accepted this, even in the face of danger. I've spent most of my life under this rule.'

He'd believed in the rule of command. Whole-heartedly.

But he'd turned a blind eye to the obvious. The Captain had been ill. Unfit. He should have done something.

'It was not your fault.' She reached across the table and took his hand. 'Look at me, Lucien. It was not your fault.'

But he might have been the only man on board who could have changed what happened.

His insides twisted as he remembered. 'He sailed right into the storm. When I finally went on deck, it was too late. The wind was blowing us closer and closer to the rocks. There was nothing to do but get people to the rowboats. That was when I knocked on your door and told you we had to abandon ship.'

'And I was with that other woman? The governess?' She still held his hand.

He ought to pull away, but she was the lifeline to keep him from drowning in guilt.

'I only caught a glimpse of her.' Had the other woman drowned? 'She handed you the reticule and ran off to get someone else.'

She tightened her grip.

'When we got on deck it was in shambles. The main mast had split. There was debris everywhere. I led you towards the boats, but before we reached them, a big wave washed over the side and plunged us into the sea. Something hit you on your head and knocked you out.'

'Is that why I cannot recall anything?' she asked.

'I do not know.' He looked up at her.

She took her hand away and poured herself another glass of wine.

He put his head in his hands. Sometimes remembering was filled with pain.

She left her chair and walked over to him. She placed her arms around him and her lips close to his ear, said, 'It was not your fault, Lucien.'

He rose from his chair and embraced her, holding her close, letting her comfort seep into him. She smelled of lavender and sea air and he wanted never to let go of her.

Even though he knew he must.

'Oh, Lucien,' she murmured against his chest.

She lifted her face to him. With her arms twined around his neck, she rose on tiptoe. Her lips were near. Tantalisingly near.

And he could not resist. He closed the short distance and crushed his lips against hers, so hungry for her, so needing her solace.

An urgent sound escaped her and she returned the kiss with a matching hunger. He widened his stance and pressed her against him. Every moment of wanting her seemed to explode into need. When had he ever needed a woman more? He could not remember. They were inches from the berth and no one would see them.

He backed her towards it.

'Yes,' she murmured. 'Yes, Lucien.'

His legs touched the side of the berth.

And he stopped. 'No. No, my lady. We will not do this.'

He eased her away from him, his body aching with protest and desire.

She was not some willing widow or tavern maid; she was an earl's daughter with her virtue intact. Her virtue assured her marriage to one of her kind. To lose it meant ruin.

She blinked up at him as if dazed. And wounded. 'I believe I want to, Lucien.'

He shook his head. 'No. You've had too much wine, that is all it is. We must keep our wits about us. This would ruin you. You would regret it.'

'I do not think so. I think I will regret stopping.' She reached for him.

He eluded her embrace and grasped her arm instead. 'Come. It is time you returned to your cabin.'

She looked petulant, ready to defy him, no doubt the aristocrat coming out in her, believing she should have something merely because she wanted it.

He put his arm around her and walked her to the door of her cabin.

He reached for the latch to open it, but she stopped him. 'Wait. We should knock. Ella and Cullen.'

Perhaps their dinner had been less complicated. The rules were different for the common folk like them. Like him. Perhaps they were free to indulge in their desire for each other. If so, he envied them.

He knocked.

The door was almost immediately opened by his new valet.

'Sir.' Cullen stood stiffly, like Lucien's men had done when they toed the line.

The valet looked as put together as he'd been before the meal. Had they not taken advantage of their privacy?

'We have finished our meal,' Lucien told him.

Ella spoke from behind Cullen. 'So have we, Captain. Our dishes are stacked.'

'I will remove them,' Cullen said. 'From your cabin, as well.'

Lucien and Lady Rebecca stepped aside so the valet could pass.

'Goodnight, my lady,' Lucien said, more stiffly than he intended. He backed away from the cabin door.

She gave him an intent look, moved towards him and reached up to touch his face. 'Goodnight, Lucien.'

Chapter Eight

~~~~~~~~~~

Claire strode into the cabin, breathing fast, her head spinning, her emotions in turmoil. He was correct. She'd consumed too much wine. It had quieted her nerves about her future—without Lucien—but had left another disorder. Of yearning.

She could not recall how it had happened, but he'd kissed her. Really kissed her. And her whole body had flared into awareness and desire. She wanted him in the most intimate way. She wanted him to touch her bare skin, as he had when he'd once undressed her. She wanted her tongue to join with his, to taste of him. She wanted—she could not even put it into words. It was too scandalous.

It was what her half-brother had accused them of. And now it was what she wished could happen.

'M'lady?' Ella looked at her with concern. 'Are you unwell?'

She put a hand to her head. 'No. I am quite well. The wine. It went to my head a little.'

'Oh.' Ella stepped towards her. 'Do you need any assistance?'

Claire waved her off. 'No. No. I will sit a moment.' She lowered herself into a chair and put her head into her hands.

'Did you have a row?' Ella asked.

Claire lifted her head quickly. 'A row?'

'A quarrel,' Ella clarified. 'Captain Roper looked very upset, and so do you.'

Weren't maids supposed to keep opinions to themselves? 'I suppose you could say we had a disagreement.'

It had been more than a disagreement. He'd stopped and she'd not wanted him to.

Ella gave her a very sympathetic look. 'Do not upset yourself. Cullen and I argue sometimes. It never lasts. It was a lovers' row, that is what it was. Or the two of you would not be so upset.'

No. She and Lucien were not lovers. Even if that was what she'd wished for. What she'd attempted.

'It is not like that,' she quickly retorted. 'He— he is my escort. Nothing more.'

The maid gave her a very sceptical look, then busied herself tidying the cabin, which needed no tidying.

Claire rested her head in her hands again.

Finally Ella asked, 'Would you like me to head on and come back later?'

And leave her alone? To her thoughts? To memories of what had transpired? The knowledge that she was probably a hoyden.

'No. Please stay.' She needed to fill her head with something else besides Lucien. 'Tell me about yourself, Ella. About you and Cullen.'

Ella stood behind the other chair, her hands resting on its back while the ship rocked gently.

Her eyes glowed. 'He is right grand, he is. My Cullen.'

Claire could not help but smile. 'Where did you meet?'

'Oh, we were just children.' Her expression sobered. 'My ma and pa were in service, but his tilled the land. I was not allowed to see him, Ma and Pa said. We were better than he was, Ma and Pa said.'

'How did you manage, then?' she asked.

'We were clever.' Her fleeting smile disappeared. 'My ma and pa came to Dublin to work and Cullen followed. When I was hired at the hotel, he found a job there, too. A low job, but he paid attention. He learned about gentlemen. He wanted to do better, he did.'

'That is admirable.'

'It is admirable indeed. But my pa did not think so. He found out Cullen was workin' at the hotel and Pa went into a tear, he did. That was when I took the chance to travel with you and Cullen came, too.'

They were running from her parents? 'How old are you, Ella?'

The maid straightened. 'I am eighteen, I am. Old enough.'

'And Cullen?'

'He is twenty.'

They were so young! Young lovers filled with hope.

How old was she? she wondered. She felt much older, but how old could she be? She could not be more than twenty or twenty-one if she were to be married? Any older and she'd be considered a spinster.

'That is a romantic story,' Claire said. Lucien would admire their determination to stay together, but she worried about what was in store for them. Life could bring hardship—although she did not know how she knew that. 'It seems like your parents would have been wiser not to try to separate you.'

'That is the right of it.' Ella nodded vigorously. 'But my pa would say, "Once a land tiller, always a land tiller." He thought he could convince me to marry a shopkeeper or one of Mr Castle's sons.' She laughed scornfully, then sobered again. 'This is Cullen's chance. No one would hire him as a valet with no experience. Not in Ireland. Not knowing where he came from. A good letter from Captain Roper will mean everything to us. Do you think the Captain will write a letter of recommendation? Could you ask him, please? Cullen won't ask, I fear. It was my idea to ask the Captain for this trip.'

Did she have any influence with Lucien? She was more a burden than anything else. And a coquettish fool.

'I will try,' she said.

She did not see Lucien until the next morning when Holyhead was in sight. Since Ella took charge of repacking her portmanteau, Claire went up on deck. Lucien stood at the rail.

Her heart skipped a beat.

She loved his erect, alert bearing, the easy way he wore his coat and buff-coloured pantaloons when other men looked stiff and uncomfortable in the same garments. His dark hair curled out from beneath his beaver hat, uncut since their rescue. He was a man secure in what he wanted, sure of his future and fully aware of his past.

So unlike her, with no past she could remember, a future filled with just as many unknowns and the feeling that she more belonged on a fishing boat than in such beautiful dresses and hats.

She took in a breath for courage and walked to his side, placing her hands on the rail.

He turned his head towards her. 'We'll dock within an hour, I expect.'

She nodded, unable to make herself speak.

Was he also thinking of the kiss? Her head

ached from the wine of the night before and she wished she could remember more clearly.

She mentally shook her head. He would not have kissed her. Every other intimacy had been initiated by her. This must have been, as well.

'What then?' she finally managed to ask.

He did not answer right away. 'We can either engage a carriage and begin the journey to London today or rest a night in Holyhead.'

Surely he did not expect her to make that choice. 'You must decide, Lucien.'

'I do not wish to ask too much of you,' he said.

He spoke to her as if the previous night had not happened, as if she'd never thrown herself at him and admitted she'd wanted to bed him. It made her angry.

She lifted her chin. 'Surely after three weeks on a fishing boat, you know I am not delicate. You offered me your escort. I do not assume that means I command you. On the contrary, I am in your debt.'

Lucien spoke sharply. 'My offer of being your escort did not mean you would have no say in how and when we travelled.' He regretted his tone, just the opposite of how he'd vowed to behave.

He'd vowed to act the gentleman, to make up for his decidedly ungentlemanly behaviour of the previous night.

Now, though, merely seeing her unsettled him

anew. The sun shining on her face, her hazel eyes reflecting the green colour of her hat, her moist pink lips.

Was it not gentlemanly of him to give her the choice, though? And what did she do? Acted as if she were not an aristocrat, as if she were the woman who'd wished she could remain on the fishing boat. What aristocratic lady wished to live on a fishing boat?

'It is your choice, Lucien,' she insisted.

So now he must guess which was better for her. To stay the night in Holyhead or to start their journey to London, a journey he had to admit he'd like to delay?

He took time to decide, but instead of thinking of carriages and inns, he savoured the faint scent of lavender that enveloped her.

Finally he forced a decision. Of sorts. 'If we can procure a carriage under such short notice, we leave today. If not, tomorrow.'

She did not respond right away. It seemed like minutes went by before she said, 'Very well.'

'But you must tell me if you become fatigued or ill,' he insisted.

'I rarely become ill,' she shot back. Her eyes widened. 'How do I know that?'

He forgot about the night before and all his other nonsense. 'Another memory?'

She glanced away and back. 'So very strange. I cannot remember ever being ill or not being ill, but I simply know I have a strong constitution.' Her eyes widened again. 'I can almost hear myself saying those words.' She looked even more pensive. 'On a ship.'

She was getting closer and closer to retrieving her past. How long would it take, he wondered, before her memory returned in full?

He smiled, hiding his unhappiness. 'See? I'll wager this will happen more. Especially when you are in familiar surroundings.'

Perhaps being in London would do it. If she had ever been in London before.

'Close your eyes and see if more comes.'

She did as he suggested, but opened them again and shook her head. 'Nothing. Emptiness.' She waved her hand. 'But, never mind. I will simply enjoy this lovely day and the excitement of docking at Holyhead and of seeing all the sights there.'

She turned back to the railing and gazed out at the land on the horizon.

The grey and green hills of the Anglesey coast soon gave way to the wooden docks of the harbour and white-stucco buildings of Holyhead and, as they came even closer, they could see the activity on the dock awaiting their arrival.

Lucien marked it all. The harbour was much like countless other harbours he'd sailed into. This time, though, he was a mere passenger with absolutely no role to play in reaching the dock safely. Soon he hoped to have another ship under his command. With luck he could gather most of his old crew. He'd be at home again.

As the ship eased its way to the dock, Lady Rebecca spoke. 'This was what was supposed to happen on the other ship.'

Where instead many died.

When it came time to disembark, Cullen and the maid appeared, Cullen carrying both his and Lady Rebecca's luggage.

'We are ready, sir,' Cullen said. 'I will collect the trunks as soon as they are unloaded.'

'Any memories of this?' Lucien asked Lady Rebecca as they stepped on to the dock.

'None. It is like I've never seen it before.' She sounded resigned.

His impulse was to ease her pain. 'It is possible you've never been here before.'

'I suppose,' she responded. 'But I must have travelled to England before this. Perhaps I even had a London Season. I must have met Lord Stonecroft somewhere. There must have been some sort of courtship.'

He ought to have asked that reprobate of a brother of hers more about the matter. It certainly would have helped her if he had.

He took her to a nearby inn to wait until Cullen and the maid collected the trunks. While there he enquired about hiring a carriage and managed to make the arrangements. It would take them at least four hours by carriage to travel over Four Mile Bridge on to Anglesey Island and across the island and on to the ferry to the mainland. They had enough daylight to do that.

The carriage was large enough for their trunks and other luggage and to seat all four of them inside. Ella and Cullen took the rear-facing seats and Lucien was very aware of Lady Rebecca beside him. Lucien was distracted from his jumbled emotions by the unrestrained excitement of the maid who could hardly remain in her seat at the sights that passed by the windows.

They passed by stucco houses with slate roofs gleaming white in the midday sun.

Ella exclaimed, 'Look!' as they passed a huge stone church.

Within an hour they had crossed the Four Mile Bridge connecting Holy Island to Anglesey and Ella actually moved so she could lean out of the window.

'I've never seen the like, I haven't!' she cried.

Lucien turned to Lady Rebecca with a silent question—did she have a memory of this?

She shook her head.

After several changes of horses they arrived at the Menai Strait where they waited for the ferry that would transport them to Caernarfon on the

Welsh mainland. The crossing was not without its hazards, Lucien knew. The strait near Caernarfon was known for its shifting sandbars. He kept his eyes open and his mouth shut as the four of them stood on the deck of the ferry, the wind blowing cool as the sun lowered in the sky.

'Look! Look, m'lady!' Ella jumped up and down and tugged on Cullen's arm. 'A castle! A real castle!' She turned to Lucien. 'Do you know what castle it is?'

It loomed high above the town around it. Old stone with crenellated towers. The town itself looked as if it were behind the castle walls.

'Caernarfon Castle,' Lucien said. 'Built by King Edward about five hundred years ago, I think.'

'It is grand.' Ella's voice was full of awe. 'Grander than any I've seen in Ireland.'

'But you've seen hardly a castle in Ireland, wouldn't you say?' Cullen smiled.

She rolled her eyes at him. 'Cullen.'

While the two servants bickered good-naturedly, Lucien stepped over to Lady Rebecca.

'No,' she answered his silent enquiry. 'I know it is a castle. I can name the parts of it, but I do not remember seeing it.'

The ferry landed without mishap and they disembarked, the carriage taking them into the town to a posting inn. Their carriage and trunks were secured and the four of them entered the inn. At

Lucien's behest, Cullen arranged for four rooms, the servants' rooms near the other two, and for a private dining room.

When the servants were about to leave them at the private room, Lady Rebecca stopped them. 'We could eat together, could we not?'

Lucien was startled at this new example of common, non-aristocratic behaviour from her.

All three sets of eyes turned to him.

'Certainly, if that is what you wish,' he responded.

During the meal Cullen kept his distance, but Ella chattered her way through each dish, detailing all the remarkable sights she'd seen that day and asking questions of what was to come.

Lucien was amused by the young maid. 'Ella, surely it is not typical of a lady's maid to be such a chatterbox. How is it you are so?'

Ella laughed. 'My pa said I was born this way. He could never do a thing with me. Believe me, he and Ma tried.' She gave Cullen a worshipful glance. 'My friendship with Cullen made me bold, I think. It always felt right to be with him, no matter what Pa and Ma said.'

When their plates were empty and some port was served, Ella stood up. 'Cullen and I will remove the dishes and prepare your rooms for sleeping.' She seemed to be trying to suppress a smile. 'Name a time we should attend you.'

She was not only outspoken; she was taking command.

'Ten o'clock?' Lucien looked to Lady Rebecca.

'That suits me,' she replied.

When they left, Lady Rebecca said, 'I believe they wanted some time together.'

Which also left Lucien alone with her.

He poured each of them some port. 'She is a somewhat unusual maid.'

She smiled. 'I agree. I am not certain how I know that, but I do agree.'

He lifted his glass to his lips. 'Any more memories?'

She scoffed. 'I don't know if I would call them memories, but, no. Nothing further.'

He leaned forward. 'I have an idea.'

Her brows rose as she took a sip of port.

He went on. 'An idea of how you might recover some memories.'

She hesitated, then fingered the stem of her glass. 'I know I should answer you eagerly, but I am a little afraid. I should remember, but I am not certain I want to.'

Perhaps that was the impediment—not wanting to remember.

She took another sip of her port. 'Shoulders back, right, Lucien? I must face this. Do tell me what your idea is.'

The idea was forming as they spoke. 'I will ask you to talk about something and we will see if any memories come.'

* * *

Claire straightened in her chair and lifted her chin. 'Very well.'

She considered downing her glass of port and asking for more to settle her nerves, but too much wine the night before had led her into trouble. Drink too much wine. Throw herself at Lucien.

'What will you ask?'

He paused, as if thinking, then leaned towards her again. 'Tell me about school.'

'School? I do not remember school.' He knew this.

'Not your school,' he said. 'Tell me about any school. What kind is it?'

'Do you mean a girls' boarding school?' she asked.

'That will do.' He gestured for her to go on. 'Tell me anything about what a girls' boarding school would be like.'

This seemed ridiculous. 'Well, there would be girls there.'

He accepted her answer with equanimity. 'And what would they study?'

She hesitated only a few seconds. 'Music, dancing, Italian, French, literature, mathematics, needlework.' She looked up at him. 'Shall I go on?'

'What would the school look like?'

'How can I know that?' she shot back.

'Make it up,' he said.

She closed her eyes. 'Red brick, at least four floors, green park surrounding, dormitory rooms with beds, one after the other, classrooms with slate boards and wooden desks and chairs.' She opened her eyes again.

'Tell me about the teachers.' He anticipated her protest. 'Make it up.'

'Very well.' She took a breath. 'Some of them are bitter and unhappy, because they have nowhere else to go, but others seem to care about the girls and want to try to help them.'

A glimpse of a smiling woman flashed through her mind.

She looked directly at Lucien. 'A woman…'

His eyes kindled with interest. 'What does she look like?'

She shook her head. 'It was too brief.'

He reached across the table and took her hand. 'Now answer this without thinking. Where is this school?'

'Bristol.' She blinked in surprise.

He squeezed her hand. 'I believe you remember a real school, one you attended. A real teacher.'

'But it doesn't feel like a memory,' she protested. 'Not like remembering the fishing boat or Dublin.'

'It is there, though,' he insisted. 'You'll have more.' He released her hand, glancing at his own as if surprised. 'Do you want to go on?'

She pressed her fingers to her temple. 'No. My head aches. Perhaps later.'

Had she remembered a real school? A real teacher?

She felt as if she were a water-filled ewer with a tiny crack growing larger and larger, but she did not want to split open. She did not want the water to spill out.

There was a knock on the door and the innkeeper entered.

'Pardon me, sir, m'lady,' the man said nervously. 'Have a problem, I do. His lordship, Lord Provey, demands a private dining room and this is the only one.'

Claire immediately rose. 'We have no further need of it, do we, Lucien?'

He frowned. 'Perhaps not.'

The innkeeper looked wretched. 'So grateful, I'd be.'

Lucien stood as well and escorted her out.

Passing them was an expensively dressed gentleman, wafting strong scent, and his three equally well-dressed cohorts.

'It is about time,' the gentleman snarled at the innkeeper. 'I expect brandy and glasses forthwith, a clean deck of playing cards and a set of markers. Hurry, man.'

The innkeeper dashed away and the men disappeared behind the room's door.

'I detest men like that,' Lucien mumbled.

Claire was not certain she was to have heard

that, but she responded. 'What sort of men? Rude, pushy ones?'

'Aristocrats.' He nearly spat out the word.

The venom in his tone struck her like a physical blow.

They walked to the hall.

Claire glanced through the window. She did not wish to say goodnight, not until she understood why he'd reacted so vehemently to aristocrats.

'It is still a little light outside. Might we take some air?' she asked.

'A turn around the yard may be safe enough.'

They walked outside. The yard which had been all abustle had quieted, although there were still hostlers moving horses into the stables. The setting sun turned the sky golden, making the brown stone of the inn glow as if lit from within. A light breeze freed the air of the scent of horses.

Claire took Lucien's arm as they walked the perimeter of the yard.

'Why did you say you detest aristocrats?' she asked at last, well aware she was one.

He frowned. 'Because they believe they are entitled to whatever it is they want.'

That sentiment rang true inside her. Was it true of herself, as well?

She countered, 'Surely not all of them.'

'Too many of them in my experience,' he stated. 'Your brother for one.'

She readily agreed with that. 'He was detestable, was he not? And that lord, the one near your village, the one your mother—'

'Viscount Waverland.' His voice tensed.

'He was detestable, too?' she asked.

'Yes. Not only in how he treated my mother, expecting her to run to him whenever he fancied her, but he expected the whole village to jump to his demands.' He made a derisive sound. 'Of course, my mother was always eager to comply. Whatever he wanted.'

They walked on, covering a quarter of the distance, before she spoke again. 'And the ladies? Aristocratic ladies, are they cut from the same cloth?'

Was she? She wanted to know.

He missed a step. 'Often the same.'

Did he believe she would become demanding and entitled when she recovered her memory?

The thought sickened her.

No wonder Lucien became angry when she'd kissed him. It must have seemed to him that she expected him to comply because it was what she wanted.

But she had wanted it.

Was she nothing but a selfish aristocrat?

'Viscount Waverland was not the only reason for my antipathy,' he went on. 'I was raised to detest aristocrats.'

'By your mother?' His father was absent, she recalled.

'Yes.'

''That makes no sense. She fell in love with one.'

He cocked his head. 'We came to different conclusions. She wanted to be one. I wanted nothing to do with them.'

And she was one of *them*. 'Something must have happened, then.'

He halted and gazed down at her with an intent look she did not understand.

Finally he spoke. 'My mother's father owned land in Ireland. He was fairly prosperous, but he was tricked into losing the property by an unscrupulous lord. My mother and her brothers were suddenly impoverished and my mother never recovered from the change in her circumstances and prospects for a good marriage.'

'What a terrible occurrence.' The poor family. No wonder Lucien felt as he did.

'That is why I was in Ireland,' he explained. 'To provide some needed funds for my uncles.'

Her heart warmed towards him. Of course. It was the sort of thing he would do. Dear Lucien.

'I should tell you more.' His tone put her aback.

'More? What more?'

He faced her directly and looked down into her eyes. 'The aristocrat who impoverished my family was the Earl of Keneagle. Your grandfather.'

She felt a chill run through her. 'My grandfather? My father's father?' Had she known her grandfather?

He kept on. 'I did not tell you before, because... well...you had enough to deal with. I feel I should have told you when we met your brother.'

Her grandfather must have been as horrible as her brother. It was a wonder Lucien could even look at her.

She wrapped her arms around herself, feeling as miserable as she could remember. 'It has turned cold. We should go back in.'

Chapter Nine

Lucien felt her withdrawal. Her pain. He was instantly sorry he had spoken. Why had he?

If he was trying to separate himself from her, he'd done a fair job of it, but it brought him no ease at all.

He shook his head. 'I should not have told you all that. I fear it has only caused you pain.'

Her muscles had stiffened. 'Better for me to know—to know what sort of a family I came from.'

Had he told her because he'd been tempted to pull her into the many shadows around the yard and taste her lips again?

They re-entered the inn and climbed the stairs to their rooms. At her doorway, he reached out his hand for her key.

She placed it in his palm and avoided a direct look at him.

He turned the key in the lock and opened the door.

All he could see in the room was the bed and

temptation flared through him. Enter her room. Taste her lips again and this time allow her to say yes.

'Shall I have breakfast sent up to your room?' he said instead.

'As you wish, Lucien,' she responded in a sad voice.

She held out her palm for the key and he returned it to her. Before he could say another word, she strode into the room, closing the door behind her.

Curse me, Lucien said to himself.

He returned to the public rooms, seated himself at a table and sent the tavern maid to bring him some brandy. A whole bottle.

He poured one glass and downed it and poured another. Sipping this one more slowly, he let his gaze drift around the room, so much like any public room of a fairly respectable inn. Weary travellers. Jocular town folk. Easy women, needing to make enough to survive. Eager men willing to pay their price.

Tucked away in a booth in the corner of the room sat his new valet and the chatterbox maid, staring into each other's eyes as if no one else in the room existed. They had at least another hour before their duties would call them away.

Too bad he could never have what they possessed. Love between equals. Strong enough that nothing or no one else mattered.

But she would always be Lady Rebecca and he would always have the sea.

He must stay the course. Bring her to London. Deliver her to Lord Stonecroft.

And say goodbye.

He downed his second glass of brandy and poured a third.

He still wished he had not hurt her so this night.

Their trip the next day took them through the mountains, and the scenic views of the peaks and valleys and lakes kept them all entertained. Lucien could hardly ignore that Lady Rebecca said as little as possible to him. Though they still sat next to each other and could not fail to touch, it was as if she were in another coach altogether.

This was an odd choice of a route, Lucien thought. The pace was slow, the horses needing to conserve strength because the few coaching inns were a greater distant apart than on busier roads.

When they stopped at an inn at midday, Lucien asked the coachmen about it.

'More direct, it is,' the coachman said. 'Saves time.'

But the man did not look him in the eye.

Twice that day they had to leave the carriage and walk so the horses could make it up a steep piece of road. This was not saving time. They should be out of this wooded, mountainous area and on to more-travelled roads.

By late afternoon, Lucien's impatience grew, even as the road narrowed and the pace slowed even further.

The carriage stopped one more time and the coachman opened the window below his perch. 'Need you to walk again.'

Lucien disembarked first and helped Lady Rebecca out. Cullen and Ella came next.

'We might as well walk the whole way,' Ella said as her feet hit the ground.

Lady Rebecca, however, had not uttered a word of complaint.

They walked ahead of the carriage, able to make more speed than the horses. When they reached the crest of the hill, they faced two horsemen aiming pistols at them.

Ella gasped.

'Your money or your life,' one growled.

The two men dismounted.

Lucien edged Lady Rebecca behind him, but kept walking towards them. 'We have little of value.'

'Stop there. Empty your pockets,' the highwayman said.

The other man's hands shook.

Lucien had faced men with pistols before when capturing enemy ships. Hesitation got men killed.

'I'll show you.' He kept approaching and made it look like he was reaching in a pocket. 'There's a pittance.'

Instead he charged the man, who stepped back in surprise, but fired his weapon. Lucien felt a sharp pain pierce his arm, but he leapt at the man, grabbing the arm with the pistol. Out of the corner of his eye, he saw Cullen grappling with the other man.

'What ho?' The coachmen jumped from the box.

'They are with them!' Lucien cried.

Lady Rebecca pulled Ella away from them and around to the other side of the road. The two coachmen rushed into the fray. Lucien held his own, but barely, and a punch to his injured arm nearly caused him to pass out. How long could he and Cullen keep this up?

He grabbed the robber by the lapels and slammed him into the coachman. Both staggered backwards, struggling to keep on their feet.

Cullen was having a worse time of it. The other robber held him while the other coachman pummelled him with his fists.

Ella let out a cry as unearthly as a proper banshee. She leapt on to the coachman's back and held on to his hair. The man swung around, trying to rid himself of her.

Lucien swung at his attacker with all his strength. His fist connected to the man's jaw with a loud crack and the man spun around and fell to the ground. The coachman charged him again and both he and Lucien tumbled over. Somehow the man's hands wrapped around his throat. Lucien tried to pry his fingers loose, but his injured arm had lost its strength.

Suddenly Lady Rebecca appeared. She threw her shawl over the man's head and jerked his head back. He lost his grip on Lucien, who rolled away, but he turned, trying to get his hands on her. Lucien came down with both fists on the back of the man's neck.

The man fell to the dirt.

Cullen freed himself and now brandished a knife, its blade gleaming as he slashed at his assailants. Ella had finally been flung off, but the man she'd leapt on took one look at the knife and yelled, 'Flee! Or we're done for.'

The man started for the horses, but Lady Rebecca ran ahead of him, waving her shawl and scaring the horses into galloping down the road.

Lucien went to the carriage. There was no way he'd allow these men to escape in the carriage and leave them stranded. He held the horses.

Lucien's assailants scrambled to their feet and stumbled off into the woods where their partners had already fled.

Lady Rebecca walked back to Lucien.

Ella had flung her arms around Cullen and was weeping loudly. 'I thought they would kill you.'

Lucien had a strong urge to hold Lady Rebecca in the same manner, but he held back.

She was breathing hard, but remained remarkably composed. 'What now, Lucien?'

'We need to leave. Right now.' He didn't want the highwaymen to regroup or return with reinforcements. 'Cullen!' he called. 'Are you able to drive the carriage?'

Ella released him.

'I can try, sir.' Cullen limped over to the carriage, climbed on to the box and took the ribbons in his hands.

Lucien turned to Lady Rebecca. 'I am going to ride on top with him. You ladies ride inside.' He opened the door and helped them in. Closing it again, he leaned in the window. 'You both did well.'

The ladies had saved them all.

Lucien climbed on the box with Cullen who flicked the ribbons. The horses started down the road.

'Are you injured?' Claire asked Ella.

The girl had not stopped weeping, but she shook her head. 'I thought they would kill Cullen. What would I do if that happened? How could I live after that?'

She put her arm around the maid. 'There, now. It is over. And you were very brave. Cullen is unharmed, is he not?'

'He was limping,' Ella whimpered.

'Well, he is a strong man. A very strong man,' she said. 'I am certain he will be right as rain in no time.'

'He is a strong man,' Ella agreed with a sigh.

Claire's heart was still pounding. The whole scene played over and over in her mind. The highwaymen pointing their pistols. Lucien rushing towards them. She'd been terrified that he'd be shot. Ella's sentiments were not unlike her own. How could she live if Lucien were killed? He was her one constant. When that man choked him, something in her snapped. She'd have killed that man if that was what it took to save Lucien.

She glanced out of the window, her senses on alert lest the attackers return. The coachmen must have set up the attack. How could they have done such a thing?

After about a half-hour they reached a road with more traffic and soon crossed an old stone bridge and entered a village that looked as if time had not touched it in a century. The carriage stayed on the main road until they came upon a coaching inn.

When the carriage turned into the inn's yard and stopped, Claire heard Cullen's voice. 'Ella, m'lady. Come quick. I need you.'

Claire opened the door and, without waiting for

the steps to be put down, jumped to the ground, Ella behind her.

Cullen had already climbed off the box. Lucien, pale as chalk, was leaning heavily on him.

'He's hurt, m'lady,' Cullen said. 'We must get him inside.'

She sprang into action. 'Ella, collect his things. Cullen, help me bring him into the inn.' She came to his other side, ready to have him drape an arm around her shoulder, but his sleeve was dark with blood.

'Lucien!' she cried.

'Started bleeding,' he said. 'Not serious.'

He looked as if he would pass out at any moment.

One of the hostlers ran ahead to alert the innkeeper who met them at the door.

'What happened?' the innkeeper asked, immediately taking over for Claire.

'We were set upon by thieves,' she answered. 'Our coachmen were part of it. He's shot, I believe.'

The innkeeper directed them to a nearby room on the first floor. She and Cullen sat Lucien on the bed. Claire very gingerly removed his coat. His shirtsleeve was bright red.

'The ball hit my upper arm.' Lucien's voice was low and strained.

She looked over at the innkeeper. 'Please send for a surgeon.'

The man nodded and left.

Cullen helped him off with his waistcoat and shirt. Claire moistened a towel from a basin in the room.

'He bled something terrible,' Cullen said.

'It is still bleeding!' She pressed the towel against his wound.

He winced.

Cullen removed Lucien's boots.

'Lucien, you must lie down,' Claire insisted.

He did as she said, closing his eyes as his head rested against the pillows. 'Need to summon the magistrate.'

'We will worry about that later,' she said.

He was so pale and weak. It frightened her.

This would not have happened if not for her. He would have already been in London by now, well on his way in his new life.

'I am so sorry, Lucien,' she whispered.

'No need,' he said. 'Just a scratch…' His voice faded off.

Claire and Cullen did all they could to control the bleeding and to make Lucien as comfortable as possible, but he clearly was growing weaker and weaker. Claire was nearly wild with worry. An hour had passed and the surgeon had still not arrived.

'Cullen, go see what is happening,' she pleaded. 'Why is the surgeon not here?'

The valet nodded and immediately left the room. A few minutes later Ella entered with some broth. 'For the Captain. The cook here said he should drink as much as possible.'

She placed the tray containing a pot of broth and a cup on the table next to the bed.

Claire poured some and put her arm around Lucien to help him sit. She lifted the cup to his lips. 'Drink this.'

She slowly poured a little of the broth down his throat. He swallowed cooperatively, but could not keep his eyes open.

His skin was hot to her touch and that worried her as much as the bleeding.

'What is going to happen to him, m'lady?' Ella asked, wringing her hands.

'He is going to recover,' she said determinedly.

Because no other option could possibly be entertained.

She could not remember attending church or saying prayers, but she prayed now that God would help him.

There was a knock on the door. It opened before they could answer and Cullen entered with a grey-haired man carrying a leather bag.

'The surgeon,' Cullen said.

'I am Mr Hughes,' the man said.

'This is Captain Roper.' Claire moved away from Lucien's bedside and the surgeon took her place. 'He's been shot in the arm. We—we haven't been able to stop the bleeding.'

Mr Hughes sat down. 'Let us see it, then.'

He removed the bloody towels Claire had wrapped around Lucien's arm, dabbed at the fresh blood and touched the wound, examining it.

Lucien roused and pulled away.

Claire went to the other side of the bed and eased him back against the pillows. 'It is all right, Lucien. It is the surgeon. Let him look at you.'

It looked as if the pistol ball had taken a slice out of Lucien's upper arm.

'Bring me some fresh water and towels,' the surgeon said. 'We'll clean the wound and stitch him up. That should do it.'

Claire held Lucien's other arm and shoulder while Cullen held his injured one. Lucien trembled in pain as the surgeon picked out pieces of cloth and small pebbles from the wound, but he did not cry out.

'It will be all right, Lucien,' Claire murmured. 'Hold fast.'

Mr Hughes poured water in the wound to wash away smaller debris. Lucien gripped Claire's hand and shook some more.

'Now we'll sew you up, young man,' Hughes said in a calm tone.

Ella stood behind Cullen, her hands covering her mouth as the surgeon stitched the wound closed. Lucien's muscles tensed and his face was pinched, as he stoically endured this last bit of pain.

Claire felt every poke of the needle, every

stroke of the thread passing through his skin as if it were happening to her. Only when the surgeon had finished, giving the wound a final dab of the towel and leaning back, did she realise she'd been as tense as Lucien.

'There you are,' Mr Hughes said. 'All done. Now let us wrap it up and all will be well.'

'Thank you, sir,' Lucien mumbled as he once more relaxed against the pillows. He gestured towards his coat, flung across a table. 'Will pay you.'

Cullen retrieved the coat and lifted the purse from a pocket, taking out some coins and paying the surgeon.

Mr Hughes packed up his things. 'He should rest a day at least. More if he still seems weak.' He glanced towards Lucien. 'Do you hear that, Captain?' he said louder.

Lucien nodded.

He turned to Claire again. 'He should have the stitches taken out in a week, assuming he's healing well.'

Claire rose and walked Mr Hughes to the door. 'Is there anything I should be on watch for? Anything that could go awry?'

The older man smiled at her. 'He will do well, I believe. Only danger is fever, but he's strong. Even fever will not beat him, I expect.'

She certainly had no intention of letting Luc-

ien out of her sight until she knew he would recover completely.

After the surgeon left, she returned to the chair
next to his bed.

'I will stay with him,' she told Cullen and Ella.
'You two go and get something to eat.'

'Shall I arrange a room for you?' Cullen asked
her.

She shook her head. 'I am staying here.'

'I will stay, as well, then,' he said. He turned
to Ella. 'You'll have a room, though. You need
your rest.'

Ella hugged him. 'You are so good to me.'

They went out of the room arm in arm.

'You should rest, too,' came a weak voice from
the bed.

She took his hand. 'I am staying with you.'

'Your reputation,' he mumbled.

'Dash my reputation,' she said. 'You did not
let go of me on the raft and I am not leaving this
room until I know you are better.'

She sat by his side throughout the night when
he thrashed in fever. She and Cullen bathed his
face with cool cloths.

Somehow she knew that fever could kill, just
as an illness or a pistol shot could kill. Or how the
sea could kill. She could not remember, though,
knowing anyone who had died. Not even the

woman on the *Dun Aengus*. Not the maid sent to accompany her. No one.

If Lucien died, though, it would be as if her whole remembered life died with him.

Chapter Ten

After fitful dreams of stormy seas and highwaymen and Lady Rebecca perishing at the hands of both, Lucien opened his eyes to a room lit by dawn peeking through the window. It took him a moment to realise where he was and what had happened.

Cullen was sprawled out in two chairs, one holding his feet, the other, the rest of him. Lady Rebecca sat next to him. Though in a chair, she rested her head in her arms on the bed's mattress. Her hair had come loose and he fingered one tendril.

She'd said she'd stay the night in his room, he dimly recalled.

He smiled. She looked peaceful in sleep, youthful and unspoiled by the events she'd endured since encountering him.

His arm throbbed and he had a powerful thirst, but he did not wish to rouse his guardians. Across the room on a table was a pitcher of water and a glass. He could reach it.

Keeping his eye on Lady Rebecca, he edged his way out of the bed, taking care not to disturb her. He wore only his unmentionables, he noticed. His chest was bare and his aching arm was wrapped in a bandage. He took his first step gingerly, pausing until the dizziness passed. Bracing himself against furniture, he made it to the water, poured himself a glass, and, still watching Lady Rebecca, drank the whole amount.

She lifted her head and sat up in surprise until she spied him. 'What are you doing?'

He put a finger to his lips and pointed to Cullen, still inhaling the even breaths of sleep. Lucien poured another glass and finished it before making his way back to the bed.

'You should not be up,' she whispered.

'Thirsty,' he said.

'You should have awoken me,' she scolded. 'I would have brought you water.'

'You were sleeping.' He winced as he climbed back into bed.

She put her hand to his forehead. 'Thank God. You are finally cool.'

Her hand felt soft and warm against his skin. 'I had a fever? That explains the dreams.'

'Dreams?' she asked.

'Fever dreams,' he responded. 'They did not

make much sense.' Except they were mostly about losing her.

Prophetic dreams, perhaps.

'Did you summon the magistrate?' he asked.

She pursed her lips. 'No, we were too concerned with keeping you alive.'

'From this?' He pointed to the bandage. 'Takes more than a scratch to kill me.'

'You lost a great deal of blood.'

Another ordeal for her to endure, he thought. 'I am sorry. I worried you.'

She reached over and brushed the hair from his face. 'As long as you mend.'

It seemed so natural to have her seated close to his bed, touching him, conversing together. He'd grown used to her presence over these eventful weeks. He did not want to part from her, but his duty was clear. Help her remember as much as she could. Return her to her life. Return to the sea.

Her hand rested briefly on his shoulder before she placed it in her lap. He might have had a feverish night, but his senses were still alive. Her touch roused him with desire and he was acutely aware of being bare chested in her presence.

'Is my bag nearby?' he asked.

'Yes.' She could not quite meet his eye. Had she felt that pang of desire, as well?

He sat up straighter. 'Could you bring me a shirt?'

She rose and walked over to the bag, opened

it and found a clean shirt Cullen had packed. She carried it to him and helped him put it on. The rest he could do when Cullen woke up.

'Are you hungry?' she whispered.

He was. Very hungry. 'I can wait for Cullen to wake up.'

'I will happily get you something to eat.'

But it was not proper for an earl's daughter to seek out the kitchens of an inn and ask for food.

'Ask Ella to do it if she is awake.' It was a maid's job.

She stood and stretched, reminding him of the Lady Rebecca of the fishing boat. Completely at ease.

'Very well. I will ask Ella to bring the food if she is awake.'

Only after she left did he realise she had not said what she would do if Ella were sleeping.

They had only procured two rooms at the inn and Ella had slept in the other one. Claire rapped lightly on the door.

'One moment.' Ella's muffled voice came through the door. She opened it. 'Oh, m'lady. It is you.'

She was dressed and the bed was made.

Claire stepped inside the room. 'I was not certain you would be awake.'

'Me? I am used to rising early.' She gave Claire a concerned look. 'How fares the Captain?'

'He is well.' It gave Claire pleasure to say so. 'His fever is gone and he is hungry.'

'And Cullen? I expected him, not you, at the door.' Her eyes widened. 'Oh, I did not mean to sound like I would not want you to come, m'lady.'

Claire held up her hand. 'I do realise that, Ella. Cullen was sleeping when I left the room. He was up with the Captain most of the night.'

The young man had been a great help, holding Lucien down when he thrashed about in the bed. He brought fresh water and towels and made both Lucien and Claire as comfortable as possible.

Ella peered at her. 'You look like you were up most of the night, too. I think you should rest. I'll fetch the food for the Captain.'

Claire glanced in the mirror. She had circles under her eyes and her hair had escaped its pins. And there were bloodstains on her dress.

'I should change my clothes.' She waved her hand. 'But that can come later. The Captain is hungry.'

'Right.' Ella headed to the door. 'I shall go to the kitchen directly.'

After she left, Claire glanced at the bed, longing to simply lie down, but she did not wish to muss it after Ella had made it so tidy. She sat in an upholstered chair and leaned her head against its back, drifting off to sleep.

Next thing she knew Ella was leaning over her. 'M'lady? M'lady? Why don't you lie in the bed?'

She shook her head. 'I'd muss it.'

'Nonsense,' Ella said. 'I'll simply make it again. You need some sleep.'

She let herself be persuaded. The maid helped her out of her dress and she climbed under the bedcovers in her shift.

When next she woke, Ella stood over her again. 'The magistrate is here, m'lady. Captain Roper would like you to come speak with him.'

She sat up and felt her hair, now half-down on her shoulders. 'I cannot go looking like this.'

'Let us make you presentable, then. Right quick.'

Ella was true to her word. The girl helped her into her other travelling dress and put her hair in a knot as quick as could be. There was nothing to do for Claire's pale complexion and dark circles.

The magistrate was the local squire, Squire Vaughn, a man in his forties.

He bowed to her. 'My lady.'

Why did this acknowledgement of her status always feel so foreign?

'Sir.' She curtsied.

She glanced over at Lucien, who was clean shaven, seated in a chair and fully dressed, wearing a clean coat draped over his injured arm. He looked very pale.

The magistrate asked each of them to tell what happened on the road and to describe the men involved.

After they spoke and answered his questions,

he said, 'I can put the word out to look for men of their description. We can check at the inn where you engaged the carriage and drivers, but, you must understand, the people may not be inclined to turn in their own. There's hardship here. Desperate people do desperate things.'

The unusually cold weather had damaged crops and led to hunger throughout the country, not to mention the unemployment and privation caused by the war.

'You do not believe the men will be caught,' Lucien said in a grim voice.

'I do not,' the magistrate admitted. 'And if I were you, I'd proceed on your trip as soon as possible. I am not saying you are in danger, but it seems to me many men must have been involved in the attempt to rob you and they all are probably worrying you'll be looking to find out who and turn them in.'

Claire could not believe this. 'But if these men are not caught, they might rob someone else. Any one of us could have been killed.' She gestured to Lucien. 'Captain Roper's injury could have killed him.'

Squire Vaughn inclined his head. 'I do understand, my lady. I am merely telling you what I think will happen.'

'But—' she started.

Lucien cut her off. 'Very well, Squire. I will take you at your word that you will try to discover who the guilty parties are. You have my direction in London. Write to me if you need me to return to press charges.'

The squire twirled his hat in his hands. 'I will do that, sir.' He turned and bowed to Claire. 'M'lady, I bid you good day.'

When the door closed behind the magistrate, Lucien rose from the chair. 'We leave today, if possible.'

'No, Lucien!' Lady Rebecca cried. 'You must rest a day. The surgeon said—'

'No matter.'

The magistrate had been very clear. By foiling the robbery attempt, they were likely in danger from the men who'd attacked them and those who aided them.

He turned to Cullen. 'Will you see if we can find drivers for the carriage or engage a new carriage and drivers to leave today?'

Cullen straightened. 'I will try, sir.' He hurried out the door.

'Ella, you can pack for us and arrange for some food to carry with us?'

She nodded and followed Cullen.

Lucien sank back into the chair.

Lady Rebecca swung around to him. 'See? You are too weak to travel.'

He rubbed his forehead. 'I am able to travel. It is nothing but sitting down.'

Once they were on Watling Street, the road well travelled since even before Roman times, the danger would be minimised. No more isolated sections of roads where they might be attacked.

She knelt down, bringing herself even with him. 'Please reconsider, Lucien. Wait one day. Will it matter so much?'

Yes. If it put her life in jeopardy one more time, it would matter a great deal.

He took her hand in his and looked into her eyes. 'Do you not realise I have been through events more treacherous than what we met on the road? I have been wounded before. I will manage, I promise you.'

She brought his hand to her lips. 'I do not wish any harm to come to you. You were so very ill during the night.'

He wished he could take her into his arms for his comfort as well as to comfort her.

'I am better,' he said in a low voice. 'It will be quite all right.'

By midday, Cullen had engaged a carriage and two coachmen who were eager for the employment.

'I'll ride above,' Cullen said. 'To watch the road.'

And to watch the coachmen.

Lady Rebecca had insisted upon purchasing several pillows and a blanket to make Lucien more comfortable and, by the time they were several miles down the road, he was glad of it. He felt every bump and rut in the road.

* * *

They travelled the whole day, stopping only to change horses and take quick refreshment. By the time they reached Shrewsbury, it was still light, but the sun was low in the sky. Shrewsbury, a market town, was still lively even at that late hour. They passed whole streets of timbered buildings that made it appear they'd travelled back to medieval England, but the inn the coachmen turned into could have belonged in Mayfair. Four storeys of red brick, it sported a gold statue of a lion above its door.

When they entered, they were greeted by Mr Lawrence, the owner and innkeeper, who set them up in two rooms, each with a closet where Cullen and Ella could sleep. By the time they climbed the stairs to the rooms, Lucien was spent, but he pushed himself, intending to arrange a private dining room.

When they reached the door of the room that was to be shared by Lady Rebecca and Ella, he took a moment to lean against the wall.

Lady Rebecca saw him. 'Lucien!' She rushed to his side. 'You ought to be lying down. You look like death itself.'

'I'm well enough,' he said, straightening again.

'No, you are not,' she insisted. She turned to Cullen. 'Cullen, take him to his room and put him into bed. This day has been entirely too difficult for him.'

Cullen dropped the portmanteaux he carried and helped Lucien to the room next door.

Lucien heard Mr Lawrence ask, 'What is wrong with him? It is not the influenza, is it?'

'Not the influenza. He was shot by highwaymen yesterday,' Lady Rebecca replied.

He could not hear the rest.

Cullen helped him undress. Lucien climbed into the bed. 'Arrange for a meal for yourselves,' he told the valet. 'Secure a private dining room. I merely need to rest a bit.'

'As you wish, sir.'

He heard Cullen leave the room and close the door behind him.

He hated feeling so weak, but, in the end, he could not fight it. He fell asleep within minutes.

Lucien became aware of sounds, a rustling in the room, but could not force himself to wake. A moment later the scent of broth reached his nostrils, as well as another scent. Lavender.

He opened his eyes.

Lady Rebecca stood next to the bed, placing a tray on a table.

She smiled down at him. 'I thought you should eat something.'

The tray held a bowl of soup, some bread and cheese. Though eating had been the last thing on his mind as they reached Shrewsbury, his stomach now cried out in hunger.

'Thank you.' He sat up. 'What of you? Did you eat?'

She nodded and draped a napkin around his neck, her fingers touching his bare skin and waking him in ways that had nothing to do with sleep.

What did it say about him that he was at ease with her even though he was dressed only in his drawers?

He'd become too close to her, obviously, which was an intimacy of sorts. Sharing the room on the fishing boat had started it, but with each step in her difficult journey, he felt more and more connected to her. At times he had to force himself to face the fact that, once she remembered everything from her upbringing, she would become an earl's daughter again.

But tonight…tonight he was simply glad of her company.

He glanced around the room. There was a table and chairs by the window. 'I'll get up. Sit at the table.'

'Very well.' She picked up the tray again and carried it over to the table.

He climbed out of bed and quickly donned his trousers and a shirt, wincing as he pulled his injured arm through the sleeve.

She must have been watching. 'How is your arm?'

Again it seemed perfectly natural that she witness him dressing. 'It is better.'

She looked unconvinced.

He sat at the table.

She took the chair opposite him. 'You have soup, as you can see. Turtle, I believe.'

He dipped his spoon into the bowl and tasted it, nodding his approval. 'It is good.' He gave her a half-smile. 'Of course, I am suddenly so hungry that anything would taste good.'

She cut him a slice of bread and a slice of cheese. Simple fare, but exactly what suited him right now. 'See? I was right. I knew you would be hungry.'

Their time together had attuned them to each other. In fact, he was so used to her company that he expected it would be wrenching to separate from her in London.

He looked up at her. 'How are you, my lady? The carriage ride must have been taxing for you as well.'

She smiled again. 'I have endured worse things.'

He could not help but smile back. 'Yes, we have, have we not?'

Their gazes caught and held.

She lowered her lashes and poured herself a cup of tea. 'Cullen learned something. There is a public coach, the Shrewsbury Wonder, that departs from this inn at five in the morning and reaches London the same day, although late at night. They have space for four passengers—'

He broke in. 'Do you wish to take this coach?'

Was she in a hurry to reach London? He'd not

thought of how she might feel about this trip. Perhaps she wanted to pursue her true life faster than he desired.

She looked surprised. 'No. I already told him no. It is too difficult a trip for you.'

Then why mention it? 'I can endure it if it is what you wish.'

Her eyes flickered with pain. 'It is not what I wish. I wish—' This time she interrupted herself. 'Never mind what I wish. I believe it is too difficult for you, but I have delayed your arrival in London by many days and I thought you should know there was a way to reach the city faster.'

'Do not say it.' He caught her gaze again. 'A couple more days will not matter.'

He hoped.

Chapter Eleven

There was so much more Claire wished to say to him, but when she looked into his eyes, the words wouldn't come. If only she could tell him how much she loathed the idea of reaching London, how much she wished she could simply stay with him.

Even if it were on a fishing boat, she would be content.

Her security. Her anchor.

But he wanted a ship, wanted to be back at sea, where he felt he most belonged. She could not stay with him. Besides, she was his family's enemy, a member of the loathed privileged class, and set to return to the world to which she was supposed to belong. More reason he did not wish to stay with her.

She hated seeing him in pain, had hated the fear he might die, the only secure part of her world. Life as she knew it—remembered it—began with him. Until his fever broke she'd been distraught with worry that he would die and her world would end with him.

And yet she knew she would soon part from him.

She reached across the table and grasped his hand. 'Have I told you how grateful I am to you, Lucien? And how sorry I am that I have put you through all this—this delay—and—and—the highwaymen and all.'

He moved a finger to stroke her skin. 'The highwaymen were not your fault, you know.'

'You would not have been in that carriage on that road if it had not been for me,' she said.

'We would not have survived the attack if it had not been for your bravery. And Ella's,' he countered.

That scene came back to her. 'Ella was so fierce and daring. She made me feel I could be, too.' She turned it around in her mind. 'I know this sounds silly, but I relish knowing I can remember what happened. Even the awful things like the highwaymen and the raft.'

And fearing him ill enough to die.

Their hands remained clasped.

'I know memories are important to you,' he said. 'And ours have been memorable.'

She felt that pull towards him, the one that made her wish to have his arms around her, his lips against hers, to have that physical intimacy that men and women desire. Those feelings that made her feel she must have been less than lady-like before the shipwreck.

If she did convince him to make love to her, she knew his sense of honour would compel him to offer marriage to her and a naval marriage was one he did not want.

She pulled her hand away. 'I am keeping you from eating and, I must confess, I am fatigued myself. I believe I should go to my room.' She stood and yawned for effect. 'Will you be all right without me?'

He picked up a piece of bread. 'I am feeling quite well, my lady. And Cullen will be here soon, I am sure.'

She walked to his side and, because she could not resist, leaned down to kiss his forehead.

'Goodnight,' she murmured.

She hurried out of the room.

Her room was right next door and she rushed inside, fearing she would burst into tears before she reached it.

They would have two more days together. Merely two.

She took a deep breath and paced the room willing herself not to weep. Weeping had never done her a bit of good—

She stopped.

That was almost a memory!

She closed her eyes and tried to imagine a time that weeping had not done her a bit of good.

Nothing came.

The door opened and Ella walked in. 'What are you doing, m'lady?'

'Trying—trying to remember something.' She wiped her eyes.

Ella came closer. 'Are you weeping, m'lady? Why are you weeping?'

'I wasn't weeping.' She'd been trying not to weep.

'Well, you look as if you were,' the maid insisted. 'Did you and the Captain have another row?'

'We did not have a row.' On the contrary. He'd been lovely with her. Tears threatened again and she blinked rapidly to force them away.

Ella put her hands on her hips. 'You had a row. But do not worry. The Captain will come around. Cullen always does and then he is sweeter than ever.'

Claire needed to correct this impression of Ella's. 'Ella, Captain Roper and I are not—not in a romantic way towards each other. I have told you before. He rescued me from the sea and has helped me ever since.'

The maid shook her head. 'You can tell me a hundred times, but I will never believe it.'

Claire had this inexplicable need to convince

her, though. 'Do you not know why I am travelling to London?'

'Because that is where the Captain wishes to
go,' Ella replied.

'No,' she said patiently. 'I am going to London
to be married.'

Ella broke out in a huge grin. 'You and the Captain are going to be married?'

'No!' A stab of pain pierced her insides.

'Then who are you to marry?' Ella asked, looking very sceptical.

Claire turned away. 'I am to marry Lord Stonecroft.'

'You are not!' Ella's voice rose in shock. 'Who
is Lord Stonecroft?'

She waved a hand. 'Some baron.'

'Some baron?' Ella repeated.

Claire turned her back to the maid. 'Here. Help
me dress for bed.'

Ella untied her laces and helped her out of the
dress.

'This Baron Stonecroft,' the maid went on. 'Is
he as nice as the Captain?'

'I—I do not know.'

Ella untied Claire's corset. 'Well, is he as handsome?'

Claire wriggled out of her corset. 'I do not
know.'

'What do you mean, you do not know?' Ella
cried. 'Have you not met him?'

'I do not know if I have met him.'

'You must know!' Ella turned her around and peered into her eyes. 'Are you ill, m'lady? You are talking nonsense.'

Claire had a sudden empathy for Ella's parents. Ella's outspokenness was unrelenting.

'It may sound like nonsense,' Claire said, 'but it is true. I know very little about Lord Stonecroft except that I was betrothed to him. I do not remember him. I learned about him in Dublin when my brother called upon me. I did not remember my brother either.'

Ella shook her head. 'I do not understand you.'

'Let us have some tea.' Claire wanted to tell Ella everything. She needed a friend right now.

There was a kettle in the fireplace, a pot, cups and milk on the table and tins of tea and sugar. Ella, still looking baffled, set about making the tea while Claire changed into her nightdress. She wrapped her Kashmir shawl around her shoulders and lowered herself into a chair at the table.

'Sit with me,' she told Ella.

Ella, a wary gleam in her eye, sat opposite her.

Claire poured tea for both of them.

'Something happened to me because of the shipwreck.' She handed Ella one of the cups. 'Captain Roper said he was taking me to one of the rowboats when a wave washed over us and swept us into the sea. I was hit on the head.' She took a sip of her tea. 'But I do not remember this.

When I woke up, we were on a raft—a door from the ship, really. And I remembered nothing about myself before that moment.'

'You lost your memory?' Ella asked.

'Yes,' Claire replied.

'Because of being hit on the head?'

'I do not know about that,' Claire said. 'I remember some things. Everyday things. How to care for myself. I know things, like about the war or about London or Dublin. I don't remember anything about myself, though. I don't remember being in London or Dublin. I don't remember reading about the war or learning anything that I simply know.'

'But-but…' Ella stammered, 'you seem like an ordinary lady.' She put her hand to her mouth. 'Beg pardon. That sounded wrong. I don't mean you are ordinary. I mean, it doesn't show.' She peered at Claire. 'You really don't remember about yourself?'

Claire sipped more tea. 'No. I know my name because Captain Roper told me my name. It never sounds right when I'm called Lady Rebecca, though.'

'G'way.' Ella's eyes grew big.

'When my brother—my half-brother—came to Dublin, he looked like a stranger to me. When he told me I was to marry Lord Stonecroft, it was as if that was the first time I'd heard it. The only people I remember are the Captain and the people I've met since the shipwreck, the fishermen who saved us, the innkeepers where we stayed, the clerks in the shops we visited.' She smiled at Ella. 'And you and Cullen, of course.'

'My poor lady!'

The young woman's sympathy touched her and tears stung her eyes again. She took another sip of tea to regain her composure.

Ella did the same, looking very thoughtful.

'So,' the maid finally said. 'You are going to London to marry this lord you don't remember?'

Claire nodded.

Ella slammed her hand on the table. 'How can you? You don't know him!'

'I don't know what else to do,' Claire admitted.

'Stay with the Captain!' Ella cried. 'Marry him!'

Her heart ached in her chest. 'He does not wish to marry me, Ella. He is going to London so that he can get a new ship.'

'No,' she said.

'He wants to go back to the sea.' Claire knew this without question. 'And even if he did not, his family and mine were enemies two generations ago. My grandfather caused his grandfather to lose his fortune and property. He would not wish to marry an enemy.'

'That is nothing,' Ella insisted. 'Cullen's family and mine have been enemies for longer than that, but what is that to us?'

'I—I became upset tonight, because we will likely reach London in two days and what will I do when I must say goodbye to the Captain? He is the only one who knows about my loss of memory.' She quickly added, 'And now you, of course.'

'I won't tell anyone,' Ella promised.

Her loyalty made Claire wish to weep all over again.

Ella set down her teacup and stood. 'I think we will be rising quite early tomorrow, so I think you should go to bed.'

Claire smiled inwardly. Her servant, a girl younger than herself—probably—was telling her what to do. 'Very well, Ella.'

'And tomorrow we'll start trying to get your memory back.'

The next morning Claire rose early, hearing Ella already moving about the room. They washed and dressed and met Lucien and Cullen for breakfast. They were on the road by eight o'clock.

Cullen again rode on the outside, but he'd already decided that the coachmen seemed like honest, hardworking men. This road would be well travelled and their coach never out of sight of some other horseman or vehicle. The possibility of another attack seemed remote.

Claire was heartened that Lucien's colour had improved. He reported feeling well, but, then, he would say that, so she watched him closely.

'I sent a messenger ahead,' Lucien told her. 'To let Lord Stonecroft know you will arrive tomorrow.'

Claire's stomach plummeted. 'I suppose that was wise.'

Parting from him was becoming more real.

When they were well on the road, Ella spoke up. 'Captain, m'lady told me about losing her memory.'

Lucien responded to her in a careful, non-committal tone. 'She did?'

'I think it must be a hardship not to remember anything about yourself,' Ella went on. 'I think we should help m'lady remember.'

He looked as if he were stifling a smile. 'I agree. How do you think we should do that?'

Ella appeared lost in thought for a moment. 'We should ask her questions.'

Claire felt her stomach clench in anxiety.

Lucien must have noticed. 'Are you willing, my lady?'

She took a couple of long breaths. 'I am willing to try.'

He turned to Ella. 'So what questions?'

Ella tapped her cheek with her finger. 'I don't know,' she finally said.

'I tried something before,' Lucien went on. 'Asking general questions. Nothing about an actual memory, just questions about life.'

Ella blinked. 'I don't understand.'

Claire's hand shook, but she wove her fingers together to disguise that fact. 'The Captain told me to talk about a school.'

The maid brightened. 'Did you remember anything?'

Claire shook her head. But she'd almost remembered.

'So,' Lucien said, 'we should ask about something different. Like…' He paused. 'Like, tell us about a house.'

'A house?' Claire felt her skin heat. She wished she had a fan.

'Yes,' Lucien said mildly, as if it was the most inconsequential of subjects.

'Do you mean like a country house?' she asked.

'Yes.' He sat up straighter. 'A country house. Describe it.'

'I don't remember a country house.' Her heart pounded.

'Imagine one. Any one,' he said. 'Remember. Do not think about it too much. Just respond.'

She released a shuddering breath. 'Like one of stucco?'

'What colour stucco?' he pressed.

She waved a hand. 'White.'

'What style?'

'Style?' She stalled.

He nodded. 'Jacobin? Tudor? Palladian?'

'Palladian,' she said. 'Tudor or Jacobin would not be stucco, would they?'

One corner of his mouth lifted. 'I would not know. Very well, we have a white Palladian country house. What does the hall look like? Remember, you are merely inventing this.'

'It is long and narrow with a wide staircase at the end and plasterwork cornices and ceiling.' She blinked. That seemed so specific.

'Very well,' he went on. 'Now imagine a room. Any room.'

A vision of a room flashed through her mind. A schoolroom. She heard a child's laughter. Her heart raced. 'A—a schoolroom. Tables, slates, books.'

Ella broke in. 'You are remembering something, m'lady!'

The vision vanished. 'But it does not feel like remembering. I cannot place myself there.'

'Try imagining another room,' Lucien suggested.

She saw a small sitting room and a man. More like the shadow of a man. Her anxiety rose until she wished she could jump out of the carriage.

'I—I cannot!' She wrapped her arms around herself.

He reached across the carriage and touched her arm. 'No matter,' he murmured. 'We will leave it now.'

'M'lady!' Ella cried. 'Do not fret so. We did not mean to upset you.'

She took a deep breath. 'I am quite restored. I do not know what happened.'

* * *

Lucien thought he knew what happened. Something she almost remembered frightened her. Perhaps it was not the blow to her head; perhaps it was fear that made her lose her memory. What else could have happened to her besides the shipwreck?

And how did he know he was not delivering her to the lion's den by taking her to London?

'I have an idea.' Ella leaned forward. 'Let us sing a song. Maybe you will remember music.'

Lady Rebecca still looked strained, but she seemed to force a smile. 'We can try.'

The maid began singing.

Yonder stands a pretty maiden,
Who she is I do not know,
I'll go court her for her beauty,
Let her answer yes or no.

Her voice was a crystalline soprano. She turned to Lady Rebecca. 'Do you know this one?

Lady Rebecca shook her head.

'Are you sure?' Ella sang more.

Pretty maid, I've come to court you,
If your favour I do gain
And you make me hearty welcome,
I will call this way again.

Ella looked at Lady Rebecca. 'No?'

'I do not remember it.' She looked distressed.

Ella sighed. 'How about this one?'

As we marched down to Fenario
As we marched down to Fenario
Our captain fell in love with a lady like a
dove
And the name she was called was pretty
Peggy-o

'I do not know that one either,' Lady Rebecca said quickly.

Lucien was glad she interrupted. That song was about a captain.

'Sing a song you know,' Lucien suggested to Lady Rebecca.

She gave him an annoyed face. 'You sing a song first.'

Before Lucien rose in rank, he'd loved singing along with the seamen as they did their work. He hadn't sung much since then.

And most of those songs the seamen sang were not fit for ladies.

He thought a moment, then remembered one that was not too scandalous.

Beauing, belleing, dancing, drinking,
Breaking windows, cursing, sinking,
Ever raking, never thinking,
Live the Rakes of Mallow—

Ella laughed with delight and he even made Lady Rebecca smile.

He finished to the end where the Rakes of Mallow married and raked no more. They married and he remembered he was taking Lady Rebecca to be married.

'Now it is your turn,' he told her, hoping she had not made that same connection.

She closed her eyes and he feared she would not find one she remembered.

But she began in a halting but rich contralto that warmed inside him like a good glass of brandy.

The hours sad I left a maid
A lingering farewell taking
Whose sighs and tears my steps delayed
I thought her heart was breaking...

'I cannot finish it.' Her eyes glistened.

With tears? he wondered. *Sighs and tears.*

'I don't remember.' Her voice cracked.

Ella put an arm around her. 'But you remembered a little!'

Ella continued to ask Lady Rebecca questions, but all that resulted in was more distress in her eyes.

'I think we should give Lady Rebecca a rest,' he told Ella. 'She'll have a headache soon enough if we persist.'

He would not be surprised if her head ached right now.

'But her memory must come back before to-morrow,' Ella cried. 'I cannot bear to leave her if it does not.'

Yes. The closer they came to London, the worse Lucien felt. He would be leaving her adrift without any tether connecting her to her past. He was in her memory longer than anyone else and everything they'd been through since the shipwreck had bound them together even more.

How was he to leave her?

Chapter Twelve

Later in the day the weather turned even colder and rain poured down, making it hard going for the horses. They were forced to stop for the day at the next coaching inn. With luck they could still make London the next day.

Cullen was soaked to the skin, not having the same coats and hats the coachmen wore. Lucien let Ella tend to him, to see he changed into dry clothes and to care for the wet ones. That left Lucien alone with Lady Rebecca in a private dining room he'd engaged.

He lowered himself into a chair. His arm ached like the devil.

'You are in pain,' Lady Rebecca said, approaching him.

He looked up at her. 'The last of the ride was a bit rough. It'll pass.'

She crouched down. 'Let me see it.'

Her face was even with his and their eyes met

briefly. Hers were filled with determination and concern. She'd fight him over this.

'Help me off with my coat, then.'

He turned in the chair and she gingerly pulled his coat over his shoulders and off his arms, taking care to avoid his wound.

His shirtsleeve was dotted with blood.

She frowned and drew the sleeve over his shoulder. Her fingers on his bare skin made him flare with desire as she exposed the bandage, red where blood seeped out of the wound.

'It is bleeding,' she said. 'I am going to take the bandage off.'

She untied the knot and unwound the bandage. Although she was gentle, it felt as if she were pounding on his arm instead of barely touching it.

He much preferred the desire over the pain.

When the bandage was off, Lucien could see that some of the stitches had been pulled apart, causing the bleeding.

She looked closely at the wound. She rose and walked over to an ewer and basin on a table in the corner of the room. She poured some water in the basin, put a towel around her arm and brought them both back to Lucien.

'Let me clean it a little so we can see how serious this is.' She moistened the towel and dabbed at the wound.

It throbbed. Lucien talked through the pain.

'I thought ladies became squeamish at the sight of blood.'

She darted a glance at him. 'I lost that sensibility when your blood soaked your coat and would not stop flowing.'

She'd been valiant at that time. 'That was a lot, I admit.'

She focused on cleaning his wound. 'This hardly signifies.' She leaned back. 'I think the bleeding is stopping. We should bandage it and you should rest that arm.'

They had been in such intimate situations these last weeks that this felt entirely normal to him, he in his shirtsleeves, his arm bared, so she could tend to him.

Tomorrow they would part.

How would he stand never seeing her morning, noon and night? He'd become so used to her.

She stood. 'I am going to find some clean bandages. I am sure the innkeeper has some.'

She walked out of the room and it seemed devoid of light without her.

It appeared as if they'd both decided to treat this last night together as if their parting was not imminent. They spent a comfortable dinner with Ella and Cullen. Ella, ever the one to spur everyone on, got Lucien to tell of some of his exploits at sea. He shared the ones fit for ladies to hear. Cullen talked of events on the farm and of coming to Dublin after knowing nothing but the farm. Ella was a gratifying audience and even Lady Rebecca seemed to relax and enjoy herself. But, then, the memories others experienced seemed to comfort her.

In the morning of their last day, the messenger Lucien had sent to Lord Stonecroft knocked at the door of the dining room where Lucien sat with Lady Rebecca, Ella and Cullen.

'I have news for you,' the man said.

'How did you find me?' Lucien asked. There must have been dozens of inns along the route he might have stopped in.

'Just stopped at every inn I could see.' He held out the envelope that Lucien had given him the previous day. 'Lord Stonecroft is not in London. He is spending the summer in Bath.'

'Bath?' Lady Rebecca exclaimed.

Bath was one of those places naval officers retired to after leaving their ships. Once most fashionable to the titled elite, it now had been replaced by Brighton where the Prince Regent preferred to spend his time.

'I thought it best to come back to find you,' the man said. 'If you want me to deliver the letter to the gentleman in Bath, I'll be off straight away.'

Lucien handed the man some coins. 'Yes. By all means deliver the letter to Bath.'

The man looked happily at the money in his hand, bowed and rushed off.

'So we go to Bath, apparently,' Lucien said.

'No, Lucien,' Lady Rebecca cried. 'You cannot go to Bath. You need to be at the Admiralty to be assigned a new ship.'

'I will escort you to Bath,' he said quietly. 'I will see you safely to where you must go. What kind of man would I be if I left you now?'

'But what will happen if you do not appear at the Admiralty?' she asked.

He did not know what would happen. He'd been absent for weeks. He wished he'd asked the messenger to wait. He'd not even informed the Admiralty that he was alive.

'It will be a longer trip than to London,' Cullen spoke up. 'Shall I go speak to the coachmen?'

'Thank you, Cullen. And if they are in agreement to transport us, see if they can be ready in half an hour.' Lucien would write to the Admiralty from Bath.

Bath echoed in Claire's mind. Golden buildings. Hills. A towering cathedral.

She held her breath. Was that a memory?

She glanced from Lucien to Ella and decided not to say anything. They would only press her and she'd disappoint them again by not remembering as they wished her to.

And likely she'd wind up with a raging headache, as well.

When they were on the road again, Claire paid close attention to the scenery outside. Would something look familiar?

Nothing did.

The weather outside was dismal and damp with a steady drizzle. It matched Claire's mood. She must still say goodbye to Lucien, if not today, tomorrow.

She tried to think of how she might feel to meet Lord Stonecroft, but her insides twisted with anxiety at that thought. Instead, she pushed herself to remember everything about her time with Lucien, from waking in his arms in the middle of the Irish Sea to tending his wound the night before.

The coachmen drove the carriage at a daring clip, jostling its passengers as it made good time on the often muddy roads. Claire worried about Lucien's wound, but he insisted it was fine. Since Cullen rode with them and sat on the backward-facing seat with Ella, Claire, next to Lucien, could not easily see Lucien's face.

They reached Bath as the sun dipped below the horizon turning everything a sombre grey. They pulled into a coaching inn called the West Gate. A letter for Lucien awaited them. The messenger had delivered Lucien's letter to Lord Stonecroft and he agreed they could call upon him the next day.

Too soon, thought Claire. But Lucien had altered his plans more than once for her sake. She must think of him.

They procured two rooms, and all were so exhausted that they retired for the night without dinner.

'Tomorrow you might meet Lord Stonecroft,' Ella remarked as she helped Claire ready herself for bed. 'I wonder what he will be like.'

Claire's anxiety about Stonecroft had settled like a hard rock inside her stomach. 'I wonder, too.'

'Do you think you fell in love with him?' Her eyes turned starry for a moment. 'You'd think you would remember someone you fell in love with. I could certainly never forget Cullen.'

'I wish I did remember.' Then she would know, too. Did she love him?

Ella helped her into her nightdress. 'What time will you call upon him?'

'I believe Lucien said eleven, by Lord Stonecroft's request.' Perhaps she would have most of the morning with Lucien.

Claire rose early and dressed in the same travelling dress she'd worn the day before, the patterned dark green one. In their fatigue last night, they'd made no plans for breakfast or for the rest of the morning. Claire wanted to spend that time with Lucien. She hoped he would knock on the door and invite her to dine with him.

Ella was busy straightening the room while Claire paced up and down, waiting to hear more bells marking the hour.

'Shall I go to his room and see what is what?' Ella asked.

'His room?' She knew precisely who Ella meant.

'The Captain,' Ella said.

'No,' she replied. 'The Captain may have other plans. I will wait until the next bells and then you may see about breakfast for us both.'

Ella folded Claire's Kashmir shawl and placed it on a chair by the door. 'I'm going to see what their plans are.'

Before Claire could protest, Ella dashed out of the room. Claire paced faster. Now he would feel obliged to spend the morning with her. She walked to the window and looked out over the street.

The buildings in their golden Bath stone felt comfortable. Familiar.

Had she been here before?

A knock sounded at the door. She crossed the room to open it.

Lucien stood in the doorway. 'Would you like to have breakfast?' he asked.

She peered at him. 'Did Ella put you up to this?'

He looked puzzled. 'Ella? No. I was simply waiting until I knew you were awake.'

She smiled.

'I am ready.' She put on her hat and picked up her Kashmir shawl and gloves.

He glanced at the shawl. 'Did you not want to eat in the public rooms here?'

'No. I—I—I assumed we would walk around the city first and see what else is here.' Although why she assumed that, she did not know.

He bowed. 'Whatever your pleasure.'

They walked down the stairs to the hall and out the main door that opened on to the street.

'I have not been in Bath before,' Lucien said.

Claire did not know why she knew, but she knew they should turn left. 'Let us go this way.'

They crossed the street and walked past the Pump Room. She knew this was where one could drink from a fountain the metallic-tasting waters that made Bath a place where people came to cure whatever ailed them. They turned again when in front of Bath Abbey and crossed another street to an area of shops.

She stopped in front of one establishment. 'We could eat here,' she said.

'You know this place?' His eyes widened.

She should have realised he would guess that she had not been simply wandering. 'It is where they sell Sally Lunn's buns.'

They went inside and ordered the sweet spongy rolls that had been served there for decades.

'How much did you remember?' he asked, tearing off a piece of roll.

'Only the places,' she responded. 'I know Bath, but I do not know why. I believe I could walk the whole of it and know each notable place, but I cannot remember ever being here.'

'None the less, it is more than you've remembered before.' His tone was encouraging.

'Why should I have been here, though?' she added. 'Did I live here? I cannot close my eyes and picture a place I could call home, but I can close my eyes and see the Crescent.'

'You remember it.' He took a sip of a mug of coffee.

'I must have been here.' She nibbled on her bun.

He leaned forward. 'Perhaps you also remembered a school in Bristol. Bristol is not far from here. It would make sense that you might have had many opportunities to visit Bath.'

How she would love to travel to Bristol and find that school. Maybe someone there could help fill in some of the blanks in her mind.

How she wished she could travel there with Lucien.

After they finished breakfast, they stepped outside again into a day that was chilly and grey, but at least not raining. Claire wrapped her Kashmir shawl around her, closing her eyes for a moment and remembering the shop where Lucien had purchased it for her. She remembered the display of all the colourful shawls and the clerk who seemed to know who she was, the scent of the fabric, the expression of approval on Lucien's face when she selected this shawl.

She still felt it was too extravagant.

But, then, it had also helped save Lucien's life.

She made herself remember that terrible day, as well. All memories, even that horrible one, were precious to her.

And it seemed all her memories involved Lucien.

If today was to be the last chance to build memories with him, she was determined to do so.

'Would you like to see the Royal Crescent and the Circus?' she asked him.

He looked directly into her eyes before answering. 'Yes. Certainly.'

She smiled, so glad he was willing to spend more time together. 'Then, come! I know the way there.'

She led him back to Westgate Street, walking to the end and turning to walk past the Theatre Royal to Queen Square. Claire was able to name each notable spot they passed.

She paused before the square, staring at the obelisk in its centre. 'The square is different,' she said. 'The obelisk—I think it used to be surrounded by a pool of water.'

Lucien touched her hand. 'You are remembering things in more and more detail.'

But what use was it if she could not put herself in those memories?

They continued to the Circus, a circle of terrace houses built in the Palladian style fifty years before and one of the most admired sites in Bath.

They walked the entire circle.

'Is it not beautiful?' she asked Lucien.

'Quite grand,' he admitted.

An older gentleman approached them. 'Roper? Is that you? As I live and breathe.'

Lucien's face lit with pleasure. 'Sir Richard!'

The two men shook hands, holding on longer than was typical.

'What the devil?' his friend asked. 'I'd heard that you'd drowned. But here you are in Bath.'

'I am indeed alive.' Lucien glanced at Claire. 'Let me present you to Lady Rebecca Pierce. My lady, this is Admiral Sir Richard Bickerton. I served on his ship in my younger days.'

'And a fine young midshipman he was.' Sir Richard grinned. He turned to Claire and bowed. 'Lady Rebecca.'

Bowing to her never felt right.

She curtsied. 'A pleasure, sir.'

Lucien and the Admiral must be full of memories of their days together.

The Admiral gave Lucien an approving look. 'Will you be in Bath long?'

Claire was eager to hear that answer.

'I am uncertain at this time,' Lucien responded.

'Tomorrow?' Sir Richard persisted. 'Would you call upon me tomorrow?' He pointed to one of the terrace houses in the Circus. 'I reside at Number Fifteen.'

'I will come, sir,' Lucien said.

The two men arranged a time and shook hands again. Sir Richard turned and bowed to Claire. 'You must come, too, my lady.'

'I—I may not be at liberty, sir, but thank you.' She did not know what tomorrow would bring.

He bowed again and went on his way.

Claire and Lucien walked on to the Royal Crescent.

'This is also very grand,' Lucien said as the buildings came into view.

'It is one of Bath's greatest attractions,' she said, although her enthusiasm had waned.

They walked on to the lawn in front of the Crescent and took in the whole expanse of terrace houses with identical front façades, built on a curve.

'My lady,' Lucien said quietly.

She turned her attention to him.

'The direction I was given to Lord Stonecroft's residence was Number Five Royal Crescent.'

Lucien watched her face fall as if disappointed at this news.

He thought she would be glad that Lord Stonecroft resided in such a desirable location.

The Royal Crescent was an imposing sight. What lady would not want to live in such a beautiful location?

She set her chin. 'I suppose this is a very good address.'

What could he say when every part of his body wanted to keep her with him longer? He was used to protecting her, that was it. But he'd posted a letter to the Admiralty, telling them he would be in London in a few days.

She smiled wanly. 'I am a bit apprehensive.'

For that brief moment she looked very apprehensive.

'I will call upon him with you,' he said impulsively.

She looked relieved. 'Will you? I was not certain.'

He had not been certain either.

She smiled again, this time bravely. 'I am sure all will be well. I only wish I could remember. I must have wanted to marry him, do you not think? Otherwise why would I have agreed?'

What was the likelihood of it being a love match? Lucien thought. Members of the *ton* married for advantage, did they not? On the other hand, what if she did love Stonecroft, and he, her? Is that not what Lucien would most wish for her?

So why did that thought bring Lucien no comfort?

'It is very hard not to know,' he finally said, but

he was not sure if he was speaking about himself or about her.

'How long before we must call upon Lord Stonecroft?' Anxious lines creased her forehead again.

He pulled out his watch. 'Two hours.'

She averted her head, almost as if the words had slapped her on the cheek.

'Do you wish to return to the inn?' he asked. Perhaps she wished to freshen up before meeting the man to whom she was betrothed.

'Only if you wish it,' she replied.

'I am content to walk,' he said.

She nodded and they turned and retraced their steps, making their way back towards the Abbey.

When they walked past one building, she said, 'This is the Pump Room. You must try the waters before you leave Bath.'

'Would you like to go in now?' he asked, wanting in these last moments together to please her.

She shook her head. 'It is always full of people and I do not wish to be around people right now.'

They walked instead to the river and watched the boats travel on its water.

'We have been through much together, Lucien,' she remarked, not looking at him. 'I must, while I have this opportunity, thank you for all you have done for me.'

He felt his throat tighten. 'You saved me, as well, remember.'

She turned and looked up at him. 'You did more than save me, Lucien.'

It was Lucien's turn to avert his gaze. 'It was my pleasure.'

Emotions he was not quite sure how to name churned inside him. Parting from her would be more difficult than he imagined.

She looked up at the sky. 'We are lucky it is not raining.'

Although rain would suit his mood.

They looked out on the River Avon again. Its expanse was so narrow in comparison to oceans, he felt as if he could jump it.

He stole a glance at her, looking lovely in her green dress and colourful shawl. The green of her hat framed her face and those changeable eyes of hers matched her clothes.

A memory of her lips against his returned to him and desire stirred inside him. He should not desire this woman of all women. Because of her status. Because of her family. Because he was delivering her to the man she was supposed to marry.

Because he needed to get back to the sea.

He pulled out his watch again. 'We should walk back.'

Chapter Thirteen

They did not speak much on the walk back to the Crescent. Claire held Lucien's arm, very aware that this might be the last time she could touch him. She again recounted her memories of him in her mind, determined not to forget a single detail.

Too soon they stood at the doorway of Number Five.

Lucien sounded the knocker and the door was opened by a footman in livery.

'Lady Rebecca Pierce and Captain Roper,' Lucien told the man. 'Lord Stonecroft is expecting us.'

The footman stood aside, holding open the door. They entered the hall with its white and black marbled floor. Straight ahead was a staircase with an arch above it. All the doorways on this floor were also arched.

It did not look like a place she had ever seen before.

'I will announce you,' the footman said.

They followed him up the stairs to the drawing room.

Claire's heart was pounding in her chest and she found it hard to breathe.

The footman knocked on the door. A voice on the other side answered and the footman opened the door. 'Lady Rebecca Pierce and Captain Roper.'

Claire stepped inside first.

Seated on a sofa was a grey-haired gentleman. He rose and gestured with his hand. 'Come in. Come in, my dear,' he said.

Could this be Lord Stonecroft?

He looked to be in his fifties. Not unpleasant in countenance, but so much older than she'd imagined.

Claire took only a step forward.

On a chair nearby was a woman near to his age.

The woman rose and crossed the room to her. 'Lady Rebecca, how delighted we are to see you. Goodness! We thought you had drowned.'

Claire turned to Lucien, grasping for a lifeline. 'This is Captain Roper. My rescuer.'

The woman smiled at Lucien. 'Captain Roper? How nice that you have brought Lady Rebecca to us.'

Lucien tilted his head. 'Forgive me. You are?'

The woman laughed. 'I am Miss Attwood. Stonecroft's sister.' She glanced to the man.

He must be Stonecroft.

'Lady Rebecca, come to me.' Stonecroft patted the back of the sofa.

She gave what must have been a panicked look to Lucien. She did not move.

'How much do you know about what happened to Lady Rebecca?' Lucien asked.

Lord Stonecroft shrugged. 'Keneagle wrote that she had not drowned and would be travelling to London. Of course, I was not in London, but the letter reached me here. Then your message came that you would be in Bath today.'

'You need to know what happened to her.' Lucien told a shortened version, glossing over the sleeping accommodations on the fishing boat. And the kisses.

'My goodness!' Miss Attwood exclaimed. 'How very dreadful.' She gestured to the chairs and sofa. 'But do let us sit. We should be getting tea.'

Claire wanted to sit with Lucien, but Lord Stonecroft patted the space beside him on the sofa. 'Sit next to me, my dear.'

She lowered herself there.

'There is one more thing you should know,' Lucien said.

'What is that, Captain?' Miss Attwood responded.

'Lady Rebecca has lost her memory.' He glanced at her, his gaze giving her strength to endure this interview. 'When we were swept out to sea, some debris struck her head, rendering her unconscious. When she woke up on the raft, she remembered nothing from before that moment.'

'Unbelievable!' Miss Attwood exclaimed.

'You remember nothing?' Stonecroft asked her.

'I know things. Like about the war. About how things work,' she explained. 'I remember places, but I cannot remember myself being in them.'

Stonecroft looked annoyed. 'You remembered we are betrothed.'

'No, my lord.' She lowered her voice. 'I did not remember. My brother told me. I do not remember anything about you.'

'Pffft!' Miss Attwood made a dismissive gesture with her hand. 'Surely this loss of memory is temporary.'

The footman brought in tea.

'Would you like to pour, dear?' Miss Attwood asked her, then looked worried. 'Do you remember how to pour tea?'

'Yes, I remember those sorts of things.' Claire reached for the teapot. 'How do you take your tea?'

They told her and she busied herself pouring the tea.

'Where are you staying, dear?' Miss Attwood asked.

'The West Gate Inn,' Lucien replied as Claire handed them each a teacup.

Lord Stonecroft's brows rose. 'West Gate, you say? No. Not the best place. All sorts stay there.'

It seemed to Claire like a fairly normal coaching inn, like many where they'd stopped on this trip.

'Stonecroft.' Miss Attwood's expression brightened. 'We should have Lady Rebecca stay here. It would be entirely respectable, because I am here to chaperon. And you are to be married anyway.'

'Yes, that would do.' Stonecroft nodded. He turned to Lucien. 'You will have her things sent here.'

Lucien stiffened. 'Only if Lady Rebecca wishes it.'

What other choice did she have? If she moved in with Lord Stonecroft, Lucien would be free to go to London.

'It is the perfect solution, dear,' Miss Attwood went on. 'Where else would you stay? Unless you have a relation here.'

Lucien replied in a taut voice, 'She cannot remember if she has a relation here. Her brother did not speak of any relations.'

Stonecroft waved his hand. 'Well, she cannot stay at West Gate Inn.'

Miss Attwood put down her teacup. 'Really, dear, you must stay with us. We have a lovely room that will be perfect for you until the nuptials take place.'

Claire's stomach clenched.

She was supposed to marry this man. She'd never expected him to be old enough to be her father. Or to seem so much of a stranger, but marrying him had been already arranged and she'd already agreed to it.

It was just so difficult to think of moving into this gentleman's house.

And being apart from Lucien.

Lucien turned to her with a troubled expression. 'Do you wish to stay here?'

She took a sip of her tea and could barely meet his gaze. 'It appears to be the best solution.'

She had to release Lucien; she knew that.

'Excellent!' Miss Attwood said. 'I will show you your room and the house as soon as we finish tea.'

Claire quickly added, 'I must have my maid with me. I insist upon that.'

'You have a maid?' Miss Attwood said. 'Was she in the shipwreck, too?'

Claire felt the pain of that poor maid lost in the shipwreck. 'No. This maid is new, but I must have her.'

Immediately she felt guilty. She'd be separating Ella from Cullen, but Lucien might not need Cullen to go to London with him. Perhaps she could also insist Cullen be employed.

'Her maid is at the inn,' Lucien said.

Stonecroft rose and walked over to a bell pull. He addressed Lucien. 'I will arrange for my carriage to take you back to that inn. You will arrange for Lady Rebecca's things to be sent back with the carriage. And this maid, of course.'

Claire felt her face heat. How dare this man command Lucien as if he were a servant!

Lucien stood. 'No, sir. I will walk back to the inn. And I dare say I will reach it before your carriage can be ready.'

Stonecroft shrugged.

All Claire could think was Lucien was leaving! She panicked inside. 'I will walk you out.'

She rose, as did Miss Attwood and Stonecroft.

No! She did not want them anywhere near her when she had to say goodbye.

'Please.' Her voice rose. 'I would like to say goodbye to the Captain alone.'

Stonecroft glanced away.

His sister said, 'Of course you would, dear. We will wait here. Come back when you are finished.'

'Good day.' Lucien bowed to them both.

She followed him out the door and closed it behind her. They were private for that moment in the hallway at the top of the stairs.

He turned to her. 'Are you certain you wish to stay here?'

No! she wanted to cry. 'It seems a good solution, does it not? It is what I was bound to do before—before the shipwreck.'

He nodded and turned to the stairs.

She caught his arm. 'I—I do not wish to say

goodbye, Lucien. After all this time—' The whole of her memory. Her only anchor.

He wrapped his arms around her and held her close and she luxuriated in the familiarity of his warmth and strength. She felt safe in his arms, as he'd kept her safe on the open sea.

He eventually released her. 'You will be able to reach me through the Admiralty. If you need me, you have merely to ask.'

If she asked him to stay with her longer, she knew he would do so. He would never abandon her. But she cared about him too much to ask that of him. The sooner he returned to London, the sooner he could be back in command of a ship, where he most wanted to be.

He descended the stairs and retrieved his hat and gloves from the footman attending the hall. The footman opened the door.

Before he crossed the threshold, he turned and looked up at her standing at the top of the stairs. Their gazes caught and Claire thought her heart would stop.

He walked out the door.

A fine mist of rain met Lucien as he stepped on to the pavement in front of the Royal Crescent terrace house. He filled his lungs with the cool air, wanting it to refresh him. But nothing eased the turmoil inside him.

He detested Lord Stonecroft.

The man was everything he despised about aristocrats. And it was not merely because he had commanded Lucien to do what he expected. He detested that Stonecroft exhibited no sympathy for Lady Rebecca having endured a shipwreck and the loss of her memory. Lucien imagined the man would have shrugged off learning of the attack by the highwaymen had Lucien told him about it.

Plus he was old. An old nobleman coveting a young, vital woman.

Stonecroft would touch her, bed her.

It made Lucien churn with rage.

But he had no right to feel such emotions. She'd made her decision to marry the man before Lucien had ever known her. It was what ladies of her status aspired to and better than to marry a man whose first love was the navy and the sea.

He and Lady Rebecca were merely attached to each other through what they'd endured together. He could admit that he'd admired her. Desired her. But they belonged in two different worlds. Once her memory returned, she would realise that.

He strode down the pavement, past the Circus where Sir Richard lived. He'd promised to call upon the man the next day. So he would not start for London this day.

He'd been pleased to see his former Captain, who had been so instrumental in making him the navy man he was. Who knew when he would ever see Sir Richard again?

One more day's delay could not matter.

He walked swiftly, and when he reached the West Gate Inn, he searched for Cullen and Ella and found them in the public rooms having refreshment.

'Have you need of me, sir?' Cullen jumped to his feet as soon as he spied Lucien.

Lucien gestured for him to sit. 'Let me join you for a moment.' He pulled up a chair and signalled for the tavern maid to bring him a tankard of ale. 'Lady Rebecca is at Lord Stonecroft's.'

'At Lord Stonecroft's? What time will she be returning?' Ella asked.

'She will not be returning. She will be staying in Lord Stonecroft's house.'

Ella's face fell. 'No!'

'She would like you to come to her,' he told Ella. 'To be her lady's maid.'

Ella frowned and looked over at Cullen. 'What about Cullen?'

Lucien had forgotten about Cullen.

Cullen's face shone with disappointment. 'I will miss serving you, sir.'

Lucien felt the impending loss harder than he expected. 'I will miss you, too, Cullen. You are a good man.'

The tavern maid brought Lucien's ale and he took a long sip of it.

He placed the tankard on the table and turned to Cullen. 'You are welcome to come with me to London, if you prefer. I can use your services until I go to sea.'

Ella gave Cullen a pained look. 'I do not want us to be separated.'

And Lucien hated the idea of separating them.

'I am not leaving yet,' he told them. 'Tomorrow I call upon my old navy commander. Perhaps he can assist in finding a position here for Cullen.'

Ella and Cullen exchanged uncertain glances.

Lucien added, 'And I intend to stay until I am certain Lady Rebecca is settled.' Where had that decision come from? He turned to Ella. 'Lord Stonecroft is sending a carriage for you and for Lady Rebecca's things. If you wish to go to her, that is.'

Lucien could not bear the thought of Lady Rebecca not having Ella with her, but it had to be Ella's choice.

She nodded. 'I do want to stay with Lady Rebecca. Not remembering things is hard on her. Someone must help her.'

Lucien felt as if he was making Ella do his duty. 'She wants you. And I would like you to be her lady's maid. You will be able to tell me if she does well there.'

Ella brightened. 'I could be a spy for you!'

Essentially, yes.

She shot up from her chair. 'I had better pack her things, then.'

Cullen stood. 'May I have your leave to assist her?'

They were facing a parting of their own of sorts, except, if Cullen found a position in Bath, they'd have opportunities to be together. 'Of course you have my leave. I'll be in my room after I finish my ale.'

Although Lucien had the feeling he would be consuming stronger spirits before the day was over.

Lord Stonecroft quickly excused himself for an engagement with some other gentlemen at the Pump Room, leaving Miss Attwood to show Claire the house. She began by assembling the servants so that Claire could meet them all.

'My dear brother spares no expense with servants,' Miss Attwood boasted. 'He hires as many as he likes and tries to select footmen who are pleasant of face and all of a similar height and build.'

Perhaps he would hire Cullen, too, then. Except he already had three footmen, a butler, a valet, two housemaids, a housekeeper, cook and two kitchen maids, as well as Miss Attwood's lady's maid. Where did they all sleep?

Would there be room for Ella? If Ella agreed to come, that is.

Miss Attwood began the tour of the house on the ground floor where Stonecroft had a respectable library and a fine dining room, as well as a sitting room and closets. The first floor had the impressive drawing room and bedrooms for Lord Stonecroft and his wife.

'You will move into this bedchamber after you and Stonecroft are wed,' Miss Attwood said, showing her the Lady's room connected by a door to Lord Stonecroft's.

The second floor consisted of two other bedrooms, one for Miss Attwood and the other, the bedchamber where Claire would stay. Behind these two bedrooms were two rooms that were sparsely decorated.

'These will be for the nursery and the governess,' Miss Attwood told her.

Claire had a flash of a table and three little girls seated around it, but the image disappeared before she could tell if it were memory or imagination. Of all of the rooms in the house, though, these two back rooms were the two in which she felt the greatest degree of comfort.

After the tour, Miss Attwood drank tea with Claire in the less formal sitting room on the ground floor.

'Have I been in this house before?' asked Claire. That might explain her reaction to the back rooms.

'No, dear.' Miss Attwood looked askance. 'Do you really not remember where you have been?'

Why would she feign what was so difficult for her?

She tamped down her irritation. She must accept these people as they were if she was going to live here. 'I remember places. Or I think I do. I knew Bath, but I have no memory of my ever having been in Bath.'

'How very strange.' Miss Attwood took a sip of her tea.

'Will you tell me, please, a little of how I met Lord Stonecroft?' Perhaps it would help spark some memory.

'You do not remember?'

Claire gritted her teeth. 'No. I do not remember.'

The older lady took another sip of her tea. 'I do not know the details. He travelled to Ireland— Stonecroft has some property there. I believe your brother arranged the introduction. He met you at your brother's country house. I was very happy to hear he'd decided to marry.'

It simply was not possible that Claire had fallen in love with Stonecroft. He held absolutely no attraction for her. And she did not seem to interest him greatly either.

How was she to marry this man?

She must find some reason to marry him, because at this moment all she wanted to do was run out the door and return to Lucien.

She felt her eyes sting and sipped her tea, blinking away tears.

She placed her teacup down. 'Tell me something of Lord Stonecroft. Why he wished to marry me.'

Miss Attwood's lips pursed. 'Well, I believe he found you suitable.'

She did not wish to set this lady against her. 'I meant, why did he wish to marry at this time?' This advanced age, she meant.

Miss Attwood hid behind her teacup again, but when she put it down, she leaned forward. 'I will tell you, only because it would pain my brother to have you ask him questions like this. I beg you will not ever speak to him about it.'

Claire nodded.

Miss Attwood spoke in a hushed tone. 'My brother was married when he was quite young. In his twenties. Our parents were against the match because she had no fortune at all and brought no status to the union. They were able to keep the couple apart, but our father died unexpectedly. My brother was free to do as he wished and he married the girl. She was a sweet thing and he was totally besotted with her.'

He'd married before. For love.

Miss Attwood went on. 'They tried to have children, but his wife could not carry babies. She lost several. Then finally she was able to carry one to term, but the birth was a terrible affair. Lasted two days and finally the baby was born, but did not live. And she died as well.' Miss Attwood's voice caught on these last words and she quickly took another sip of tea. 'As you can imagine, Stonecroft was desolate.' She cleared her throat. 'That was nearly twenty-five years ago.'

'How very sad,' Claire said.

'Yes,' Miss Attwood agreed. 'Very sad. Poor Stonecroft has never recovered, really, which is why you must never speak to him about this.' Her voice turned severe.

Because it made him remember? Some memories can be unbearable, Claire thought. But it was so much worse to have no memory at all.

'You want to know why Stonecroft wishes to marry now?' the older lady challenged.

Claire stared at her.

Miss Attwood did not wait for her reply. 'He needs an heir. I convinced him so.' She finished her tea and poured another cup. 'Otherwise everything will go to his cousin's son, who is a perfectly responsible young man, but much too distant a relation and Stonecroft's cousin married an actress, you know, so the family is less than respectable.'

So Stonecroft's parents were not the only ones who considered one's birth important.

'But why did he choose me?' she asked. 'Surely there are many English ladies who would be honoured to be his wife.'

'Indeed so,' agreed Miss Attwood. 'But he

wanted someone whose family had no connection to his wife, nor any knowledge of her.'

Nor any memory of her?

The older lady leaned closer to Claire. 'I hope
you do not have any romantic notions, dear. Stonecroft will be good to you, but his heart will never
be engaged. He's made that perfectly clear.'

Because he loved his wife so much, he has no
more love to give to another?

'I do not have romantic notions,' None she
could remember, that was.

None except one unattainable one.

Chapter Fourteen

Claire finished her tea. 'Might I retire to my room? I would love a rest.' She had not done anything exerting, but she desperately wished to be alone.

With her memories.

'As you wish.' Miss Attwood stood wearily and started to escort her to the door.

Claire stopped her. 'Please do not feel you have to accompany me if you would rather stay. I can find the room myself.'

The older lady sat down again. 'Thank you, dear.'

Claire walked back to the hall and climbed the two flights of stairs to the bedchamber she must call hers.

At least until she must move to the room next to Lord Stonecroft.

She opened the door and a surprised Ella gave out a cry. 'Oh, m'lady. You startled me so.'

Claire rushed over to her, taking both Ella's

hands in hers and squeezing them. 'I am so happy to see you, Ella! No one told me you had arrived.'

'Yes, a little while ago.' Ella smiled. 'The housekeeper said I was to unpack your trunk.'

Claire released her. 'Did you meet the other servants?'

'I think so. I suppose I will find out if I met all of them when I appear for a meal.' Ella turned to the dressing room with its clothes press and cupboard. 'I was putting everything in here. Will that do?'

'Certainly.' Claire watched her unpack the trunk with its lovely clothes purchased by Lucien. Her heart ached.

'So,' the outspoken Ella started asking as she lifted another dress from the trunk, 'what is this Lord Stonecroft like?'

Claire's ache intensified. 'He is older. Old enough to be my father, easily. But there is nothing to object to in him.' Those last words seemed to echo as she spoke them, as if she'd heard them from someone else's mouth.

'Old enough to be your father?' Ella cried. 'He must be ancient. Fifty? As old as fifty?'

She shook the strange sensation away. 'Quite as old as fifty.'

'Did you remember him at all?' Ella asked.

'Not at all.' The cold Bath stone with which the Crescent and the Circus were built was more familiar to her.

'Are you going to marry him?' the maid pressed.

Claire's hands rose in a futile gesture. 'It is what I am supposed to do.'

'Yes,' mumbled Ella. 'And I was supposed to marry some well-to-do merchant.'

There was a knock on the door and it opened before Claire could acknowledge it.

Miss Attwood walked in. 'I was informed your maid had arrived.'

Claire swallowed a retort about respecting her privacy. 'Miss Attwood, may I present Miss Ella Kiley, my lady's maid.'

'Kiley?' Miss Attwood's brows rose. 'You are Irish, then?'

Ella curtsied respectfully. 'I am Irish, ma'am.'

'Miss Attwood is Lord Stonecroft's sister,' Claire explained to Ella. 'She runs his house for him.'

Ella curtsied again. 'Ma'am.'

'She is very young for a lady's maid,' Miss Attwood said in disapproving tones.

'Perhaps,' Claire responded. 'But I am well satisfied with her.'

'Have you been told where you will sleep, girl?' Miss Attwood asked.

'In the attic, ma'am,' Ella replied.

'No!' Claire broke in. 'I want her to sleep in the dressing room here. There is plenty of room for a cot.'

It jarred Claire to order anything to be as she wished it to be, but she could not allow Ella to be squeezed into the attic with all the other female servants.

Miss Attwood's brows rose. 'If you insist, dear.'

'I do.' Claire nodded. 'It is what I wish.'

'Very well.' Miss Attwood turned to leave, but stopped. 'Dinner will be served at six. Stonecroft prefers country hours. And he prefers to dress for dinner.'

'I understand.'

After Miss Attwood left, Ella expelled a breath. 'Whew! She makes me quake in my shoes.'

'I have not yet taken her measure,' Claire said. 'She seems very kind one minute and somewhat intolerant the next.'

Ella's eyes widened. 'I will watch out for her. And for the housekeeper. She is a dragon.'

Ella's forthrightness made Claire want to hug her, but she suspected an unguarded tongue could cause the girl trouble in this house.

'Remember, you answer to me, not to the housekeeper,' Claire told her. 'You must tell me if you have any problems at all.'

Ella laughed. 'Do not fear, m'lady! I'll tell you.'

Claire smiled in return, so happy she was no longer alone.

Claire went down to the drawing room before six o'clock to await dinner being announced. Both Lord Stonecroft and Miss Attwood were already there.

Stonecroft rose as she entered. 'Lady Rebecca,' he said cordially. 'May I offer you a glass of claret?'

'Thank you, sir,' she said.

She sat on the sofa where she'd sat before when she and Lucien had been in this room. Stonecroft handed her the claret and sat next to her, as she'd expected.

'I hope you have settled in.' His words were polite, but his tone flat.

'Yes, my lord,' she responded.

'And is all to your liking?' he asked.

'I am quite comfortable.' Although she'd rather be dressed in men's clothing mopping fish guts off the deck of a fishing boat.

He turned to his sister and talked of the people he'd met with that day. The names meant nothing to Claire. The conversation swept over her.

Dinner was announced and he escorted her to the dining room. Its formal table was set with three places. Stonecroft sat at the end and Claire and Miss Attwood adjacent to him. Miss Attwood asked him more about his afternoon meeting. Claire sat quietly and relived the meals she'd shared with Lucien, Cullen and Ella.

Eventually Stonecroft noticed her. 'There is an Assembly two days hence. Would you care to attend?'

'If you desire me to,' she responded.

'You had only one trunk delivered,' Miss Attwood said. 'Was your ball gown among the dresses in that trunk?'

'I have no ball gown.' Claire gestured to her clothes. 'This is my best dress. Will it do?'

Miss Attwood's brows shot up. 'No, it will not do.'

Stonecroft looked annoyed. 'For God's sake, get her what she needs, Honora. Have the bills sent to me.'

'We cannot have a ball gown sewn in a day,' his sister shot back.

'Pay whatever they wish, but she should have decent clothes.'

Claire glanced down at the beautiful dress she wore, the dress Lucien bought for her, the most beautiful dress she could remember ever wearing. She loved this dress.

She straightened in her chair and glanced from one to the other. 'You do realise that all my possessions, all my clothes, were lost in the shipwreck, do you not?'

Stonecroft merely looked down at his food.

Miss Attwood appeared contrite. 'Of course, dear. We had not taken that into consideration.'

They all ate in silence for a while until Stonecroft spoke again. 'I have an engagement tonight. I will be home late.'

Miss Attwood asked who he would see and the two of them again spoke about people Claire did not know. Or, rather, people she might have once known, but could not remember. Claire contented herself with remembering the second-hand shop and trying on dress after dress and seeing which met Lucien's approval. What a lovely memory.

When dinner was done, Stonecroft excused himself and left the room. Claire and Miss Attwood sat for a time in the small sitting room for yet another cup of tea.

The next morning Claire rose early, but Ella was already awake and full of information.

'Breakfast is served in the small drawing room at eight o'clock,' Ella told her. 'But apparently Miss Attwood doesn't rise until ten and then she eats in her room.'

'Do you think I am expected to eat at eight?' she asked.

'Oh, I think you might do as you wish, but the servants are all trying to figure out if you are going to create lots more work for them or not,' she responded. 'I've told them how agreeable you are, but they don't believe a word I say, because I am Irish.'

Claire bit her lip. 'I hope they will not be unkind to you.'

Ella smiled. 'I'll manage it.'

'I suppose I should appear at breakfast at the appointed time.' Claire had already washed and donned her shift.

Ella helped her with her corset, petticoat and her sprigged-muslin day dress.

'Just dress my hair plainly,' Claire said.

'Not too plain,' Ella insisted.

So she wound up with curls around her face.

She wore the pearl pendant Lucien had purchased for her, fingering the cool smoothness of the pearl and remembering when he insisted upon buying it for her.

When Ella declared her ready, she stood and eyed the Kashmir shawl, wanting to wrap herself in it and the memories it evoked, but instead she chose a lighter one they'd purchased at the second-hand shop.

She walked out of the room, but instead of heading for the stairs, she paused, looking at the doors to the two unused rooms. She stepped to the one that would be the nursery and opened the door. She could almost hear little girls laughing.

There would be a table and chairs and children seated at the table writing on slates or reading books. Had she dreamed this? It did not seem any more real than an invented story, but the image had come a second time.

She closed her eyes and tried to see herself in the vision, but nothing came.

She turned and walked back to the hallway and down the two flights of stairs.

'Good morning,' she said to the footman attending the hall.

He bowed. 'Good morning, m'lady.'

Would she ever feel right about being bowed to?

'Breakfast will be in the back sitting room,' he added helpfully.

As she had known from Ella. 'Thank you.'

When she reached the sitting room another footman bowed and opened the door for her.

A table had been set up in the middle of the room and a sideboard was filled with food. Lord Stonecroft glanced up from his newspaper. He stood, watching her every move as she approached the table as if to check she was all in one piece.

'Good morning, sir,' she said.

'You are up early,' he responded.

'I tend to rise early.'

He gestured to the sideboard. 'Shall I prepare you a plate?' His tone was unenthusiastic.

'Please sit and continue reading your paper.' She went to the sideboard. 'I will serve myself.'

The footman who had attended the door now stood at the ready to place the food on her plate for her.

She chose some toasted bread and slices of ham and cheese and sat opposite Lord Stonecroft. The footman poured her some tea.

Stonecroft was still watching her.

It made her heart race in anxiety, but she did not wish her nerves to show.

She lifted her chin. 'Am I not dressed properly, my lord? You keep staring.'

He quickly looked down at his food, but his gaze rose again. 'Your dress is out of fashion, but you look well in it.'

'I thank you for the compliment.' Such as it was. She spread some butter on her bread.

She'd told Stonecroft and his sister that she'd lost everything in the shipwreck. Had he no interest in how she had any clothes at all to wear?

She'd tell him anyway. 'I cannot remember the clothes I lost or what is in fashion. When we reached Ireland, I had to wear a dress the innkeeper's wife provided. It was very generous of her. It was also very generous of Captain Roper to buy me my present clothing at a second-hand shop in Dublin.'

She loved every item Lucien purchased for her.

He glanced up. 'A second-hand shop? Clothing discarded by its owners?' His gaze assessed her anew. 'Second-hand clothes will not do. Order whatever you need from the modiste and when we go to London, you will be able to fill your wardrobe with the latest fashions.'

The food tasted like dust in her mouth. She did not need sympathy for what she'd been through, but she certainly wished to see some semblance of feeling from him.

She had to force herself to keep eating.

Had this man been understanding with his beloved wife? Had he seen her sorrows? Soothed her disappointments? Comforted her in her losses?

She had promised not to ask.

He appeared to be reading his newspaper, but

he spoke again. 'Shall I stop by the Abbey and arrange to have the banns read?

Her head snapped up. That would mean marrying in three or four weeks. 'So soon?'

He gave her a severe look. 'You were supposed to arrive two months ago.'

It became difficult for her to breathe. 'My lord, the delay was not my fault. I was in a shipwreck. And I cannot remember anything but these last two months. I do not remember you. I did not remember my brother. I did not know my name. Everything but these last two months is like an empty slate—' An image of a little girl writing on a slate flashed through her mind. Again. And it was gone so quickly she did not know if she'd really experienced it.

'Oh, come. You must remember something,' he said.

'Nothing connected to me. I have been in Bath before. I know this, because I knew of the Circus and the Crescent and how to walk here, but I cannot remember ever being here.'

'That does not make sense to me,' he said.

'It does not make sense to me either!' she cried. 'I want time to recover. I want to have my memory back. I do not want to have the banns read until my memory returns.' She surprised herself by speaking so forcefully. It seemed out of character.

He frowned. 'Very well. We will wait. But I do hope you will not announce to the whole of society that you have lost your memory.'

'I have no wish to speak of it to anyone,' she said. But she would expect to receive more sympathy from others than Lord Stonecroft showed.

He wiped his mouth with a napkin and rose. 'If you will excuse me, I must leave. My sister will see what can be done about your wardrobe.'

He bowed and walked out.

That morning Lucien walked to the Circus and knocked at Number Fifteen. His head ached and his mood was foul. Not the best way to meet an old friend.

The door opened and he followed a footman to Sir Richard's study. The Admiral shot to his feet upon seeing Lucien.

'Prompt as ever, eh, boy?' Sir Richard grinned and pumped Lucien's hand.

He invited Lucien to sit and poured them both a brandy, although the hour was early and Lucien had consumed enough brandy from the night before.

'Now let me know all about how you are alive and about that lovely lady you were with yesterday,' Sir Richard insisted. 'I am disappointed she is not with you.'

How was Lucien to tell of Lady Rebecca? 'First tell me how is your wife? In good health, I hope.'

'Very good health, thank you. She is visiting her sister in Brighton. Taking part in all that Brighton frivolity. Not for me at all.' He seemed unconcerned about his wife's absence. 'Now about the Lady Rebecca…' He lifted his glass to his lips.

Lucien told him about the shipwreck, about saving Lady Rebecca and himself from drowning. He told of their rescue by the fishing boat and about escorting her back to England.

'Remarkable story,' Sir Richard said. 'Remarkable.'

'There is more.' Lucien decided to tell Sir Richard about Lady Rebecca's amnesia. He could trust this man. 'But I must have your word that you will not speak to anyone about this.'

Sir Richard's brows rose. 'You have my word.'

'Lady Rebecca was knocked unconscious from debris from the shipwreck. When she woke, she had no memory. She remembers nothing of her life before waking on the raft. I thought it would be temporary, but so far she has not recovered it.'

'Nothing?' the Admiral asked.

'Nothing. She did not remember her brother. She does not remember being betrothed.'

'Betrothed?' Sir Richard frowned. 'To whom?'

'Lord Stonecroft.'

'Stonecroft?' Sir Richard's voice rose. 'Why, he is as old as I am.'

'You are acquainted with him?' Lucien asked.

'Acquainted. Yes.'

Lucien leaned forward. 'Then tell me what you think of him.'

The Admiral shrugged. 'He is a decent sort. Pays his gambling debts. Not one to chase skirts.

A bit...' He looked as if he was searching for words. 'A bit standoffish, if you know what I mean.'

If he meant an autocratic stiff-neck, Lucien knew precisely what he meant.

Lucien took a sip of his brandy. 'I—I feel a duty to Lady Rebecca.'

'A duty, you say.' Sir Richard looked amused.

'A duty,' Lucien insisted. 'Because of her amnesia. Because of the shipwreck. I feel a responsibility to make certain she is where she belongs. I delivered her to Lord Stonecroft. She is residing there, but I find I cannot leave until I know she is well settled.'

'Leave? For where?' the man asked.

'For London. To the Admiralty,' he responded. 'I was promised a ship.'

'A ship?' Sir Richard's brows knitted. 'That would have been months ago. You realise they would believe you dead?'

'I wrote to them.' Only recently, however.

'My dear boy, the navy is ridding itself of ships. Like your *Foxfire.*'

There would not be many commands to be given, he meant. 'I know. But I cannot leave now. Not until I know how Lady Rebecca fares.'

Sir Richard gave him a knowing glance. 'This lady has become important to you.'

'We have endured much together,' Lucien admitted. 'But she is the daughter of an earl and eventually she will remember how that matters to her. And I am determined to have another ship.'

'Even if all you can get is a merchant ship?' his friend asked.

Lucien lifted a shoulder. 'I want the navy.'

Sir Richard poured Lucien and himself more brandy as their conversation turned to their experiences in the war.

Finally a clock chimed. They'd been talking for three hours.

Lucien stood. 'I should leave. I am overstaying my welcome.'

Sir Richard rose as well. 'It has been my delight to converse with you.'

He walked Lucien to the hall where Lucien retrieved his hat and gloves. Lucien then remembered Cullen. He'd forgotten to ask Sir Richard about finding a position for Cullen.

It felt too late to do so now.

They shook hands once more and Lucien turned to leave.

Sir Richard stopped him with a hand on Lucien's shoulder. 'Wait, my boy. I have an idea. Come stay with me. I am rattling around in this house alone; I would welcome the company.'

He started to tell Sir Richard that it would be too much of an imposition, but then he realised it was the perfect way to show Cullen's worth. 'I have my valet with me.'

'A valet?' Sir Richard laughed. 'We can accommodate a valet. You would do me a favour to be my guest.'

'Perhaps...' Lucien said.

Sir Richard gave his shoulder a fatherly pat. 'I have always thought of you as the son I wished God had given me. I would delight in having more of your company.' He lifted a finger. 'Consider this. There is to be an Assembly in tomorrow night. It is the sort of event Stonecroft attends. I would wager he will be there with your Lady Rebecca. You may come as my guest. It will provide you the chance to see for yourself how she gets on.'

Lucien nodded. 'Then I am grateful to accept your kind invitation.'

'Excellent!' Sir Richard beamed. 'Come to me with your valet before the day is out. I have no plans. I will tell Cook to prepare a meal for two and to expect another servant at the servants' table.'

'I will make the arrangements as soon as I return to the inn.'

This might be the very way he could see the three people newly in his life settled. Their welfare—especially Lady Rebecca's—had become important to him.

Chapter Fifteen

The night of the Assembly arrived and Claire wore a blue silk dress with a gauze overdress trimmed in lace. It was lovely, but, because Miss Attwood directed everything about its creation, Claire felt as if it was more hers than Claire's. The seamstresses were putting the final touches on the gown while Ella arranged her hair under the watchful eyes of Miss Attwood. When she finally donned the dress and put her pearl earrings in her ears, Miss Attwood declared her ready.

She and Miss Attwood walked into the drawing room where Stonecroft waited for her. He again gave an assessing scan of her from top to toe, but this time his eyes revealed an admiration she found equally disturbing.

'I am pleased you are prompt,' he said, looking over her again. 'Of course your jewels are lacking.'

'I only possess the pearl pendant and earrings,' she said.

Miss Attwood wrung her hands. 'Oh, dear. I did not give jewellery a thought. Shall I run upstairs and select some of mine?'

'No time,' Lord Stonecroft said. 'The sedan chairs are waiting.'

'Sedan chairs?' Claire could not imagine making men carry her such a short distance. The Upper Assembly Rooms were right behind the Circus.

Stonecroft escorted her to the hall where two footmen stood ready to help them on with their outer garments. Claire wore the cloak Lucien had purchased for her.

Lord Stonecroft eyed it disapprovingly. 'Is that from the second-hand shop?'

It was a perfectly serviceable red cloak made of a good quality wool. 'All my clothing was once worn by someone else, my lord. Except this gown, of course.' And her Kashmir shawl.

One of the footmen held open the door.

'We should not need such outer garments in the summer.' Lord Stonecroft gestured for her to walk out first. 'It is unseasonably cold.'

The footmen followed them out.

In the street were two sedan chairs, white with gold embellishments and a crest on each side. She assumed the crest was Stonecroft's. Four burly men stood next to the chairs. One of the footmen helped her climb into the second chair.

She hated the trip to the Upper Assembly Rooms. So silly to be carried a few streets away.

When the chairmen put down the chair in front of the Assembly Rooms, Claire opened the door and exited herself, so eager was she to be out. She waited at Lord Stonecroft's sedan chair until he emerged.

'What sort of event is this?' she asked as she took his arm and they walked to the door.

'A private party,' he responded.

They entered and walked through the ballroom, a huge room lit by five magnificent crystal chandeliers. At one end was a balcony where musicians would play for a ball. Here and there in the room groups of people stood in conversation or sat in the chairs that lined the walls.

Claire could almost imagine music and lines of dancers, but she could not remember ever being there.

In the Octagon Room tables were set up and men and women were intent on their card play. Only a few looked up as they passed.

The Tea Room was the actual setting for the party and the hostess stood near the entrance receiving greetings from the guests. She was of an age with Lord Stonecroft.

He brought Claire over to her. 'Lady Milliforte,

may I present Lady Rebecca Pierce, daughter of the Earl of Keneagle.'

Claire curtsied.

'Earl of Keneagle, you say?' Lady Milliforte asked.

'An Irish peer,' Stonecroft explained.

'Delighted to meet you, Lady Rebecca,' the woman said kindly.

'Thank you, ma'am,' Claire said.

Stonecroft leaned towards Lady Milliforte. 'No formal announcement has been made, but Lady Rebecca has consented to be my wife.'

'Oh?' Lady Milliforte looked at her with more interest. She turned back to Stonecroft. 'Well, Jonas, I am glad you have at last come to your senses.'

'I am telling only my dearest friends,' he said to her.

'I do understand.' She smiled from Stonecroft to Claire. 'I am gratified to be so considered.' She patted his hand. 'Is Honora with you?'

'Not tonight,' he responded. 'You know how my sister abhors crowds.'

'This is not a crowd,' she exclaimed.

Claire thought there were plenty of people there to make it a crowd, but she did not listen to the rest of their conversation. Obviously they were close friends to be using given names, but she could tell no more than that.

Lady Milliforte took Claire's arm. 'Let me present you to my husband, Lord Milliforte.'

The Baron was conversing with two other gentlemen who stepped away. He and Stonecroft exchanged pleasantries. Another old friend, Claire surmised.

She felt quite separate from the people surrounding her. Perhaps if she had her memory she would recognise the names and titles of these people. Most seemed to be contemporaries of Lord Stonecroft. There were very few guests who looked to be around Claire's age. It seemed odd to her to be around so many older people.

Was that a memory of sorts?

Lady Milliforte tapped Stonecroft on the shoulder. 'Jonas, introduce Lady Rebecca around. She must not know a soul.'

But she did know someone.

A gentleman in naval uniform strode over to her. 'Good evening, Lady Rebecca,' he said cheerfully.

'Sir Richard, how lovely to see you again.' He was connected to Lucien and that made her feel less alone.

Stonecroft turned, then, and stepped away from the host and hostess. 'Sir Richard.' He nodded in greeting.

Sir Richard laughed. 'You are wondering how I know this young lady, are you not, sir? Captain Roper introduced us the other day.'

Claire's insides fluttered at the mention of Lucien. She wanted to ask the Admiral if Lucien had called upon him, as they'd arranged. Did he know if Lucien had left for London?

He must have done, she thought depressingly.

Stonecroft took her by the elbow. 'If you will pardon us, Sir Richard. I wish to introduce Lady Rebecca to my friends.'

'I do not mind at all,' Sir Richard said, although Claire thought Stonecroft's words were rude. Sir Richard winked at Claire. 'I trust we will meet again, my lady.'

'I do hope so,' she responded.

Stonecroft took her around the room and introduced her to many people. She tried to remember each one, but he pulled her to another group before she could fix the names in her memory.

He brought her to yet another older lady, whose costume was more colourful than most with a turban that she wore slightly askew.

'Lady Rebecca Pierce?' the lady cried. 'Not *the* Lady Rebecca Pierce?'

'I—I am not certain what you mean,' Claire responded.

'I was just reading about you!' Her voice rose. She turned to those people standing near her. 'Everyone! She is here. This is Lady Rebecca Pierce who was thought drowned in the *Dun Aengus* shipwreck!'

It seemed as if all eyes turned to her.

Stonecroft frowned. 'How do you know this, my lady?'

'It was in the *Morning Chronicle*. From London,' the lady said. 'Did you not receive the *Chronicle*?'

'I read the *Post*,' he said.

'What did the article say?' another lady asked.

'That she was swept out to sea and rescued by a fishing boat. Everyone thought her dead and then she appeared in Dublin.' The lady's eyes grew larger. 'But her rescuer is here! I met him not a few moments ago.' She stood on tiptoe and called, 'Captain Roper? Captain Roper?'

Claire felt the breath knocked out of her.

He was here. He had not left.

'Someone calls me?' The crowd parted and Lucien appeared.

The lady took his arm. 'This is the man who rescued her! Captain Roper is also a war hero. Captain of the *Foxfire*. Is that not grand?'

'Lucien,' Claire murmured.

His gaze was on her. He smiled.

'Do tell us of the shipwreck!' one of the ladies cried. 'What happened?'

Half the room was attending. Lucien described being swept out to sea and finding the door to use as a raft.

'Were you not terrified?' another lady asked Claire.

'It was very frightening,' she admitted, leaving

out the extra terror of not knowing who she was or how she came to be in the middle of the sea. 'The Captain kept me calm.'

They asked more questions about the fishing boat. 'It must have been horrible to be stuck with all those fishermen for all that time.'

Claire answered. 'Not at all. They were the kindest, most generous people I have ever met.' Or could remember. 'I adored each one of them.'

Some of the faces looked approving, but others, including Lord Stonecroft, looked horrified.

When Lord Stonecroft had walked her around the room introducing her, most of the guests showed polite interest, but learning she was rescued from drowning in a shipwreck by the handsome young Captain made her and Lucien objects of great interest.

The few younger ladies present and some of the older ones flocked around Lucien, as well they should. He was a true hero. None of them could comprehend just how heroic he had been; saving her in so many ways. Her heart felt full to bursting at the mere sight of him, but it was excruciating not to be in his company, sharing everything with him.

Lord Stonecroft approached her with a petulant look. 'If I might have your leave, I will retire to the card room.'

'You must do as you like,' she responded.

It did not take long after that for people to drift

away, attracted by other conversations. Claire found herself alone. With a glance to where Lucien still was surrounded by admirers, she walked to one of the chairs set against the wall.

And forced herself not to look at Lucien.

Lucien noticed the minute Lord Stonecroft left her side. He watched her walk to the chairs and sit by herself.

What sort of gentleman would leave a lady alone?

Lady Rebecca certainly looked the part of an earl's daughter at this entertainment. The gown was obviously new and looked lovely on her. The pale blue under the sheer overdress shimmered in the candlelight from the chandelier. She looked composed as Stonecroft walked her around the room and gracious when he introduced her to someone. And only slightly uncomfortable when she was questioned about the shipwreck.

He'd never expected the story they gave to the Dublin reporter would reach London and Bath. Or that it would have been greeted with such interest by these people.

Lucien had been proud of her praise of the fishermen, even though she might have answered differently if she had remembered her life before the shipwreck when fishermen would have been a class way below hers.

Had she been worried they would question her about before the shipwreck? All that she did not remember? Although she looked so poised, perhaps she knew she could handle those questions even about what she did not remember. She looked as if she'd settled in quite well.

As soon as he could, he extricated himself from the ladies who were much too enthralled by something any man would have done in the same situation.

He made his way over to Lady Rebecca. 'May I sit with you?'

She looked up in surprise, but her eyes turned warm when she saw it was him. 'Please do.'

He sat next to her. He'd become so used to being at her side over these last weeks that he'd felt out of kilter since leaving her at Stonecroft's.

'How is your shoulder?' she asked.

He touched his wound and winced. 'It is healing.'

Her expression became concerned. 'I hope you are taking care of it.'

'Cullen makes certain of that,' he said.

She smiled at that.

'I thought you would be off to London by now,' she said after a pause.

He would travel to London as soon as he knew she would do well.

But he said, 'Sir Richard has made a house guest of me. I believe I'll keep him company for a while. I hope Sir Richard will help Cullen get a position here in Bath.'

'Ella will be pleased.' She smiled. 'We will be practically neighbours, will we not?'

He'd missed her smiles these last two days.

'But what of getting a ship?' she asked.

'I've written to the Admiralty.' He changed the subject. 'How are you faring?'

'Well enough.' She took a deep breath. 'Although I cannot shake the feeling that I am out of place.'

He gazed at her. 'You look like you were born and bred to be right here, in this sort of company.'

Her cheeks flushed with colour. 'Miss Attwood would have it no other way, I am certain.' She added, 'Neither would Stonecroft for that matter.'

'Has he been good to you?' Lucien had intended to be less direct.

'I should have no complaints.'

Which made him suspect she did have complaints. 'What complaints should you not have?'

She glanced away as if considering how to answer. 'He is a bit too concerned about what I wear. Apparently I am to have an entire new wardrobe.'

'Is that not what any woman would desire?' he asked.

She tilted her head. 'It seems so extravagant. There is nothing wrong with the beautiful dresses you bought me in Dublin.'

'They are out of fashion, I suspect,' he said. 'Otherwise why would anyone give them away?'

She waved a hand as if saying that was a trifle.

'Other than that complaint?' he persisted.

'It is just strange.' She turned her gaze on him. 'I suppose because we have spent so much time in very humble places—except the hotel in Dublin, of course. The only rooms in which I feel comfortable are unfurnished ones, the ones meant to become a nursery or a schoolroom.' Her gaze turned intent. 'I have this strange thought of little girls at a table in a schoolroom. Do you suppose that is a memory?'

He sat up straighter. 'It might be. Do you think you are remembering a part of your life?'

She shook her head. 'It feels like I am simply imagining it.'

A violin began playing Haydn in the balcony, joined by another violin, a viola and a cello.

'Do they dance at these affairs, I wonder?' she asked.

He certainly did not know. 'I am less accustomed to events like this than you must be.'

Lucien had no great fondness for dancing, but this night he wished he might dance with her.

'How—how long might you stay in Bath?' she asked.

It depended on her. 'I do not know. A few days perhaps.'

'Look at the two of you.' The lady who had first recognised him as the rescuer from the shipwreck in the newspaper stood in front of them. She sat down. 'What a bond must be formed between you when you survive such danger!'

Yes. A bond. Lucien agreed.

'Captain Roper will always be important to me,' Lady Rebecca told her. 'I wish his happiness above all things.'

The lady patted her hands. 'That is so dear.' She clutched one hand and squeezed. 'Now you must tell me the reason you are in the company of Stonecroft, though. There are quite a few of us who are pining to know.'

Lady Rebecca did not answer right away. 'I suppose you could say Lord Stonecroft is courting me.'

The woman grinned. 'We thought so! About time. He's been a widower for over twenty years. He is a good catch, my dear. Doesn't gamble much. Doesn't carouse. Has a respectable fortune.'

'So I understand,' Lady Rebecca responded.

He also seemed to think anyone below him in status was his to command, Lucien thought. And he lacked empathy about her loss of memory. Would he ever care what Lady Rebecca endured?

Lucien hoped she would have the courage to stand up to Stonecroft if he ignored her wishes or her needs. This Lady Rebecca had courage not seen in many men. Lucien hoped she would not lose that courage when her memory returned.

Which he thought could be imminent. Lady Rebecca's thoughts of a schoolroom could mean cracks had formed in the wall around her memory.

Other guests walked over and joined the conversation with them. The chance to be alone with her had disappeared.

Servants began setting up the room for supper and when the supper was called Lord Stonecroft emerged from the card room and found Claire sitting with Lucien.

He acknowledged Lucien with a slight nod and extended his hand to her. 'Come, Lady Rebecca. Let us be seated for the supper.'

She rose, but turned back to Lucien. 'Take care, Captain.'

He nodded. 'And you, as well.'

After Stonecroft led her a few steps away, he said in a snappish tone, 'Did you keep company with Captain Roper all this time?'

'Not all the time,' she replied. 'He joined me where I was seated.'

'With that newspaper piece, you must be careful. Respectable ladies are not written about in newspapers. It is only a matter of time before someone suggests something more scandalous between you and this Captain.'

She bristled. 'Do not speak ill of the man who saved my life.'

'I am not speaking ill,' he retorted, his voice low. 'I am saying that people gossip.'

'I cannot stop people from gossiping.' Really. What did he think?

A footman held the chair for Claire and they sat down. They were seated at the hostess's table.

'I am not happy that you were written of in a newspaper like the *Chronicle*,' Stonecroft went on.

She shot back, 'When we told the story to the reporter from the Dublin paper, how were we supposed to know it would appear in the *Chronicle*?'

He looked aghast. 'You spoke to a reporter?'

'Better he know the real story than to have one he made up.'

He was annoying her greatly.

If she looked at Lord Stonecroft through his sister's eyes, she could see something to admire about him. The warmth between him and Lady Milliforte lent credence to that impression. But with her he seemed condescending and overbearing. Perhaps if she recovered her memory, she would remember something she had liked about him. So far, the only redeeming quality she knew he possessed was the love he'd had towards his first wife.

She tried to keep that in mind as she ate the supper and answered more questions about the shipwreck, this time from the gentlemen seated at the table.

Stonecroft frowned through the whole conversation.

After the supper was done, Stonecroft turned to Lady Milliforte. 'Iona, may we have your leave? I am quite fatigued.'

They were leaving? It seemed early. She'd hoped for another chance to speak with Lucien.

'Of course, Jonas,' Lady Milliforte responded. 'So lovely of you to come and to bring your Lady Rebecca with you.' She turned to Claire. 'I hope we see more of you, my dear.'

Claire put down her glass of wine. 'Thank you, my lady.'

She rose and Stonecroft led her out of the room. There was no chance to even say goodbye to Lucien, although her gaze caught his as she passed by.

They walked through the Octagon Room and the magnificent ballroom to the entrance of the Assembly Rooms where she retrieved her red cloak, the one that was not good enough for Stonecroft. They again climbed into the detestable sedan chairs and she was carried the short distance to the Royal Crescent.

When they entered the house, Lord Stonecroft looked shrunken and even older than before.

He turned to her. 'May I escort you to your room?' He sounded weary.

She took his arm.

As they ascended the steps, he said, 'I should not have taken you away from the party so early. I was not thinking you might want to stay longer.'

This was close to an apology. It helped.

When they reached the first floor she said, 'If you are fatigued, you need not take me to my room. I can leave you here.' No need for him to climb another flight of stairs.

'Very well, I will say goodnight to you here.' But rather than walk to his room, he took her hand and leaned towards her, placing his lips on to hers.

The only kisses she remembered were Lucien's. Lucien's lips lit a fire inside her that made her wish to abandon all propriety. Lord Stonecroft's kiss left her cold. As soon as she could, she drew away from him.

'Goodnight, sir,' she said. She turned to the stairs and hurried up them before he had a chance to kiss her again.

She walked swiftly to her bedchamber door and opened it.

Ella stood up from one of the chairs. She rubbed her eyes. 'You are back?'

Claire untied her cloak and handed it to Ella. 'Early, I know.'

Ella took the cloak from her hands. 'I'll fold it and put it away.'

'I have something else to tell you,' Claire said. 'Lucien did not leave Bath. He is staying in the Circus with a naval admiral he once served with. At least for a few days.'

'The Circus?' Ella asked from the dressing room.

'The buildings built in a circle,' she explained.

'Oh! I remember it! That is close by.' Ella skipped back to the bedchamber. 'The Captain said he might ask a friend to help Cullen find a position.'

This made Claire happy. She had no wish to separate the two lovers. 'This means Cullen will be nearby. We must devise a way to let him know that you can see him whenever you wish.'

'Whenever I wish? Thank you, m'lady.' She danced over and hugged her, but let go quickly. 'What about the Captain? Will you see him again?'

How she hoped. 'I suppose, if he attends the same functions as Lord Stonecroft, I might.'

Ella untied the laces of the net overdress and carefully lifted it over Claire's shoulders. She draped it over a chair while she helped Claire out of the silk ball gown.

'Perhaps I might see Cullen tomorrow,' the girl said excitedly.

'I have no idea what tomorrow brings,' Claire said. 'But any time I have no need of you, you are free to see Cullen.'

When in her nightdress, Claire climbed beneath the covers of this bed that felt stranger to her than the berth in the fishing boat. She did indeed not know what tomorrow would bring. When she was with Lucien, she could at least know he would be with her. But now, not only was her past a *tabula rasa*, so was her future. Her future seemed empty of anything worth anticipating.

Chapter Sixteen

A week went by and Claire's life settled into a routine of stultifying boredom. Because of her newfound notoriety Lord Stonecroft received more invitations than he was accustomed to, although at that time of year the entertainments were all very like Lady Milliforte's party, with all the same people.

That meant she often saw Lucien and watched him become a sought-after bachelor among the younger unattached ladies.

Stonecroft often took the waters for his health, so he frequently bathed in the waters, leaving Claire and his sister to promenade in the Pump Room where his sister met her friends and liked to pass much of the day.

This day Miss Attwood was in a tête-à-tête with Lady Milliforte. Claire wandered over to the fountain where a server filled glasses with the medicinal water of the hot springs. She accepted a small glass of the water and put it to her lips. It smelled of rotten eggs and tasted like liquid metal.

As unpleasant as the taste and smell were, they were familiar. She'd tasted the waters before, she realised. She closed her eyes and an image of herself laughing with other young ladies flashed through her mind.

A memory!

It had no context, no attachment to anything but the taste and smell of the waters, but it made her heart beat faster. She'd experienced a memory!

'Lady Rebecca, surely you do not need the waters. You are the very picture of health.'

She opened her eyes to see Sir Richard, Lucien's Admiral friend.

'I tasted it for a lark,' she said. 'How are you today, Sir Richard? Are you here for the waters?'

He smiled. 'I am here in hopes of meeting a lovely young lady and, look! I have done so.'

'You flatter me,' she said.

His expression turned serious. 'And how do you fare, my lady?'

She had the sense he was asking about more than the state of her health. And, perhaps, asking for his friend.

'Oh.' She sighed. 'I shall do well enough.'

The truth was, she was ever more clear that marriage to Lord Stonecroft would not do. The life he offered her was as desolate as the blankness of her mind. She felt more like a piece of furniture in his presence than a betrothed woman. And when he did look upon her as a person, it was merely to point out some way he disapproved of her.

She had the money her brother had given her. It provided her some means to do something else besides marry Lord Stonecroft.

She still had the recurring image of children in a schoolroom. She'd dreamt of it the night before and it gave her the notion that she could support herself as a teacher in a school or as a governess. All she needed was to find someone who would recommend her. Lucien had been convinced that she'd remembered a real school in Bristol when he'd questioned her. Perhaps she could find it and they would remember her.

'Yes,' she repeated to Sir Richard. 'I shall do well enough.'

The Admiral looked sympathetic, but he changed the subject. 'I suspect you are wondering where our mutual friend is right now.'

She felt her cheeks turn warm, but she tried to cover up by smiling. 'I suspect you might tell me whether I wondered or not.'

'He is at the West Gate Inn,' Sir Richard responded. 'He is speaking with yet another newspaper man, this time from a newspaper here in Bath.'

'Oh, dear, I do hope the reporter will not wish to interview me,' she said. 'Lord Stonecroft finds it unacceptable for a lady to be written of in a newspaper.'

Sir Richard turned to the door. 'Ah. Here he is.' He waved a hand to get Lucien's attention.

Lucien walked towards him and Claire saw his gait falter for a step when he spied her next to his friend. Was he disappointed to see her? Her spirits sank.

'Sir Richard.' He nodded to his friend and turned his gaze on Claire. 'Lady Rebecca.'

She made herself smile. 'Hello, Lucien.'

'So,' Sir Richard said, 'was the reporter satisfied with your interview?'

Lucien rolled his eyes. 'I hope so. I believe he was disappointed there was little to tell that had not appeared in the London paper.'

'Will he try to interview me, as well?' she asked.

'I discouraged him from doing so.' His gaze rested softly on her. 'How are you, my lady?'

'I—I am well, Lucien.' She wanted to tell him of her memory, but how could she? 'All is well.'

Miss Attwood strode over. 'There you are, dear. Last I saw, you were at my side.'

'I had a fancy to drink the waters, ma'am. And then I met my friends.'

No doubt Miss Attwood would tell her brother that she had been speaking with Lucien in a public place. Stonecroft had taken to warning her that people would talk if she and Lucien were too often seen together.

'Well, we should go,' Miss Attwood said. 'Stonecroft sent me a message that he has some business to attend to. He will meet us back at the Crescent.' She nodded to Lucien and Sir Richard. 'Good day, gentlemen.'

Claire felt her anger kindle. Both Miss Attwood and her brother expected she do whatever they wished when they wished it. But, at this moment, defying Miss Attwood would serve no purpose and would only risk a scene.

Still, she wished for more time with Lucien.

'Good day,' she said, hoping her tone was not too resentful.

They started to walk towards the door when a man approached. The reporter, perhaps?

He broke into a smile and opened his arms. 'My dear! I have found you at last!'

An inexplicable sense of dread engulfed her. Was this someone she should know?

He went on. 'Ever since I learned you were in Bath I have frequented the Pump Room and other places hoping to locate you.'

She drew back. 'I fear you mistake me for someone else, sir.'

'No, it is you, I know that now!' He gave her an entreating look. 'Are you not happy to see me?'

He spoke with a hint of an Irish accent. Was he someone she knew in Ireland?

Her knees shook and she did not know what to do or say. She did not remember this man, but should she? Would this encounter expose what she'd hidden so successfully from all but a few, that her mind was disordered, that she had amnesia? How long before that on dit reached the newspapers?

Lucien saw the red-haired man approach Lady Rebecca. He watched her recoil and immediately strode over to her.

'Do you need assistance, Lady Rebecca?' he asked.

'She is not Lady Rebecca,' the man protested. 'She is—'

Lady Rebecca broke in. 'He has mistaken me for someone else. I tried to tell him he was wrong.'

'He has been quite rude,' added Miss Attwood. 'Speaking to us without an introduction.'

Lucien placed himself between the man and the ladies. 'Perhaps you should leave, sir.'

'But I need to speak to her,' the man argued, trying to move around him. 'It is what I have come all this way to do.'

Lucien blocked his way and used his greater height to loom over the man. 'You are distressing these ladies. You need to leave them. Now!' He kept his voice low, but commanding.

The man backed up. 'Very well.' He bowed. 'I

see I cannot speak with you here, *Lady Rebecca*.'
He put a strange emphasis on her name.

He strode off.

Sir Richard joined them. 'Are you all right,
Miss Attwood?'

'What a strange creature,' she said.

While Sir Richard engaged Miss Attwood,
Lucien stepped aside with Lady Rebecca. 'He
alarmed you.'

'I was afraid he was someone I should remember,' she whispered. 'I did not want all of Bath society to know about—about—me.'

Lucien nodded. 'I understand.'

She took a breath and pressed a hand to her
chest. 'I am relieved, though. He thought I was
someone else. That was clear.'

Sir Richard interrupted. 'I do not think these
ladies should walk home alone, do you, Captain?'

'No, he may be waiting for them outside.' He
looked at Lady Rebecca. 'We will see you home
safely.'

Sir Richard offered Miss Attwood his arm,
leaving Lucien just where he wished to be. With
Lady Rebecca. They left the Pump Room and
started up Barton Street.

Lady Rebecca slowed her step so that they
lagged enough behind Sir Richard and Miss
Attwood that their conversation could be private.
'Lucien, I had a memory.'

'A memory?' Perhaps this was the start.

'In the Pump Room. Just a little while ago. I drank the waters and I distinctly remembered the smell and taste. I knew I'd tasted it before.' Her voice was quiet but excited. 'And then the memory came. I remembered laughing with other girls and I knew them. Or I had the sense that I knew them. It was very fleeting, but I remembered being in the Pump Room.'

He squeezed her hand. 'I told you that you'd get your memory back.'

'It is a little thing, though.'

'You probably came to Bath as a schoolgirl,' he said. 'Makes sense if you were at a school in Bristol. It is not that far.'

'I wonder if I would have more memories if I travelled to Bristol and found that school.'

It was on the tip of his tongue to offer to take her there, but he'd be delayed even longer from getting a ship.

Besides, Stonecroft should be taking her to Bristol and helping her regain her memory.

'Where is Stonecroft today?' he asked.

She waved her hand. 'He was taking the waters. It helps his arthritic knees, he said.'

They walked without talking for a while and were quiet enough to hear Sir Richard regaling Miss Attwood with some tale. Lucien glanced around, making certain the man who'd bothered her was not in sight.

Lady Rebecca broke their silence. 'That man alarmed me, Lucien.'

'You must let me know if he bothers you again.'

She turned to him with a wan smile. 'So you can rescue me once more?'

He ought to remain in Bath until he was certain that man would not distress her further.

'When do you go to London?' she asked.

'Soon,' he replied. 'I should go soon.'

'Will you let me know when you plan to leave?' she asked. 'I would like to say goodbye.'

'I will.'

They reached Queen Square.

Miss Attwood turned around and called to Lady Rebecca, 'Do not lag so! Come up here.'

They could no longer be alone. From then they said little to each other.

When they reached the door to Number Five Royal Crescent, Lucien faced her. She extended her hand and he clasped it. They held on for a moment longer than was needed to say goodbye.

'Thank you again, Captain.' He missed hearing her call him Lucien.

'I am at your disposal.' He released her hand.

The footman opened the door and the ladies went inside.

Sir Richard clapped Lucien on the shoulder. 'I do not comprehend why you fail to simply tell that lady of your regard for her.'

'It is very difficult to explain,' Lucien said as they walked to the Circus.

He did have a great regard for her, he admitted to himself. He was concerned for her happiness, but knew it could not be achieved with him.

'She is recovering her memory,' he told his friend. 'Being among people of her class may have been the catalyst. She will not want a mere captain when she remembers who she is.'

'Falderal,' Sir Richard said. 'You overrate status and titles and such.'

'Overrate them?' Lucien shot back. 'I despise what status and titles do to people. You've met them. They believe they deserve whatever they want merely because they want it. It is inconsequential what more humble people need. They think nothing of moving villages so the view from their estate is more picturesque. Or they ruin a life for a moment of pleasure—' He stopped, realising he was ranting.

'Might I remind you, boy, that I have a title?' Sir Richard's tone was kind.

'That is another matter entirely,' Lucien said defensively.

Sir Richard laughed.

As they reached the door to Sir Richard's house, Lucien said, 'Yours is not a very elevated title, Sir Richard.' He slanted his friend a glance and smiled.

Sir Richard clapped him on the back. 'You are a hopeless prig.'

Sir Richard's point was not lost on Lucien, though. Was it possible he put too much importance on titles and status? Sir Richard was the opposite of what Lucien abhorred. He was generous and accepting of all kinds of people from all walks of life. Was he merely a rare exception? Or was Lucien wrong to cut all aristocrats from the same cloth?

None of this mattered, though. Because Lucien wanted to be back at sea where he belonged. He missed the rhythm of navy life, the way every man mattered and everyone depended on each other. He missed the scent of the sea air and the rocking of the ship. He missed knowing his duty to his ship, his crew and his King.

All that afternoon Claire had flashes of the man who had approached her at the Pump Room. She did not know why he returned to her thoughts or why the instances were so fleeting that she could not hold on to them to make sense of it.

She told Ella about the man. And about Lucien once again coming to her aid.

'You must watch out for that fellow,' Ella said. 'I have a premonition he will not be good for you.'

'You have a premonition?' This was the first Claire heard of Ella having premonitions.

'I have premonitions, I do,' insisted Ella. 'My grandmother had the sight, too.'

Then Claire wished Ella could tell her when she would get her memory back and when she should make her break from Stonecroft.

* * *

Ella had helped Claire dress for dinner. There was a concert at the Upper Assembly Rooms this night so she wore yet another dress that the modiste in Bath had made for her, another dress chosen and approved by Miss Attwood.

It was pretty enough, a lilac satin with silver embroidery along the hem and neckline. Miss Attwood lent her amethyst earrings and a matching necklace.

When she entered the drawing room before dinner, Lord Stonecroft's gaze swept over her as a man might look over a horse he wished to purchase.

He turned to his sister. 'The dress is very fitting. You did well.'

His sister smiled. 'Thank you. The modiste did wonders to work so quickly.'

Stonecroft never complimented Claire directly. He seemed determined not to do anything that would endear him to her.

Dinner was announced and they went to the dining room.

As they began the first course, Stonecroft said, 'Honora tells me that you engaged with a strange man at the Pump Room today and nearly made a spectacle of yourself.'

Claire glanced at Miss Attwood before responding.

The woman's brows knitted and Claire was

fairly certain Lord Stonecroft was distorting what he'd been told.

'Are you certain you understood what happened, sir?' she finally said.

She thought she saw a guilty look flit across his face before his expression turned bland again. 'Suppose you tell me what happened.'

'A man came up to me and professed to know me, but I did not know him.' That was the gist of it.

Stonecroft gave her a steady look. 'You did not know him or you did not remember him?'

A wave of anxiety washed through her. He'd homed in on precisely what she'd feared. 'I did not know him. He mistook me for someone else.'

'I do not like this. Strange men speaking with you.' He took a loud sip of his soup. 'It does not look seemly.'

'The contact was quite brief,' she said, trying not to let her irritation show. 'Captain Roper intervened and sent the man away.'

He pointed to her with his spoon. 'That is another thing. You and Roper. You spoke privately together.'

'In the Pump Room surrounded by everyone else who was there,' she retorted.

'And on the walk home?' His brows rose.

She had spoken privately to Lucien. She lifted her chin. 'Yes. I did engage in conversation with Captain Roper as he and Sir Richard escorted us home in case the stranger reappeared.'

The next course was served. The food at Stonecroft's dinner table was bland in taste and unimaginative. Boiled fish, stewed chicken, boiled vegetables, small tarts for dessert.

That she observed that fact meant she must have eaten finer food elsewhere. Of course, the food on the fishing boat had been nearly the same every night and she'd found no fault in that.

'Honora believes you spend entirely too much time with that Captain Roper,' Stonecroft went on.

She glanced at Miss Attwood again. This time it seemed that had been what the woman had told her brother.

Claire straightened in her chair. 'If I see Captain Roper at the Pump Room or at an Assembly or a concert, or on the street in Bath, I will speak to him. I will never snub him or avoid him. And you well know why, my lord.'

Because he had saved her life and was once her life and now deserved a life of his own.

Lucien was not in the habit of attending concerts. Concerts usually were more about the elite wanting to see and be seen. However, Sir Richard had learned from Miss Attwood that she, Stonecroft and Lady Rebecca would attend this night and Lucien was concerned that the stranger would be there, too, and would try again to approach her.

The tea room was set up for the concert, but the Octagon Room was filled as well, its tables filled with card players, another aristocratic pastime which Lucien disdained. Sir Richard joined some friends who sat near the middle of the room, but Lucien stood in the back where he could watch who entered and left.

Lord Stonecroft entered with Lady Rebecca on his arm and his sister following close behind. The Baron looked as arrogant as the other times Lucien had seen him. Miss Attwood greeted her friends with a tight smile. Lady Rebecca looked remote, as if her thoughts were anywhere but on the concert and the people attending.

She did not appear content and that worried him.

Stonecroft chose seats near the front of the room.

Lucien was reasonably certain they had not seen him. From Miss Attwood's eagerness to separate them earlier, that was probably a good thing.

Gradually the seats filled and the din of the many voices sounded in his ears. Lucien scanned the crowd many times to be certain the stranger had not arrived unseen by him.

Soon the musicians entered and took their places. The soloist, a soprano, was introduced, and a tenor who'd been trained by Rauzzini, the Italian castrato who'd made much of his fortune singing in Bath.

The soloist sang the 'Exsultate, jubilate' which Mozart was supposed to have composed for Rauzzini—or so the introduction said.

The music and soloist's voice were pleasant,

but Lucien's attention remained on the door. Finally he saw a man slip in. The stranger. He watched the man look through the crowd. He walked part way up the side of the room. Lucien knew the moment the man spotted her. He paused and his posture tensed. He smiled and returned to the back of the room. Lucien watched him from the opposite side. He would probably approach her during the intermission when refreshments would be served.

When the soloist finished and the applause ended, the audience stood and some left their seats, Stonecroft and Miss Attwood among them. Lady Rebecca remained where she was, sitting alone.

The stranger started to walk towards her. Lucien quickly crossed the room, intending to intercept him and escort him out. But the stranger spied him and turned back, mixing in with the crowd. Lucien could not reach him. He saw the man leave the room and he quickly followed. When he reached the door the man was already across the Octagon Room. By the time he made his way across that room, the stranger had quickened his step and was nearly at the other end of the ballroom. Lucien sprinted to catch up. Outside a cold drizzle darkened the streets. Lucien quickened his pace and caught the stranger by the collar.

'Wait!' he ordered. 'I want to know who you are and what business you have with Lady Rebecca.'

The man squirmed under his grip. 'Let me go!'

'Answer me first.'

The man struggled. He and Lucien spun around as he tried to escape. Lucien's injured shoulder ached with the strain of holding on to the man.

One of the Assembly Rooms attendants emerged from the building. 'What goes here?' he shouted.

The stranger cried, 'He is trying to rob me!'

The attendant hurried towards them.

'I am not robbing him,' Lucien said.

'Help me!' the stranger wailed.

The attendant reached them.

Lucien said, 'I want to question him.'

The attendant was close enough to see his face. 'Captain Roper?' He turned to the stranger. 'This is Captain Roper. He is not a robber, sir. He is the Captain of the *Foxfire*. What is this?'

Lucien's notoriety came to his assistance, apparently.

The stranger stopped struggling. 'Very well. I will tell you. Make him let me go.'

Lucien loosened his grip, but did not release him. The man took advantage, though, and pushed against him, knocking Lucien off balance. The stranger wrenched away and fled down the street. Both the attendant and Lucien dashed after him, but he disappeared in the dark streets behind the Assembly Rooms.

Lucien uttered a low curse.

The attendant breathed hard. 'What—who was he?'

'That is what I wanted to discover.' Lucien also needed to catch his breath. 'I believed he means to do harm to a lady.'

'Which lady?' the man asked.

'Lady Rebecca.'

'Ah,' the attendant said knowingly. He must have been aware of the connection between Lucien and Lady Rebecca.

They walked back to the Assembly Rooms.

When they reached the door, Lucien stopped him. 'Let us not speak of this. I do not wish to alarm anyone unnecessarily.'

'Very well, sir.'

Lucien returned to the tea room where the concert had resumed, but he remained in the back, avoiding encountering Lady Rebecca. When the concert was over, he followed Lady Rebecca and her party in their sedan chairs back to the Royal Crescent, just to make certain that the stranger did not accost her.

When the chairmen dropped them off in front of Lord Stonecroft's door and Lady Rebecca was safe inside, Lucien walked back to Sir Richard's.

One thing he knew—he would not leave Bath until he was certain Lady Rebecca was safe from this strange man's interest in her.

Chapter Seventeen

The next morning Claire had planned to sleep late and miss breakfast, the time of day she was almost certain to be alone with Lord Stonecroft, but she woke even earlier than usual.

From the nightmare that plagued her over and over during the night.

She'd dreamed about the red-haired stranger who'd approached her at the Pump Room, disturbing dreams mixed with the vision of the little girls at a schoolroom table. He loomed over her in the dream and the sense of danger woke her each time.

The sun was up, though, and leaving her bed was less undesirable than risking one more nightmare. She padded over to the dressing-room door to peek in on Ella, but the girl's cot was empty and neatly made. The maid must rise before the sun.

She walked back to the bureau and poured water from the pitcher into the basin. With a nice piece of scented soap—soap Lucien had purchased for her—she removed her nightdress and washed herself.

She'd donned her shift and was brushing her hair at the dressing table when Ella walked in.

'Oh, you are awake early, m'lady!' Ella carried a pail of coal over to the fireplace. 'And looks like you are half-dressed, as well.'

'I could not sleep more.' No need to tell Ella of her nightmares. She'd only hear more about premonitions. And she did not wish to worry the girl.

'What dress would you like to wear today?' Ella asked, crossing over to the dressing room.

She'd like to wear the sprigged muslin that Lucien had bought her, but did not wish to hear Stonecroft's complaints. 'Any one of the new walking dresses.'

Ella chose a blue printed cotton that the modiste had delivered the day before. 'You might as well wear this new one.'

After Ella helped her into the dress, she again sat at the dressing table. 'Arrange my hair simply today, Ella. I do not feel up to a fussy do.'

'Whatever you say, m'lady.'

She put Claire's hair into a knot atop her head, but could not resist pulling a few curls out to frame her face.

Claire went down to the sitting room where breakfast was served and was not surprised to see Stonecroft already seated there.

'Good morning, sir,' she said.

He stood and gave her an assessing scan. 'Good morning.'

'Please sit,' she said.

Each day started the same.

She chose her food from the sideboard and sat opposite him as she had every day of the past week. She was no closer to knowing this man— or he, her—than she had that first day.

Was this what the loss of love did to a man?

She wanted to feel something for Stonecroft, but it became more and more evident that his guard would never be lowered. As she nibbled on her toasted bread, she again ran through her plan to run away to Bristol where, if she could not find herself there, she could at least find someone who knew her and could perhaps help her find employment.

'It is time to announce the banns,' he said behind his newspaper.

She glanced up at him. 'My lord, I have asked—'

'I know what you have asked.' He lowered his paper. 'But I fail to see what recovering your memory will do to alter the matter. At present there is entirely too much talk about you and your rescue. Perhaps your Captain Roper will leave Bath if you are a married woman. Then the talk will cease.'

So that was it. 'Captain Roper is not your rival, sir, I assure you.'

'I believe he has aspirations.'

Her brows rose. 'Aspirations?'

'To wed into the aristocracy,' he said.

She almost laughed. 'Oh, no, my lord. I can assure you he has no wish to marry into the aristocracy. His attachment to me is merely one of duty.'

He gave her a sceptical and patronising look. 'He is everywhere you are,' he said. 'Even at the concert last night. A man of his background certainly would not come for such elevated music.'

He'd been there? She'd had no idea. 'I did not see him.'

Stonecroft lifted his paper again. 'Nevertheless I will have the banns announced next Sunday.'

That left her three days to make her decision and take action.

She stood. 'If I may have your leave, sir.'

'As you wish.' He did not stop reading his paper.

She rushed out of the room, past the stony-faced footman who'd heard the whole exchange. In the hall she looked around, feeling as if the walls would close in on her. She hurried up the stairs to her bedchamber.

Ella was straightening the room. 'M'lady. That was a quick breakfast.'

'Where is my Kashmir shawl?' She opened the bureau drawer. 'I am going to take a walk before I turn mad.'

Ella stepped into the dressing room and emerged

carrying the shawl. 'Are you walking with Lord Stonecroft?'

'No.' She wrapped herself in her favourite possession. 'No one. I just need some air.'

'Wait a moment, then,' Ella said. 'You should not go alone. I will go with you.'

They put on hats and gloves and walked down to the hall.

'If Lord Stonecroft or Miss Attwood should ask for me, I am taking a walk,' she told the footman in attendance.

'Yes, m'lady.' He opened the door for her.

Like all days of that summer, the air was chilly. The sky was grey, but it did not look like rain was imminent.

'Do you want to walk through the fields?' Ella asked.

'Not with the cows grazing there.' The green fields in front of the Royal Crescent were a piece of the country in that city, but Claire did not want to view the Crescent. She wanted to escape it. 'Let us wander the streets.'

They walked to Church Street towards Cottles Lane, away from the Crescent.

'So, what is this about, m'lady?' Ella asked.

'Nothing.' She knew Ella did not want her to marry Stonecroft, but her emotions were too raw to discuss. 'I am restless, is all.'

As they turned on Cottles Lane, Ella gripped

Claire's hand. 'M'lady! I think a man is following us.'

Claire immediately thought of the stranger, the man in her dreams. Though an occasional carriage or sedan chair passed them, there was no one else on the street. They quickened their pace and when Claire had an opportunity, she turned and saw the man, who stopped abruptly.

It was the red-haired man from her dreams.

'He is the man who approached me at the Pump Room,' she told Ella.

'Oh, I do not feel easy about this.' The girl shuddered.

They came to an alleyway connecting Cottles Lane to Rivers Street.

'Come with me!' Ella cried.

They raced down the alley and ran to Rivers Street, ducked down another alley and another until they reached the mews to the Circus. Ella guided them through the mews to the back entrances of the terrace houses.

She knocked on one of them. 'This is Sir Richard's house. The servants know me because of Cullen.'

One of the kitchen maids answered the door and saw it was Ella. 'Oh, it is you.' The girl then spied Claire and looked puzzled.

Ella pushed them both past the girl and entered the house. 'We were out for a walk, Lady Rebecca and I, and a man was following us. Is Sir Richard here? Or Captain Roper?'

The kitchen maid curtsied. 'I am sure I do not know, miss, but best you take her ladyship above stairs and ask there.'

'Come on, m'lady,' Ella said. 'I know the way.'

She took her up the servants' stairs to the hall where a surprised footman rose to his feet from the chair where he ought not to have been seated.

'Miss Kiley? You'll be wanting to see Cullen?' He also noticed Claire. 'Beg pardon, ma'am.'

'We need Sir Richard or Captain Roper. Tell them it is Lady Rebecca and Ella.'

'Sir Richard went out,' the man said.

'Then Captain Roper,' Ella demanded.

The footman nodded and hurried up the stairs. A few moments later he returned with Cullen in tow. 'Captain says he will meet you in the drawing room directly.'

Cullen looked concerned. 'What is it, Ella? What has happened?' He glanced at Claire. 'Lady Rebecca, I forget myself.' He bowed to her.

They no sooner entered the drawing room than Lucien appeared. He walked straight to Claire. 'What has happened?'

She wished she could fall into his arms.

'I am sorry for the intrusion, Lucien. Ella brought us here,' she said. 'We were on a walk and that stranger from the Pump Room started following us.' She did not wish to show him how shaken she was.

'That stranger.' His voice dipped. He turned to Cullen. 'Would you and Ella arrange for some refreshments to be brought to us? And find some refreshments for Ella, too.'

Cullen nodded and he and Ella left the room.

He led Claire to a sofa and sat next to her. 'I do not comprehend this. You told him at the Pump Room that you were Lady Rebecca, not the woman for whom he searched. Why is he persisting?'

'Could he be in my memory?' she asked him. 'I dreamed about him.' Frightening dreams. 'If he was in my memory, it would make sense.'

He stood and rubbed his forehead. 'I need to find him. Talk to him. I almost had him—' He broke off.

'What do you mean, you almost had him?' What had he done?

He paced. 'I attended the concert last night. He was there, but noticed me approaching and ran out. I chased him. Had him in my grip, but he managed to get away.'

So he had been at the concert, like Stonecroft said. 'Lucien, did you attend that concert because of that man?'

He shrugged. 'It occurred to me he might seek you there.'

'You were watching over me, then.' As he'd done since she'd woken up on the raft.

He did not respond, but his expression told her yes.

She stood and faced him. 'Are you staying in Bath because of me?'

He glanced away.

She put her hand on his arm. 'You are delaying your trip to the Admiralty because of me.'

He met her gaze, but still did not answer.

More than anything she wanted him to stay with her. More than anything but his happiness, that was. And his happiness was being at sea. Suddenly she could see how selfish she'd been to want him to stay.

'You must not remain in Bath for me, Lucien.' Her guilt cut into her. 'I have burdened you enough.'

He frowned. 'A few more days will not matter. I want to find this man first. Make certain he is no threat to you.' He glanced towards the door. 'Wait here a moment.'

Before she could say another word, he strode out of the room.

Lucien went in search of Cullen and Ella, finding them below stairs in the servants' room.

Cullen rose at his entrance. 'Sir?'

'I want you both to go out, wander around and look for that man,' Lucien told him. 'If you can, bring him to me. If not, find out where he is staying. It is time we discovered what his business with Lady Rebecca is.' He turned to Ella. 'Will you be comfortable doing that?'

'Yes, sir!' She smiled and gazed up at Cullen. He nodded.

As he left the room, he encountered the footman carrying a tea tray with biscuits. 'I'll take that,' he said.

He carried the tray to the drawing room and placed it on the table in front of Lady Rebecca. 'I've sent Cullen and Ella out to look for the stranger. My guess is he is still wandering around in hopes of discovering where you are.'

She poured the tea for him, not needing to ask him how he liked it, after all the time they'd spent together.

She took a biscuit. 'I did not have much breakfast.' After eating it, she said, 'Perhaps he is simply mistaking me for someone else. Maybe he is not a threat at all.'

She sounded as if she were trying to convince herself not to worry.

'Let us hope Cullen can find him and we'll discover for sure.'

She took another biscuit.

Sitting here with her felt comfortable. They had spent so much time together since the shipwreck that it felt strange not to be in her company.

'How are you faring?' he asked after a time.

'Besides this matter with the stranger. The truth, please.'

She placed the biscuit on her saucer. 'I am trying to accustom myself to my situation.'

'That is no answer,' he said.

She stared into her tea for a time before speaking. 'Stonecroft is not cruel. Neither is Miss Attwood. No one is unkind. I do wish for more time, though.'

'More time?'

She released a breath. 'Lord Stonecroft says he will have the banns announced beginning this Sunday, but I am not ready for it.'

Lucien stiffened. 'Then you should stop him.'

'Yes, I should do that,' she said without conviction.

Meaning she would not stop him, he thought. Meaning she intended to go along with the plans made for her.

She glanced around the room. 'I should return to Lord Stonecroft's house.'

He did not want her to go, but he extended his hand. 'I will escort you.'

She picked up her shawl and allowed him to help her up. Theirs gazes locked for a moment and he kept hold of her hand. But he released it as soon as she stepped away from the sofa. When they reached the hall he told the footman, 'I am walking Lady Rebecca home. If Cullen returns, tell him to wait for me. I'll be back shortly.'

When they left the house, Lucien scanned the area. There were a few people about, but none looked like the stranger. Some of the people they passed, people he'd met at the various entertainments he'd attended, greeted them.

'I suppose we will be gossiped about,' she said, glancing back at them.

'Will that distress you?' he asked.

'No.' She slanted him a look. 'I know you have always behaved honourably towards me. You've proved it over and over.'

He, on the other hand, remembered almost taking her to bed and almost giving in to his desire for her.

They reached Stonecroft's house.

'Do I knock?' he asked.

'Yes,' she responded. 'I am not really a member of the household.'

He sounded the knocker and stepped away.

A footman answered and seeing it was Lady Rebecca, opened the door wide for her.

She turned back to Lucien. 'Thank you once again, Lucien.'

'Promise me you will not venture out alone,' he said.

'I won't.'

He started to turn away, but turned back. 'I will let you know what we discover.'

She nodded and disappeared inside the house.

As Lucien turned towards Church Street, he

spied a man who quickly ducked behind some buildings. The stranger. And now he knew where Lady Rebecca lived.

He ran to the spot where he saw the stranger disappear, but there was no sign of him.

'Blast!' Lucien swore.

When Claire walked inside Stonecroft stood in the hall.

'Do you mind telling me what you are about?' His voice was stern, but his eyes showed no more interest or emotion than any other time.

She would not tolerate being scolded like a child. She removed her hat. 'I took a walk with my lady's maid and we saw the man who approached me at the Pump Room following us. We were near the Circus so we knocked upon Sir Richard's door.'

He raised his brows. 'And where is your lady's maid?'

'She is with the Captain's valet. Captain Roper asked them to try to search for the man and discover who he is and where he is staying.' She started to climb the stairs.

'So, you were with Captain Roper.' He followed her on her heels up the stairway.

Had he not heard the most important part? That this stranger was following her?

She could not keep the annoyance from her voice. 'Captain Roper escorted me so I would not have to walk alone when there is a stranger who might threaten me.' She turned to face him. 'What else would you have had me do?'

He pursed his lips. 'I merely want the talk about you and Captain Roper to end.'

She continued up the stairs. 'And what of this man who is following me?'

Did that not matter to him?

He responded, 'You said he believes you are someone else. There is no reason to think he wishes you harm.'

How could he be certain of this?

When they reached the first floor, he said, 'Come to the drawing room. I wish to speak with you.'

She gritted her teeth as she followed him to the drawing room. He gestured for her to sit.

She chose a chair. 'Well?'

He remained standing. 'As you know, I expect you to produce an heir. That is the reason for our marriage. That is why I want the banns.'

Had she agreed to that?

'If you discussed that with me before, I do not remember it.' She drew an irritated breath. 'You have said nothing to me since. You want the banns, but I believe you do not understand how difficult it is for me not to have any memory of those agreements we made about marriage. I want to remember those things before posting the banns.'

'It is ridiculous to wait.' He paced in front of her. 'You do not need a memory to get with child. It is not as if you have other choices. How many offers do you expect to receive at your age?'

She disliked having to look up at him. 'You see, sir, I do not know my age. That is what I am trying to make you understand—'

He waved an impatient hand. 'You are twenty-three, if your brother told the truth about it.'

Twenty-three was old enough to be considered a spinster.

'I have no idea what my brother told you.'

'I suppose your birthdate is in the documents your brother sent to me when we reached a settlement.' He stopped pacing and leaned down to her. 'If you are planning to cry off, or if you are the sort to engage in affairs, I beg you tell me now. I have wasted enough time.'

A wave of guilt washed through her. Should she simply tell him now that she would not marry him? She did not know what to do.

She stood and faced him. 'Sir, I have no idea if I am the sort who has affairs.' She certainly had experienced wanton impulses with Lucien. 'I do not know at all what sort of person I am.'

He took a step back. 'Well, you can show me by staying away from Roper.'

Her face warmed with anger. This man failed to hear or consider anything she had to say. She'd had enough of being at the mercy of men who expected her to do what they wanted and did not listen to her.

Where had that thought come from?

Once in her room, she could not sit still.

She'd promised Lucien she would not walk out alone, but staying inside would drive her mad. The streets would be busier at this time of day. It should be safe enough.

She needed to discover how to reach Bristol. Once in Bristol she could find the school she had attended and from there beg them to find her work. Her recurrent dream about little girls seated at a school table must mean something. If it was school that could crack open her memory, she must find that school.

She put on her hat again and, before she could change her mind, walked out of the room, down the stairs and to the hall.

'I am going out again,' she said to the footman in the hall.

'Going out?' He sounded surprised.

'Yes. To the shops.' She walked to the door.

He stepped quickly to open it and she hurried into the street.

Chapter Eighteen

Lucien had tried to follow the stranger, but by the time he reached the buildings where he'd seen the man, he'd disappeared. He walked the streets around there, but did not see him again.

He started back to Sir Richard's, hoping Cullen and Ella had had better luck.

As he neared Brock Street from Church, he saw Lady Rebecca walking swiftly towards the Circus. Alone.

What the devil was she doing? She'd promised not to venture out.

He took a breath, but didn't hesitate. He followed her at some distance.

She walked past the Circus on to Gay Street, but paused and glanced around. When she spied him, she looked alarmed at first, but then stood her ground and waited for him to catch up to her.

'Lady Rebecca—' He was vexed with her.

'I know. I know,' she responded. 'I promised not to go out alone.'

'Then why are you?'

She averted her gaze. 'I have errands…'

He crossed his arms over his chest. 'You will have to do better than that.'

She returned an obstinate look.

'Tell me.' He softened his voice. 'What would make you take a chance like this? It must be something important. Because I know you are not a fool.'

She lifted her eyes to him briefly, then looked away. 'I want to find out how to go to Bristol. I'm convinced if I can find my school, my memory will come back.'

'Can you not ask Stonecroft to take you?' he asked. 'He would want your memory restored, would he not?'

Her gaze met his again. 'He thinks my memory loss a trifling matter.'

Lucien fell silent for a time as they walked down Gay Street together.

Finally he said, 'I will take you to Bristol. There are coaches to Bristol from the West Gate Inn.'

Her step faltered. 'Oh, Lucien. No. You need to go to London, not Bristol. It might take me several days to locate the right school.'

Yes. He should go to London, but how could he? He could not leave until he knew she was safe.

The sky that had been grey for days darkened even more and fat drops of rain pattered the pavement.

Lucien glanced up at the clouds. 'Quick. Let us find some shelter. It will be pouring in a moment.'

They dashed behind the buildings on Trim Street and found a garden doorway that provided a semblance of shelter.

The shower grew thicker and Lucien put his arms around her to help keep her out of the rain in the small space they occupied. Their bodies were pressed together.

'Lucien.' She sighed and rested her head against his chest.

'Like on the raft,' he murmured. 'I must hold you to keep you safe.'

He savoured the feel of her in his arms, one more moment in so many they had shared together.

She touched his shoulder. 'How is your wound? I have not asked these several days. Does it still pain you?'

'Very little,' he told her. 'Sir Richard's surgeon examined it and removed the stitches. It is healed over.'

He'd missed the warmth of her, the scent of her. Something shifted inside him about her. Could he be happy without her? He was no longer convinced that she could be content with Stonecroft, who was so indifferent to her needs.

They did not speak, but clung to each other like they had on the raft. Perhaps that was the way to get through life, he thought. Clinging together.

The rain shower stopped as abruptly as it had begun and Lucien reluctantly released her.

'I—I believe I should return to Lord Stonecroft's,' she said. 'You have told me how to find a coach to Bristol, so I do not need to go further.'

'I mean it, that I will take you to Bristol, if you wish it,' he repeated.

She looked up at him and brushed the raindrops from his shoulders. 'I will think about it.'

He offered his arm once more. 'I will walk you back.'

They stepped around puddles behind the buildings and returned to Gay Street.

'You know you took a risk leaving the house by yourself,' he told her. 'I saw the stranger when last I left you. That is why I was still out. I searched for him to no avail.'

'I thought there would be enough people out to keep me safe,' she said.

'Do not take another chance like that, my lady. Not until we know more about this man and his interest in you.'

They walked several steps before she answered, 'I will be cautious.'

It was not precisely a promise to do as he said. He must try to discover this man some other way. He'd check the inns in Bath and see if a man of his description was staying there.

They continued past the Circus until eventually they reached the Crescent.

He sounded the knocker. 'Again I say goodbye to you, my lady.'

She took his hand in hers and smiled. 'Again I say thank you, Lucien.'

The door opened and Lord Stonecroft stepped out. 'Captain Roper, I would speak with you.' He stepped aside so Lucien could enter.

Lady Rebecca gave Lucien a distressed look. He tried to return her a reassuring one, but certainly nothing good could come from this meeting. 'Very well, sir.'

'Lady Rebecca,' Stonecroft said in a stern voice. 'You may go upstairs and change into dry clothing. I will speak with you later.'

With one more glance at Lucien, she did what Lord Stonecroft ordered.

Lucien followed the man into a library right off the hall. The books on the shelves looked as if they'd not been removed in a decade and the chairs and sofa were arranged in perfect symmetry. Only one chair looked inviting, a large leather chair that sat behind a desk embellished with gilt.

Stonecroft turned and faced him. 'What are your intentions towards Lady Rebecca?'

At least the man was forthright. 'Intentions? As from the beginning, to see her safe and well.'

Stonecroft walked to a cabinet and took out a decanter and two glasses. He poured brown liquid into both and handed one to Lucien.

Stonecroft took a sip of his before speaking

again. 'You being so frequently in her company causes talk. That whole shipwreck story just adds fuel to the flame. It was bad enough you were written of in the newspapers.'

'The shipwreck happened,' Lucien said. 'Our rescue was news.'

'Having one's name in the newspaper makes people talk.' Stonecroft grimaced. 'I find it distasteful.'

Lucien's spine stiffened. 'You, sir, are more concerned with how people talk than the traumas Lady Rebecca endured. Even now she suffers from her loss of memory. It affects her greatly.'

Stonecroft sneered. 'You talk like a lover, Roper. I took you at your word that nothing improper occurred between you and my fiancée—'

Lucien raised his voice. 'Heed me, Stonecroft. Lady Rebecca needs consideration. That is more important than newspapers and gossip.'

Stonecroft lifted his chin like a petulant child. 'Do take note of who you are speaking to, Roper.'

'I know precisely who I am speaking to,' Lucien shot back.

Stonecroft sputtered. 'You are disrespectful, sir!'

'Show some respect for Lady Rebecca,' Lucien countered.

Stonecroft's face turned haughty. 'Your association makes people speculate about impropriety over dinner and cards. Still, I am willing to marry her, but I dislike scandal above all things. I demand you honour my wishes in this matter.'

Lucien's voice rose again. 'You demand?'

'Yes. I demand you stay away,' the man said. 'Leave Bath. You cause me nothing but trouble here.'

Stonecroft was still missing the point.

'What of this stranger stalking Lady Rebecca?' Lucien asked. 'What will you do to protect her?'

Stonecroft shook his shoulders. 'I will marry her. When she is my wife no man will dare trifle with her.'

That was a ridiculous statement.

Lucien set down his glass, untouched, next to Stonecroft's. 'I find your lack of concern for the lady who is to be your wife reprehensible, sir. You care nothing for the danger that may lurk out there for her. Or for the ordeal she has endured. Or for her loss of memory.'

Stonecroft's face turned red. 'You dare to lecture me?'

Lucien countered, 'I merely state what should be obvious to anyone who has a regard for her.'

Stonecroft fumed. 'I believe I know what is best for her and for the children I will beget with her.'

Lucien directed a steely glance at the man. 'If Lady Rebecca needs my assistance, I will always come to her aid. If I see her at an entertainment or on the street, I will greet her and speak with her.

I will also decide when I leave Bath and it will never be because you commanded me to leave.'

He turned away from the man and walked out the door.

Claire had delayed going upstairs, wanting to know what Lord Stonecroft had said to Lucien.

As she waited on the first floor, looking down on the hall, Miss Attwood came down from the floor above.

'Lady Rebecca, what on earth has been happening this morning? First I am told you and your maid go out, then you come back without her—and in the company of Captain Roper—then you leave again, alone this time and again return with the Captain. What is all this?'

She had half a mind to tell Miss Attwood everything. About how her brother was pressuring her to have the banns read before she was ready. How he was discounting the difficulty she experienced over the loss of her memory. How unconcerned he was about the stranger who'd approached them.

'I desired a walk after breakfast and Ella went with me,' she said instead. 'We noticed that the stranger who bothered us yesterday was following us and we fled to Sir Richard's house. Captain Roper was the only one at home. He walked me back.'

'And your maid?' Miss Attwood asked.

'She and Captain Roper's valet went in search of the stranger.'

She frowned. 'The other servants tell me that maid of yours is always running off to Sir Richard's. Did you know there was some carnal attachment between her and that valet? You'd best be wary. That girl will be increasing in no time and, I tell you, Stonecroft will not tolerate a servant in his household with low morals.'

Now they were casting aspersions on Ella?

'Miss Attwood, Ella is a fine young woman.'

'I believe at my age I may know more about servants and what can happen than you. I am simply warning you. If you want her to stay as your lady's maid, you ought to sever these goings on right now. Nip them in the bud.' She made a gesture with her fingers as if she were doing that very thing.

On the contrary, Claire thought. She should encourage Ella to go after as much happiness as she could, because in a moment everything could be washed away.

Claire climbed one step of the stairs leading to the second floor. 'If you will excuse me, I must change out of these wet clothes.'

She fled to her bedchamber and was surprised to find Ella there.

'Oh, m'lady.' Ella removed her hat and eyed Claire's wet clothes. 'I just came in. Where were you?'

'Captain Roper and I got caught in the rain.'

Ella seemed to accept that explanation.

What was Claire to do about Ella? She could not take her along to Bristol. Claire would be lucky to find a way to support herself; she certainly did not want to spoil Ella's chances of good employment. And she did not want to separate Ella from Cullen. At least one of them should be happy. She would leave an excellent reference for her and trust that Lucien would help her find a position.

She pulled the hat off her head. 'You can help me change into dry clothes.'

'Of course, m'lady.' She took the shawl and draped it over a chair and came back to undo Claire's laces. 'Cullen and I almost caught up to that strange man, m'lady.'

'You did?' Her heart pounded faster.

'We saw him standing on the field in front of these houses. Cullen ran after him and almost caught up to him, but he disappeared into the shrubbery.'

The stranger must know where she lived. Was he watching the house at this very moment? She shivered at the thought.

She was trapped in this house with Lord Stonecroft and Miss Attwood, who both considered her a mere means to an end—the means by which Stonecroft's heir would be born. Neither cared much for her beyond that and beyond how she appeared to their society.

Well, if she could endure a day and night on a

raft at sea, three weeks on a fishing boat and the loss of all her possessions—and her memory—she could endure three more days with these people.

Because she was determined to make her escape before Lord Stonecroft had the banns read.

Lucien spent the rest of the morning and half the afternoon asking at inns in Bath to discover the identity of man who'd accosted Lady Rebecca. The only possibility he'd found so far was the White Hart. No one remembered the redhaired man, but the inn was large enough that the stranger could be staying there without anyone's notice.

He visited the West Gate Inn last.

The innkeeper remembered him. 'Captain Roper, a letter just arrived for you from London. You save me sending a man to bring it to you. Wait a moment.'

The man disappeared into another room and returned with the envelope.

'Thank you.' It was from the Admiralty, but Lucien had to put it in a pocket. 'I am searching for a man,' he said and described the stranger.

The innkeeper said, 'I do not recall such a man, but ask the hostlers and in the public room. Someone else might have seen him.'

While Lucien queried every inn worker he could find—to no avail—the letter burned in his pocket. He sat at a table in the public room, a tankard of ale in front of him when he finally opened it and read.

Dear Captain Roper,
The Admiralty is delighted to hear of your survival and rescue and we are eager to have the hero of the Mediterranean return to service.

Most ship assignments were of necessity made in your absence due to important action in Algiers. There is one more opportunity.

The HMS Gaius *is ready to sail to the Baltic Sea, but its Captain must be on board by September the tenth. If you can reach our offices by September eighth and be ready to sail by September tenth, the ship is yours.*
Yours respectfully,
Melville
First Lord of the Admiralty

Lucien folded the letter and put it back in his pocket.

September the eighth. Two days away.

If he could get passage on the mail coach, he might reach London in a day. There was time. He could do it.

If he left the next day.

Lucien walked slowly back to the Circus. The weather had turned to drizzle, but he did not heed it.

If he left for London tomorrow, it would be without making certain that red-haired stranger did not endanger Lady Rebecca and without taking her to Bristol.

He'd be abandoning her in a time of need, the way his parents had abandoned him.

But it might be his only chance to get a ship.

He reached Number Fifteen in the Circus. Sir Richard was at home.

Sir Richard encountered him on the stairs. 'Good God, Roper! You've been caught in the rain, have you not? You'll catch your death.'

Lucien forced a smile. 'After the weather we've both endured on our ships, I doubt a little dampness will hurt me.'

Sir Richard smiled. 'Well, change into some dry clothes and come have a brandy with me. I'll be in the library.'

Lucien continued up the stairs to the guest room he'd been given. Cullen was there, brushing one of Lucien's coats.

Cullen. What was he to do about Cullen?

'Sir! I am glad you are back at last,' the valet said.

Lucien started to take off his jacket. Cullen hurried over to assist him.

'I went to some of the inns in Bath. Trying to find the stranger.' Lucien felt his waistcoat. It seemed dry enough. He sat and took off his boots.

'Ella and I saw the man when we were out,'

Cullen said. 'He knows where Lady Rebecca lives. He was watching the house from the field in front of the Crescent.

'I saw him, too. Just for a second. He ran off before I could reach him.'

'Do you think he means Lady Rebecca harm?' Cullen asked.

Lucien lifted a shoulder. 'There is a big risk assuming he does not.'

'That is what I thought, too, sir.'

The young man helped Lucien into a dry coat. He put on a dry pair of shoes and walked down to the library.

'Ah, just in time,' Sir Richard said. 'I was about to pour the brandy.'

This room was a huge contrast to Lord Stonecroft's library. Books were stacked on tables and laid sideways on the shelves. The furniture was aimed more at comfort than symmetry. Sir Richard spent a great deal of time in this room and it showed.

'So your valet said our red-haired gentleman has been seen around Lord Stonecroft's residence.' Sir Richard handed Lucien a glass of brandy. 'You have let Lord Stonecroft know?'

'He knows,' Lucien said in a tight voice.

Sir Richard's brows rose. 'What does that tone mean?'

'He is more concerned with gossip and reputations than whether some stranger poses a threat.'

The older man nodded. 'It is you he wants away from her, then.'

'Because people talk if we are seen together.' Lucien imitated Stonecroft's speech.

Sir Richard lifted his glass to his mouth. 'I am sure people do talk.'

Lucien's eyes flashed. 'I cannot control what people think or say.'

Sir Richard leaned back in his chair. 'You handed her off to him, my boy. You say that is for the best. You have to let go of her, then. She is the responsibility of another man now. Not you.'

Lucien had run out of time to help her.

'There is nothing you can do except cause her more trouble as long as she is with Lord Stonecroft,' Sir Richard went on.

Lucien downed his brandy in one gulp. 'It is a moot point. I had a letter from the Admiralty. I can be given a ship, but I must appear at the Admiralty by September the eighth.'

'September the eighth!' his friend cried. 'That is two days' time.'

'I can make it if I catch the mail coach tomorrow.' Lucien frowned. 'So Stonecroft will have what he wishes. I will be gone.'

Sir Richard poured Lucien a second brandy.

'I have one favour to ask of you,' Lucien said.

'Ask it and I will comply if I can,' his friend replied.

'Cullen. He needs work. I'll write a good recommendation and leave him enough money to tide him over for a while, but will you help him?'

Sir Richard sipped his brandy. 'I'll do all I can. I may even hire him myself, I'm that fond of him. In any event, he may live here until the matter is settled.'

'I am very grateful.' At least Cullen would be off his conscience.

He and Sir Richard lapsed into an uncomfortable silence, during which Lucien mulled over his worries about Lady Rebecca. After a time spent staring into his glass, Lucien looked over at his friend.

Sir Richard was sound asleep.

Lucien drank the rest of his brandy and set the glass on the table. He rose quietly and left the library. Once in the hall, he hurried up to his room.

He flung open the door. 'Cullen! I have a favour to ask of you.'

Chapter Nineteen

Claire sat in front of her bedchamber window, staring out at the sunless day. She wondered if she could beg off from attending dinner and so avoid being in Lord Stonecroft's company or that of his sister.

There was so much to think about. The stranger. Lord Stonecroft. Ella.

Lucien.

Much less painful to plan her escape.

She did not know the departure time for the coach to Bristol, so the best she could hope for was to be at the West Gate Inn early in the day. Perhaps no one would think to look for her there until she was safely on her way.

She had ink, pen and paper in her bedchamber so she could write her letters without having to ask for those supplies. She'd write to Lord Stonecroft and to Ella, also leaving her a favourable letter of recommendation and instructions of what to do with her belongings. She'd leave Ella money, too, of course.

She must pack. Only what Lucien had purchased for her, though. She wanted none of the dresses Lord Stonecroft wanted her to wear. She would pack a portmanteau for the trip to Bristol and fill her trunk with the rest of her clothes and hope Sir Richard would agree to keep it until she knew where it could be sent.

Her disappearance would cause more talk among Bath society, a situation that would likely upset Stonecroft more than her crying off. Well, Lord Stonecroft and Miss Attwood would merely have to weather that small storm.

She must write to Lucien.

What would she say to him? Thank him one more time. Release him from any further obligation to her. Tell him she hoped he'd get his ship. That she hoped he could again be free and happy once he was back at sea. Be in a place he felt he belonged.

Ella entered the room, interrupting Claire's thoughts.

The girl looked distressed. 'M'lady, Cullen is below stairs. He says the Captain wants to see you right now!'

Claire rose from her chair. 'Has something happened?'

'I do not know,' Ella cried. 'I only know that Cullen said the Captain can't simply call on you, because of his lordship, so he wants you to come with Cullen and meet him outside in the garden.'

Claire had never been in the garden, had never seen the back door to the house, nor accessed the garden from the outside.

'I cannot leave by the front without the footman knowing.' And risking the stranger seeing her if he was watching the house. 'How am I to reach the garden unseen?'

'I do not know,' Ella admitted. 'Cullen is waiting at the bottom of the servants' stairs, but if you go out that way, you have to pass the servants' hall and the kitchen. That is the way I leave the house when I am to visit Cullen and where he comes to visit me.'

'Then if you go out with Cullen, no one will remark on it?'

'Oh, they will remark on it,' Ella said with feeling. 'But what good will it do for me to go to the Captain?'

'Not you. Me. We will exchange clothes and they will think I am you.' Where had this idea come from? 'I'll wear your shawl and cap. I'll hide my face some way. They will think I am you. They know you have my permission to see Cullen whenever you want.'

'That is why they remark upon it,' Ella said, but she was already untying Claire's laces.

They hurriedly changed into each other's

clothes. Claire covered her hair with Ella's cap and draped the shawl around her head.

'Cullen is waiting at the bottom of the stairs?' she asked.

Ella nodded.

Claire had never been below stairs where the servants' rooms and the kitchen were, but she descended the servants' narrow and steep stairway until she reached its lowest level.

Cullen turned at her approach. 'Ella?' He sounded surprised.

Claire revealed her face.

'Oh, m'lady.' He bowed. 'You fooled me. That is good. I was puzzling how to get you to the Captain.'

'If I fooled you, we should fool the servants.' She looked up at him. 'Do you know what has happened? Ella made it sound urgent.'

'I don't know.' He looked sheepish. 'I'll have to be askin' you to take my arm, m'lady. I hope you don't mind.'

She smiled at him. 'I do not mind at all.'

She wrapped her arm though his and walked close to him, as Ella usually did. He led them down the hallway to the back door.

When they passed the kitchen, he called out, 'I'll be having her back in time for dinner.'

'You had better,' the housekeeper shot back. 'Or she'll not eat.'

When they reached the outside he stepped away from her.

'The Captain will be by the outbuildings back here.'

She and Cullen crossed the garden to where the outbuildings stood and where Lucien could be seen pacing back and forth. When he spied her he strode over to her.

'Lucien, what has happened?'

He took her hand and led her to a relatively private spot between two small storage sheds. Cullen waited a short distance away.

All her senses were on alert. 'Tell me, Lucien, what is wrong?'

His expression was as serious as she'd ever seen it.

'I could not call at the house, not after that encounter with Stonecroft.' He was unsettled.

Her Lucien was never unsettled.

'Was he dreadful to you?' she asked.

'I care nothing for that.' His face filled with anger. 'He is an abominable man. Everything I abhor in an aristocrat.'

'I know,' she said quietly.

'But never mind that. I am—' He faced her, holding her upper arms. 'I am leaving. Tomorrow. I heard from the Admiralty. I will get a ship if I can reach London in two days' time.'

This was what he'd counted upon.

This was really and truly goodbye.

'That is wonderful, Lucien,' she managed to reply. 'I am so happy for you.'

Inside her heart was breaking. She might never see him again.

He released her. 'I promised I would say goodbye.'

She reached up and touched his face. 'I appreciate that.'

'If you need me, though—'

She placed her fingers on his lips. 'Do not say it. You must have your ship.'

'But there is the red-haired stranger.' His brow furrowed. 'And you need to go to Bristol.'

'I'll go to Bristol. Perhaps I'll hire Cullen to come with me.' Although she wouldn't. Because when she went to Bristol she wasn't coming back.

'There will be other ships,' he went on. 'I will stay if you need me.'

Oh, how she needed him! But even more she needed him to be happy.

'I will do well enough,' she said. 'You must go.'

'You will marry Stonecroft?' He spoke the name with scorn.

She skirted around the truth. 'That is the plan.'

'But earlier you seemed distressed by the idea,' he protested. 'You did not want him to have the banns read.'

She still did not.

'That was because I want to wait until my memory comes back.'

'He cares nothing for that.' He raised his voice.

'I know.' She fought to keep her emotions under tight control. 'He does not understand.'

His expression turned earnest. 'Lady Rebecca, he cares nothing for you.'

'And I care nothing for him, but at least I'll gain a home of my own to manage. Children. Comfort and security. Status—' She stopped herself. It felt like she'd spoken such words before.

He looked as if she'd struck him across the face.

'What about the stranger?' he asked stiffly.

'I'll be careful, Lucien. No more running out alone.' Except when she made her escape.

'Then this is goodbye,' he said.

She put her arms around him and hugged him close to her. For the last time. 'Goodbye, Lucien,' she murmured.

His muscles were taut, as if he were anticipating an attack, but he relaxed and hugged her back. They remained in that embrace for a long time, reluctant to let go.

But let go they must. Claire released him first.

He stepped back. 'I have not told Cullen yet. You are first.'

'I will not say anything.' Her throat constricted. And her heart was shattering.

'Cullen!' he called.

The valet hurried over to them.

'You can return Lady Rebecca to the house.'

'I'll do that, sir,' Cullen said. 'Come, m'lady.'

Claire let Cullen lead her to the door, but she turned for one last glimpse of Lucien.

He opened the door for her. 'Thank you, Cullen,' she said.

Cullen looked confused and concerned, but he did not ask her what had happened. 'Tell—tell Ella I'll see her when I can.'

Would her decisions and Lucien's separate those two? She prayed not.

'I will.' She touched his arm. 'You are a good man, Cullen.'

Before breaking down completely, she covered her face with Ella's shawl and entered the house, hurrying by the kitchen and the other rooms.

The housekeeper's voice trailed after her. 'You had better not be late for dinner!'

Lucien waited for Cullen to walk back to him. 'You are at liberty, Cullen. I am going into town. Tell Sir Richard I'll miss dinner. I'll be back late.'

'I will tell him, sir.' Cullen's expression was questioning, but Lucien was in no mood to explain.

He walked off, his pace brisk. He should have told Cullen he was leaving on the morrow. Given the young man some warning. Too late now. He'd speak with him when he returned to Sir Richard's.

Why was he feeling so desolate? He wanted a

ship and he would get one. This was always what should have happened.

He passed several of the people he'd met at the Pump Room and at various entertainments. They all greeted him warmly. Decently.

Perhaps not all aristocrats were like Stonecroft or Lady Rebecca's brother or his mother's viscount lover.

The lady who had first recognised him as the Captain rescued from the shipwreck spied him and crossed the street to speak with him.

'Captain!' she called. 'Are you all on your own tonight? Come with us. We are having a few friends for dinner and would love to have you come.'

She was on the arm of her husband, who nodded his agreement. 'Should have sent an invitation. Have Sir Richard come, as well. Nine o'clock.'

It was kind of them.

'I cannot tonight,' he responded. 'But I am honoured you would invite me.' He meant that.

'Another time!' the lady called as they proceeded on their way.

Lucien wanted to find the most humble tavern in Bath, a place where no one would know him. He planned to drink until this ache inside him disappeared.

Saying goodbye to her, leaving her to marry Stonecroft, had ripped him to pieces.

* * *

Claire had run up the servants' staircase, but stopped before reaching the second floor, her emotions finally overtaking her. She'd taken deep breaths and fanned her face to keep the tears from flowing. Her insides felt as if they'd broken into sharp shards, the pain was so great.

The pain of saying goodbye to the man you loved.

Because she loved him, she had no other choice. To ask him to stay would have been the height of selfishness.

With a fragile sense of control she climbed the rest of the stairs and returned to her bedchamber.

Ella, who had been standing at the window overlooking the garden, swivelled around. 'I was watching, but I couldn't see anything. What did he want, m'lady?'

Claire forced a smile. 'He is leaving tomorrow. He came to say goodbye.'

Ella's eyes widened. 'No. He cannot leave.'

Claire put down the shawl and took off Ella's cap. 'He must. He is a captain in the navy. He belongs on a ship at sea.'

Ella looked distraught. 'Did Cullen know that?'

'No,' Claire said. 'The Captain wanted to tell me first.'

Claire presented her back to Ella so that she could untie her laces and also so Ella would not see her blink away tears. Claire turned around and did the same for Ella.

'I suppose you could dress me for dinner,' Claire said. Although how she would manage to sit through dinner with Lord Stonecroft and Miss Attwood she did not know.

'I do not see how you can be remaining so un-affected!' Ella cried.

Claire met her eyes. 'I am affected. But I've known from the beginning that I would have to say goodbye.'

'I think you could have made him stay,' the girl grumbled.

'Yes. If I did not care for him so much,' Claire responded.

She held her emotions in check while Ella helped her into a dinner dress and rearranged her hair.

With that complete, she said, 'You may do as you please, Ella. I will not need you until time for bed. Say ten o'clock?'

Ella pursed her lips before speaking. 'As you wish, m'lady.'

When the girl left the room, Claire allowed her tears to flow.

That night at dinner Lord Stonecroft never mentioned the red-haired stranger or his conver-sation with Lucien. Instead he and Miss Attwood discussed the people they had seen that day and what they were planning to do the next day. Claire was glad they paid no attention to her, but she attended to the times they planned to be gone the next day.

'You are very quiet tonight, Lady Rebecca,' Miss Attwood said in a kind tone. 'Are you not feeling well?'

'Perhaps a little unwell,' she replied. 'I was caught in the rain.'

She glanced over at Stonecroft to see his reaction. He merely kept eating.

Miss Attwood peered at her from across the table. 'I do believe you look a bit pale. You should take care. Do not exert yourself.'

Claire had no doubt she was pale.

Miss Attwood gave her a concerned look. 'I would ask you to accompany me to the Pump Room tomorrow, but if you are unwell…'

Claire's spirits rose a slight fraction. Tomorrow would be her chance to leave.

A pain stabbed her heart. Her whole life was about to change again. She hoped she could hold on to the memories. The memories of being with Lucien.

Perhaps she would glimpse him tomorrow at the West Gate Inn. Perhaps she'd see him board the coach to London.

It was something to hope for.

Chapter Twenty

The next morning Claire did not have any difficulty convincing anyone that she was unwell. She'd hardly slept and her eyes were red from weeping into her pillow so Ella would not hear.

'Should I ask Miss Attwood if we should send for a physician?' Ella asked her worriedly.

'No. No.' Claire managed a wan smile. 'I have no fever. I am certain the stress from yesterday has merely left me fatigued. I intend to spend the day in this room.'

'Do you wish to stay abed?' the girl asked.

'I am not so ill!' she insisted. 'I'll simply have you put me in one of my old dresses in case I wish to see if the library has a book worth reading.'

She chose one of the travelling dresses, hoping Ella did not think it an odd choice.

As Ella finished arranging her hair, Claire told her, 'I will not need you here today. Not at all. Spend the day with Cullen, if you can.'

Cullen's future was uncertain now. Ella would soon learn hers was as well.

'But if you are not feeling well, I should stay here,' Ella protested.

Claire took the girl's hands in her own. 'I tell you, I am not ill. I just need rest. Go. Be with Cullen. He will need your support.'

Ella looked uncertain. 'If you think so.'

'I do.' She shook her hands in emphasis.

Ella stepped back. 'I could go now, I suppose.'

'Yes. Go now.'

'I'll just put some of your things away.' She started to tidy the room.

Claire rose from her chair. 'I'll do that. It will give me something to do. You could ask Cook to send breakfast up to my room. That would be very nice.'

'I'll do that, m'lady.' She skipped into the dressing room and picked up her hat and shawl. She hurried to the door. 'Is there anything else?' she asked before leaving.

Claire took one long look at her, committing her image to memory. 'Only one more thing,' she murmured.

'What, m'lady?'

Claire smiled. 'Enjoy your time with Cullen.'

Ella grinned. 'I will!'

As soon as Ella left, Claire went over to the desk and took out paper and ink. She began writing a letter of recommendation for Ella.

Before she finished a footman brought up a breakfast tray. Though she had no appetite, she made herself eat. She did not know when she would have another chance.

Then she returned to her letters. The one to Stonecroft was by far the easiest, because she was certain he did not care about her, nor she, him. She wondered what he would have been like if his wife and child had lived. Whatever part of him that had died with them was a part for which she might have developed a fondness.

Ella's letter was difficult. She was saying good-bye to her only woman friend.

It turned out she did not need to write Lucien at all. That was almost harder than putting pen to paper for him. She wrote a letter to Sir Richard instead, begging him to look out for Cullen and Ella.

When she finished she was in tears again. This time she let herself weep openly, because she was alone on this floor and no one would hear. She'd heard Miss Attwood leave a while ago and peeked out her door to see that she'd taken her lady's maid with her. Lord Stonecroft was to have left very early. Both would be out until late afternoon.

When her letters were completed and her tears dried, she opened the desk drawer and placed the letters inside for safe keeping until she was ready to leave. Nothing else left to do but pack her trunk and portmanteau.

She went into the dressing room and found the

small bag Lucien had purchased for her that first day in Ireland. As she packed one other dress, one nightdress and the brush, comb, hairpins and other essentials Lucien had bought her, she had the sense of packing like this once before. Not while with Lucien. Some other time, a time of packing with a sense of urgency. It was not quite a memory, but almost one and she had an inexplicable feeling of dread.

A knock on the door made her jump.

She walked into the bedroom. 'Yes?' she called through the door.

'M'lady?' It was one of the footmen.

She opened the door.

'A Lord and Lady Brookmore here to call on you,' he said.

Who? 'Did they say what they wanted?'

Was she supposed to know a Lord and Lady Brookmore? She'd not met them in Bath, she was certain. She'd worked very hard to remember all the names of people she'd met.

'They did not say, m'lady,' he responded. 'But they said it was very important they speak with you. They will wait all day to speak with you if necessary.'

'Very well. I'll be down directly.' Was this someone from her past? 'Are they waiting in the drawing room?'

'They are.' He bowed and left.

She took a deep breath and started down the stairs.

The footman announced her.

'I will not need you,' she told him.

He bowed again and continued downstairs to attend the hall.

She stepped into the room.

A lady and gentleman, more her age than the Stonecrofts, stood.

'You wished to speak with me?' she asked.

The lady's face was obscured by a veil over her hat. Neither she nor the gentleman said anything. The lady walked towards her.

And lifted her veil.

Lucien had time to kill before the mail coach left. He woke early and took a long walk, turning in his mind everything that had transpired between him and Lady Rebecca. Everything on the walk reminded him of her, of when she'd led him through the streets of Bath, knowing all the buildings, but not knowing why. Even the passers-by reminded him of her.

A gentleman and lady passed him on his way back to the Circus. The lady reminded him of Lady Rebecca. Not her face, because it was obscured by a veil, but otherwise she had the look of Lady Rebecca.

So had another woman, though, who did not look anything like Lady Rebecca, but her laugh reminded him of Lady Rebecca's laugh, the first thing that had attracted him to her.

He'd been drawn to her from the start, from the

moment of hearing that laugh. She was unlike any other woman he'd known with her courage and her vulnerability.

He'd told himself what he admired was caused by her amnesia. He'd convinced himself she'd turn into a haughty aristocrat as soon as she remembered who she was. Now he was not so sure. There was an essence of her that could be genuine.

He'd done a lot of thinking since the day before. Turned out he was not able to drink away his emotions. Instead he'd nursed his second tankard of ale for several hours. A man had to be a very sorry sort, if he lost even the solace of drink.

He kept telling himself how glad he was to be getting another ship, but inside he only felt loss.

He returned to Sir Richard's house and handed the footman his hat and gloves. 'Do you know where Cullen is?'

'Believe he and his Ella are visiting below stairs, sir,' the man replied. 'Shall I send him to you?'

'No.' Lucien might as well speak to Ella, as well. 'I'll go down to them.'

He found them in the servants' hall eating biscuits and drinking tea.

Cullen jumped to his feet. 'Sir! Do you have need of me?' He wore a wounded expression.

'Sit, Cullen,' he said. 'I want to talk to you both.'

Ella piped up. 'He already knows, Captain. I told him.'

Lucien felt a stab of guilt. 'Forgive me, Cullen. I meant to tell you last night.'

'Do not fret, sir,' Cullen said in a stoic tone. 'I knew you would be leaving sooner or later. I've packed for you.' He looked like he'd lost his best friend.

Which was rather like Lucien felt when he thought about the young man.

'Are you sure you must leave?' Ella asked.

Was he sure? 'Yes. I need to leave today or lose the chance to get a ship.'

'Because I am worried about Lady Rebecca,' Ella went on. 'She says she's not ill, but she looks so pale and her eyes are all red. I think she is sick, but she doesn't want a physician and I do not know what to do.'

Sick? Lucien felt an immediate impulse to run to her, send for a doctor. Something. Anything.

Cullen spoke up. 'I told Ella Lady Rebecca is probably just upset. Red eyes usually means a fit of weeping. Or, at least, that's what it always meant on my sisters.'

She'd seemed composed the day before when he'd said goodbye. Had something else happened?

'Did she say how she felt?' he asked.

'Unwell, is all.' Ella toyed with her teacup.

'I do not know what to say.' He sat in one of the chairs and picked up a biscuit from the plate.

Ella rose this time. 'Shall I find you a cup, Captain? Would you like some tea?'

'No, stay here a moment. I want you both to

know I am leaving Cullen a year's wage, just to help tide him over until he gets a new position.'

'That is kind of you, sir.' Cullen's voice thickened.

Ella sat down again. 'I do not think you should leave. Not with my lady sick and that mad man out to harm her and all.'

'She's to marry Stonecroft, Ella,' he said in a patient tone he did not feel. 'It is not up to me to help any more.'

'She can't marry that old man!' Ella cried. 'He is as cold as stone. You have to stop it.'

His insides twisted in pain. 'It is what she wants, Ella. She told me.'

'Well, she doesn't mean it!' She lowered her head into her hands. 'She simply can't.'

Cullen put his arm around Ella. 'Now, do not you become upset.'

Lucien stood again. 'I should speak with Sir Richard.'

'Yes, sir,' Cullen said in depressed tones.

Lucien walked away with Ella's voice echoing in his mind.

She doesn't mean it.

Claire stared into a face that looked exactly like her own, so alike the lady could have stepped through a looking glass.

'You look like me,' she whispered.

'Claire! It is me! Yes, I look like you. I am so sorry. So sorry. I thought you had drowned.

I saw you get washed overboard! I thought you were dead!'

Claire's head started to pound. 'You were on the *Dun Aengus*?'

'You know I was!' the lady cried.

Claire held up a hand. 'Wait. Are you my sister?' She didn't know she had a sister, especially not a twin sister.

'What sort of question is that?' the lady cried. 'Of course I am not your sister.'

The gentleman spoke. Lord Brookmore. Was that name familiar? 'Something is wrong, Becca. Let her speak.'

Becca? Did he mean Rebecca? Who was he talking to? Let who speak?

She lowered herself into a chair. 'Forgive me. I cannot stand.'

The woman who looked like her—Lady Brookmore—pulled a chair close to hers, with an expectant look on her face.

Her husband chose another chair nearby. 'We read about you in the newspaper. About your rescue after the shipwreck. I assure you, we have not come to cause you any trouble. None at all. But there is something you must know—'

Claire pressed her fingers against her temple. This was like waking up on the raft all over again. In a world she did not know. With people she did not recognise.

'I—I don't remember,' she said.

'You don't remember?' Lady Brookmore cried. 'How can you not remember?'

Claire lifted her gaze to the face so like her own. 'When I woke up. After the shipwreck. I—I did not remember anything.'

'You forgot the shipwreck?' Lord Brookmore turned to his wife. 'I have seen that before. Soldiers injured in battle. Afterwards they can't remember it.'

Claire pressed her temples harder. 'You do not understand. I remember nothing from before waking up on the raft.' In Lucien's arms. 'Not who I am. Not my family. Or my home. Not you. Or what I had done the day before or the month before or ever before.'

Understanding dawned on the woman's face. 'Then you think you are—' She broke off and turned to her husband. 'She thinks she is—'

He leaned towards Claire. 'You did not know your name?' he asked gently.

Claire shook her head. 'No.'

'Someone told you that you were Lady Rebecca?'

'Lucien.' Her head pounded. 'I mean, Captain Roper.'

'The man who rescued you,' he stated.

She nodded.

'Oh, Claire! You don't remember?' Lady Brookmore cried.

'I know how to do things. I remember facts.

I could even lead Lucien all around Bath, but I have had only one memory and that was fleeting. I remembered drinking the waters here in Bath, but nothing else.'

Except that sinister figure in her dreams. And the little girls doing their schoolwork.

She turned to Lady Brookmore. 'Why do you call me Claire?'

'Because that is your name,' Lady Brookmore said in a low voice full of sympathy. 'You are Miss Claire Tilson.'

The name did not surprise her, but neither did it feel real.

Lady Brookmore continued. 'And I am Lady Rebecca Pierce.'

Chapter Twenty-One

Claire thought her head would burst. Lady Brookmore's words echoed over and over in her mind, *I am Lady Rebecca Pierce.*

The lady continued, 'We met by happenstance on the packet boat. Like this, suddenly seeing each other's faces. It was remarkable and we spent time together to try to understand it all.'

'Are we related?' Claire asked.

'We never found any connection,' Lady Brookmore went on. 'We are not related. It is merely a fantastic coincidence, but it was a little like finding a long-lost sister. We spent most of the voyage together, talking as if we were sisters. I was headed to London to marry Lord Stonecroft and you—you were travelling to the Lake District to be governess to Lord Brookmore's nieces—'

'No. No,' Claire broke in. 'I was not dressed as a governess.'

Lady Brookmore blushed and she lowered her

head. 'We swapped clothing. To fool people. I dressed you in my clothes and everyone thought you were me. Even—even Nolan, the maid sent with me.' Her voice cracked. 'The maid who drowned.'

A maid! The maid her brother—Lady Rebecca's brother—spoke of.

Could this be the truth?

'Then I am this Claire Tilson? A governess?'

'You are the daughter of a vicar. Your mother died when you were young, or when you were born. I don't remember. Your father sent you to school. When he died, you became a governess.'

She pressed her temples again. 'Was this school in Bristol?'

'Yes,' her likeness said. 'Yes, it was.'

She started to believe this. Even though she did not remember, these facts did not unsettle her. The name did not alarm her. She'd been more alarmed to think she was Lady Rebecca.

'Everyone thinks I am Lady Rebecca.'

'And you can stay Lady Rebecca for all I care.' The lady's voice thickened with emotion again. 'I pretended to be you. I woke up after a fever and—and Garret—' She glanced over at her husband. 'Garret was there. He thought I was you. And, because I did not want to be me, on my way to marry a man who cared nothing for me, I let him and everyone think I was you. I am so sorry, Claire. I thought you were dead.'

Claire turned to Lord Brookmore. 'I was supposed to be your governess?'

'To my nieces. Yes,' he responded.

She looked from Lady Brookmore to Lord Brookmore. 'You pretended to be the governess, but now you are married?'

They shot each other adoring looks. 'Yes,' they said in unison.

How lovely for them.

So unlike a marriage with Stonecroft would be, a marriage that would never occur.

She held a hand against her forehead. 'Forgive me. I do not remember any of this, but it makes a certain sense.' She gazed from one to the other. 'Am I truly Claire Tilson, a governess?'

They both nodded.

'Then what do we do now?' she asked.

'You have not married Lord Stonecroft,' Brookmore said. 'I assume the footman would have addressed you as such if you had.'

'No, I have not married him.'

'Do you want to?' Lady Brookmore—Rebecca—asked. 'Because I remember you thought marriage to him would bring me security. A house of my own to manage. A place in society. Children. It is all right with me if you want to.'

She'd said almost those exact words to Lucien.

'How can I marry him?' Not that she still intended to. 'I cannot sign the register as Lady Rebecca if I am not she. Did you marry as Claire Tilson?'

'We went to Scotland to marry,' Lady Brookmore responded. 'I married as myself. We're going to make up some story about why Garret will call me Rebecca, but otherwise we'll simply let people think what they will.'

'How did you know about me? That I'd be here?' Claire asked.

'We read about it in the *Morning Chronicle*,' Brookmore said. 'We knew it must be you, because, of course...' He inclined his head towards his wife.

'Honestly, I would never have pretended to be you if I'd had any idea you could be alive.' Lady Brookmore looked distressed again.

Claire had no feelings at all about this woman impersonating her. She certainly could not have assumed that governess position. 'It hardly matters.'

'If you wish to marry Lord Stonecroft and remain Rebecca Pierce, you are welcome to. I will not cause you any trouble over it. I do not need to be Rebecca Pierce any more, now that I am Lady Brookmore.' She cast another loving gaze at her husband.

'I will not marry Lord Stonecroft,' Claire admitted.

'There is another matter we must tell you about,' Lord Brookmore broke in. 'Warn you about. It is the reason we sought you out.'

That sense of dread that hovered in her dreams returned. 'Warn me?'

He leaned forward to explain. 'Before you became governess to my nieces you were a governess in Ireland. That is why you were sailing from Ireland to England on that packet boat.'

She was not from Ireland?

'You were governess to the young daughters of Sir Orin Foley, a baronet, and his wife,' he went on.

The little girls at the school table, the ones who appeared in her dreams?

His wife took up the tale. 'Sir Orin apparently developed a romantic attachment to you.'

'A romantic attachment?' Had she been wanton after all?

Lady Brookmore quickly added, 'Oh, we do not think you returned his sentiments. We believe you were running away from him.'

'How do you know all this? Did I tell you all of it?' That seemed unlikely. Surely she was more private than that.

'No. He came for you at Brookmore House,' Lord Brookmore explained.

'He thought I was you,' his wife said.

'We have reason to believe he is a danger to you,' he added.

'He tried to kidnap me!' Lady Brookmore told her.

'And he said that his wife died,' Lord Brookmore went on, 'which we thought was very convenient. He came to take you away with him because he was now free to marry you.'

'We think he may have killed his wife!' Lady Brookmore cried.

Then that sinister figure in her dreams might have been real? And that figure might be the man who was probably watching the house this very moment?

No. It could not be. 'But if he thought you were me, why would I be in danger here?'

'We feared he would find out as we found out. From the newspaper,' Lord Brookmore said.

'I had to tell him I was not you. I told him my real name.' Lady Brookmore looked distressed again. 'If he reads that newspaper, he'll realise that the Lady Rebecca in the article is probably you. If we found you, he could find you.'

Claire stared at the room's window, facing the green field across from the Crescent. 'Tell me. Does this Sir Orin have red hair?'

'Yes!' Lady Brookmore said.

'Then he has already found me.'

Claire explained her encounters with the red-haired stranger and the Brookmores were convinced it was Sir Orin.

What these people told her about herself settled comfortably inside her, but she still did not remember any of it. Worse, it made her feel that what happened to her while she'd thought herself Lady Rebecca had been nothing more than a fantasy. Would it become so unreal she would lose her memories of the fishermen, the innkeepers, the store clerks in Dublin? Ella and Cullen?

Lucien.

She was more determined than ever to find her school in Bristol. The Brookmores offered to accompany her, but she declined. Being with them distressed her. More people telling her who she was and what she did not remember.

Lord Brookmore insisted upon hiring a carriage for her and that offer she accepted.

They also devised a way for her to leave the house without Sir Orin knowing it. She and Lady Brookmore would exchange clothing and Claire would leave looking exactly like the woman who called upon her. When she was safely on her way to Bristol, he'd come back for his wife.

Claire brought Lady Brookmore up to her bedchamber.

'I am nearly ready to leave,' she told her.

She glanced in the full-length mirror in the room and saw them both reflected in it.

Lady Brookmore stood at her side. 'We compared our images in a mirror on the ship.'

Claire could not remember.

As they helped each other change dresses, Lady Brookmore said, 'It must have been terribly difficult for you to not remember your past.'

'It has been a challenge,' she responded. 'Tell me about what happened to you, though.'

While they arranged their hair, Lady Brookmore told about her experiences as Claire, about Brookmore's dear nieces, about the house and estate and its people there.

'I learned I am a terrible governess,' the lady added.

They looked in the mirror again, this time dressed as each other.

Lady Brookmore put an arm around Claire's shoulders. 'If not for this remarkable resemblance and for meeting you on that ship, I would never have met Garret. Because of you, I have the greatest happiness I can imagine, being his wife.' She leaned her head on Claire's. 'Thank you, Claire.'

Without this remarkable resemblance Claire would have never met Lucien and though she now experienced a great sadness, she would never regret knowing him.

Claire finished packing the portmanteau and walked over to the desk.

'I have letters. One for my maid. One for Stonecroft. And one for Admiral Sir Richard Bickerton.' She took them from the desk drawer and put them on top of the desk where Ella would be sure to find them.

Claire picked up Lady Brookmore's hat and placed it on her head. Lady Brookmore arranged the veil.

'Wait a moment.' Claire realised she'd almost left her Kashmir shawl behind. She draped it over her arm. 'I am ready now.'

They returned to the drawing room where Lord Brookmore waited.

He looked at them side by side. 'Remarkable.'

He kissed his wife goodbye and picked up Claire's portmanteau. 'I'll arrange her a coach to Bristol and I'll come back for you.'

His wife smiled. 'In the meantime I'll pretend again to be Claire.' She turned to Claire. 'You must write to us at Brookmore House. Tell us how you are doing. Let us know if you ever need anything. Anything.'

She hugged Claire.

Claire left the house with Lord Brookmore, for the last time, playing Lady Rebecca.

Lucien paced the floor of his bedchamber.

She doesn't mean it.

Ella's words echoed in his mind, repeating over and over.

He'd not even thought of speaking to Sir Richard like he'd said. Instead he left the house and walked down Gay Street towards Queen Square, turning on Back Lane and entering the Gravel Walk. The Gravel Walk ran behind one section of the Circus and at its top opened up into the field facing the Royal Crescent.

Lucien stood and stared at that magnificent example of Bath architecture, but he was not admiring buildings. He was hearing Ella's words.

She doesn't mean it.

Could it be that she, Lady Rebecca, was lying to him about planning to marry Stonecroft? Was she weeping because Lucien was leaving her with no other choice?

The footman attending the hall went in search of Lady Rebecca.

When he returned, he said, 'Her ladyship is resting and does not wish to receive callers.'

'She'll see me.' He straightened and used his Captain's voice. 'Tell her I will search this whole house until I find her and she listens to me.'

His message landed firmly. The footman's eyes grew large and he hurried up the stairs again.

He returned shortly. 'She will see you in the drawing room.'

Lucien climbed the stairs and entered the room where he'd developed that first instant dislike of Lord Stonecroft.

She was alone in the room and turned at his entrance. 'Captain Roper?'

Captain Roper? Something was off. 'You become formal now, my lady? You've used my given name almost since you've met me.'

'Well,' she said uncertainly, 'tell me what is so urgent you had to interrupt my rest.'

Good God. She sounded like an aristocrat.

'Something's wrong...' He could not place it.

A nervous look crossed her face, but she steeled it into something haughty. 'I am still waiting to hear the reason for this visit.'

He came closer. The light from the window illuminated her face. He could not place his finger on it, but something was wrong.

But he went on. 'I came to urge you to reconsider your decision.'

That distressed expression returned. 'What decision?'

He changed tack. 'Ella said you were ill. I came to see for myself.'

The lines in her forehead smoothed. 'Oh, I am quite recovered. Not ill at all. There is no cause at all to be concerned.'

She started to show him the door, but as she passed him, he took her arm and stared directly into her face.

'Release me this instant!' she cried.

He did not release her. 'You are not…' No, it was impossible.

He let go in confusion.

She sank down in a chair. 'Sit, Captain Roper. I have something to say to you.'

'That you are not her,' he said. 'You are not her.'

It was impossible, but that was the only conclusion he could make.

'That is correct,' she admitted. 'I am not her, but I am Lady Rebecca. And I will explain it all.'

Chapter Twenty-Two

Claire stood in the hall of the White Hart, waiting until the coach that Lord Brookmore had hired was ready to pick her up. The coachman had said it would be only minute, but she waited a great deal longer. She held the Kashmir shawl in her arms like a blanket.

She was Claire Tilson, a governess, a woman without relations, alone in the world. She certainly felt alone at this moment. She must become used to this new identity, though. It must be the true one. All the bits and pieces flitting through her mind, her dreams, what Lord and Lady Brookmore told her about herself, were like pieces completing a puzzle. Everything fit.

Everything was there except her memory.

And Lucien, of course. He'd become a part of her—a part of a fictitious Lady Rebecca. He never knew her at all. And now he was gone.

The pain of losing him stabbed at her heart once more. She closed her eyes, trying to bear it.

'Claire Tilson?' a man's voice spoke.

Expecting word of her coach, she lifted her head and opened her eyes.

But it was not a coachman. It was the red-haired stranger. Sir Orin Foley.

He smiled. 'It *is* you.'

Before she could rise to flee, he sat down next to her and pressed something sharp against her ribs.

'This is a knife,' he explained in an eerily calm voice. 'Make a sound and I will push it through your skin.'

She clutched her shawl.

'I thought that was you,' he went on in that mild tone. 'Not the other one. She would not have walked back from the Royal Crescent with a portmanteau, now, would she? And she wouldn't have answered to your name.'

He had been watching her, both at the house and here.

'I was quite surprised to see the other one show up here. In the same inn as I, no less. Then imagine my surprise when they walked precisely where I was bound.' He laughed. 'It did not take me long to surmise what was afoot. An attempt to fool me again.'

The hall of the inn was not without other people about, but everyone seemed preoccupied with their own affairs. No one noticed the look of alarm on her face, her silent pleas for help.

'Now.' He became firm. 'You will stand when I stand and come with me. We will go to my room until I figure out how to take you back to Ireland where you belong.'

He walked her to a deserted staircase and together they climbed to the third floor. When they reached it, Claire attempted to pull away.

The knife cut through her dress and pierced her skin. She ceased her struggle.

They walked down a long hallway.

'How fortuitous it is that they provided me with such a secluded room,' he remarked.

The hallway was empty and quiet.

He painfully gripped her arm while he worked the key in the door. The room was sparsely furnished. One bed. One chair. A bureau. He shoved her on to the bed and walked towards her, like the sinister figure of her dream.

Her head pounded and she closed her eyes.

And the memories came.

First of him trapping her in rooms of his country house, trying to seduce her, forcing her to kiss him, fearing that he would force more on her. Then other memories. It was like starting a book at the end and flipping the pages back to the beginning, to her childhood, her father smiling at her, her playing in the churchyard.

She doubled over with the onslaught. How

ironic that she would be given back her memory at a time when her life could very well end.

But not if she could help it. She'd endured too much to let this man rob her of life.

'You have gone to a great deal of trouble to find me, Sir Orin.' She kept her voice calm.

He laughed again, a crazed look in his eyes. 'You must know I would do anything for you, my dear Claire.'

'Then let me go.'

He looked wounded. 'I can never let you go. I need you. My children need you. Their mother died, you see.' He made a smirk, then a sad face.

'I am so sorry to hear of your wife's death,' she said. 'Such a dear lady. Had she been ill?'

He smirked again. 'Not ill.'

A shiver went up her spine. Perhaps he had killed her.

This man was inhuman. 'How could you have left your children after they lost their poor mother?'

He had never paid the children much mind. She remembered—she *remembered*!—he was far more interested in her, the governess, than his own daughters.

He waved her words away as if they were inconsequential. 'Oh, my two sisters came to take care of them. They are spinsters, poor as church mice, and quite devoted to the girls. And to my son, though he is at school most of the time. They will be happy to live off my wealth and I am delighted for it, because it freed me to search for you. We can be married quickly, my dear Claire. In Scotland, perhaps.'

She would escape long before Scotland, she vowed. 'But I have had a better offer, Sir Orin. Yours does not signify.'

His expression darkened. 'That Captain? What can he offer you that I cannot?'

He thought she meant Lucien? If he were here, Sir Orin's life would be in danger.

But Lucien was not here, so she must fend for herself.

'Not the Captain,' she said scornfully. 'He has no title, after all. I meant Lord Stonecroft. He is a baron and that would make me a baroness. And he would marry me properly. In church.'

Sir Orin looked wounded. 'I am a baronet. That is almost as high. Besides, I have better things to offer you than some old man.'

His eyes raked her and she remembered when she'd first seen that look on his face. After that narrow escape she had confided in his wife and they hatched a plan for her to leave in secret.

His poor wife.

She lifted her arm and felt where the knife had cut her. Blood had seeped from the wound.

'I think you should release me, Sir Orin, and court me properly. After your period of mourning is up, that is.' She stood.

He pushed her back down. 'And have you marry that feeble Baron first? Never!'

She clutched her shawl and thought of Lucien. Her rescuer. She was alone now, though. She remembered now just how alone she was. But she also was not the same defeated person as that governess who'd first stepped on the deck of the *Dun Aengus*. She'd gained strength and courage. Lucien had taught her both.

Lucien listened to this unbelievable tale Lady Rebecca told him and he believed it. She fit the picture of the Lady Rebecca he imagined would emerge if his Lady Rebecca—Claire Tilson—regained her memory.

Although Lucien rather liked this version as well, aristocratic or not.

When she finished, he said, 'I believe you.'

She looked relieved.

'There is something I should tell you, though.' This time he would not hold back. 'We have a connection, you and I, and it is not a happy one?'

'A connection besides Claire?' she asked.

'Yes.' He took a breath. 'Your grandfather tricked my grandfather out of his property in Ireland. He impoverished my mother's family.'

She averted her gaze. 'That horrible man. I detested my grandfather. He was vindictive and cruel.' She looked back. 'Rather like my half-brother, as a matter of fact.'

He went on, 'That is why I travelled to Ireland and was returning on that packet boat. I went to provide financial assistance to my uncles. They'd struggled for many years and this year has been the hardest.'

Her expression turned sympathetic. 'I am so sorry for it. You must let me know if there is anything I can do to help them. My Garret would certainly understand.'

He was greatly surprised at her reaction. 'I am actually in a good position to help them.'

She sighed. 'You should have known my father, though. He was the dearest man.' She regarded him quizzically. 'And why are you here, Captain? Why did you call on Claire today?'

'Because I realised I wanted her more than I wanted a ship.'

She looked puzzled.

'I love her more than the sea.' It was that simple. 'The sea has been my life heretofore, but today I had a choice to make. Return to the sea and probably never see her again, or return here and convince her not to marry Stonecroft.' He turned serious. 'To marry me instead.'

'Did she tell you she would marry Stonecroft?' she asked.

'Yes.' And he'd hated her saying it. 'Last night when I thought I needed to say goodbye.'

She leaned forward and touched his arm, much

as her likeness would have done. But her touch did not set his senses on fire.

'She is not marrying Stonecroft,' the lady said. 'She is leaving today by private coach to Bristol, to find her old school and see if they will help her procure another governess position.'

'Leaving?' He must stop her. Or join her.

A footman interrupted to announce Lord Brookmore.

Lucien and Lady Brookmore both stood.

Brookmore walked directly to his wife and kissed her.

Then he noticed Lucien. 'I beg pardon. I did not know you had a caller.' He looked at his wife with a question in his eyes.

'Do not worry, Garret,' she said. 'He knows. Garret, this is Captain Roper. You know. The Captain who rescued Claire? I have just told him everything.'

'Lord Brookmore.' Lucien nodded.

'Garret.' She grasped his arm. 'The Captain is in love with Claire. Please tell us she has not left yet. He must see her.'

'I left her waiting for the coach to be ready,' he responded. 'There won't be much time.'

She pushed him. 'Go, then. You and the Captain. I will follow as soon as I find a hat and gloves.'

'What about Sir Orin?' her husband asked. 'He will think you are Claire.'

Lucien broke in. 'Tell me where she is. Follow later if you must.'

'I left her waiting in the hall of the White Hart. The hall attendant will know if the coach left or not.'

Lucien started for the door, but it opened again and Lord Stonecroft stood in the doorway.

'See here, Roper. I told you to stay away!' His face was puffed and red. He noticed Lord Brookmore and turned to Lady Rebecca—Lady Brookmore. 'Who the devil is this?'

Brookmore stepped forward. 'You do not remember me, sir? I am Brookmore. We were introduced in Lords.'

Stonecroft looked him up and down. 'What the devil are you doing here?'

Lucien refused to wait. 'I've had enough of you, Stonecroft. Step aside and let me by.'

Stonecroft sputtered. Lady Brookmore laughed and Lucien pushed the man aside.

He rushed out of the house and ran all the way to the White Hart. At this late morning hour, there were many people on the streets, especially near the inn which was right across from the Pump Room. He did not care who saw him.

He slowed only when he reached the door of the White Hart. He strode in, looking around. He did not see her, but beside an empty sofa sat her portmanteau, the one he'd purchased for her. He scanned the hall frantically.

A footman approached him, one of the men he'd spoken to the day before when he'd enquired about the stranger—Sir Orin Foley. 'Captain Roper? Remember that man you were asking about? I believe I saw him today. Right here, actually. A little while ago. With a lady.'

'I know his name now.' Lucien's heart pounded. 'Can we find his room?'

'We will ask the attendant.'

Claire frantically looked for some means of achieving her escape, especially as he came to sit next to her on the bed. She spread her shawl across her lap.

'Let me show you why you cannot marry that old man. Why you must marry me instead.' He face came nearer, until his lips touched hers.

She forced herself to remain still, but she gathered her shawl in each of her hands and pulled it taut. When she did not flinch from his kiss, Sir Orin became bolder. His hands moved to her breasts and she tolerated his fingers kneading into her flesh. Pretending she found it pleasurable she slid her hands, still holding her shawl, up his chest. When she reached his neck, she threw the shawl over his head and pulled him to the side. He tumbled on to the floor. She scrambled off the bed and ran for the door.

He had forgotten to lock it.

She threw open the door and ran down the hallway. He'd regained his feet, though, and was right on her heels.

He caught up with her at the top of the stairs. Remembering Ella's wild fight with the highwayman, Claire pulled Sir Orin's hair and pushed her fingers into his eyes.

'Stop this! Claire!' he yelled.

She kneed him in his groin and he let go momentarily.

'I'll kill you!' he growled.

He charged her.

Using the banister to assist her, she flung herself against the balustrade just as he reached the top step. He tried desperately to grab her, but she pressed herself against the balustrade and his hands slipped off her body.

With a cry of rage and fear, he tumbled down the long flight of stairs. Claire pressed her hands against her ears at the horrible sound.

She collapsed on to the step, clutching a baluster and afraid to move, but also afraid he'd rise up and come after her again. Other voices sounded. Someone bounded up the stairs. She closed her eyes, fearing another attack.

'Claire?'

Not his voice.

She opened her eyes.

Lucien crouched down beside her. 'It is all over,' he murmured, taking her into his arms. 'He won't hurt you again.'

* * *

Within an hour Claire was seated with Lucien, and Lord and Lady Brookmore, in the innkeeper's office at the White Hart Inn. Also present were the magistrate and coroner who had sought their testimony. By mutual agreement, they held nothing back, telling the two men the whole story. No more secrets, even though they knew their story would likely become public.

The magistrate was dumbfounded. 'By God, this sounds like one of the novels my wife and daughters rave about.'

No, too unbelievable to be a novel. Claire would not have believed it had she not lived it.

The coroner placed both hands on the desk. 'The man's death was obviously accidental. We should not need any more from you about this.'

'Those poor little children, both parents gone.' Claire remembered the darling little girls and their brother. Perhaps they were better off with devoted aunts to care for them instead of an insane murderer for a father.

She wrapped her shawl tighter around her. Her lovely Kashmir shawl. She'd insisted on returning to Sir Orin's room to get it, this shawl that had saved Lucien from the highwayman and her from Sir Orin.

She glanced at Lucien. 'I remember the children now. I think I remember everything.'

He took her hand and held it in his.

They were all dismissed and when they came out of the office, Sir Richard, Ella and Cullen were waiting for them in the hall.

Ella ran up to Claire and hugged her. 'Oh, m'lady!' she cried.

Cullen had Claire's portmanteau.

Introductions were made and Sir Richard invited everyone to his house where they could dine in some privacy. They walked together as a group.

When they reached Sir Richard's house, Claire said, 'I should call upon Lord Stonecroft and Miss Attwood. I believe I owe them some explanation.'

'I'll go with you,' Lucien said.

'We have already told him the whole story,' the real Lady Rebecca said.

Would it do any good to tell him to open his heart to some lady who would appreciate him? Perhaps not today. She was still reeling from learning the truth.

And finally having her memory restored.

Lucien took her arm. 'If you all do not mind, I would like to walk with Lady—I mean—Claire on the Gravel Walk.

Ella and Lady Brookmore grinned.

'We do not mind at all,' the lady said.

Lucien led Claire away from their companions and they were soon rewarded with the privacy for which the Walk was known.

Claire smiled. 'I remember walking here when I was a girl.'

He put his arm around her. 'Your memory is back. You are whole again.'

'I wish it had been returned to me differently.' Not because of an attack by a mad man.

They walked in silence for a few steps, before Claire stopped. 'Lucien, are you certain you will not regret giving up this ship?'

He faced her. 'I know I will not regret it. When it came down to it, losing you was more intolerable than losing a ship.' He smiled. 'I have become too used to you, I suppose, and I cannot imagine my life without the woman I fell in love with.'

She put her arms around his neck. 'When do you think that happened?'

He cocked his head. 'When you were mopping up fish guts, I think.'

She rose on tiptoe. 'I thought I merely depended on you. It took saying goodbye to you to show me I loved you.'

He lifted her closer so that her lips were inches from his. 'It took the fish guts for me.'

He closed the short distance between them and kissed her.

Epilogue

❦

December 1816

Captain and Mrs Lucien Roper came in the back entrance of their country house laden with evergreens, holly and mistletoe to decorate the house for their first Christmas together.

They had settled where Lucien had begun life, in a property near the Lancashire village where he'd spent his lonely boyhood. It had been Claire's idea for them to settle there so he could reconcile with the parents who had so overlooked his needs as a boy. The end of the war had forced his father, the Admiral, to retire. Lucien's parents were truly together for the first time. It was not without its rough waters, but it helped that Viscount Waverland had abandoned Lucien's mother, now that she was older.

To Lucien's surprise, there were villagers who remembered him and who welcomed him home.

So even if his parents did not pass muster, Lucien had the sense he belonged.

Claire was more optimistic about having his parents near. She, who'd never known her mother and, with her memory restored, newly grieved the loss of her father, considered any family connections as precious.

Their property was a modest farm with sea views that helped Lucien feel connected to where he'd spent most of his life. His prize money provided them a comfortable living and enabled him to employ servants and other workers who would have faced unemployment and hardship if he'd not hired them. The farm was a new challenge to Lucien, but he also had his eye on other ventures. Their proximity to Liverpool piqued his interest in investing in shipping or shipbuilding or even radical new ideas such as ships run by steam engines.

But that was all for another day. Today he was content to remain at home with Claire.

They left their snow-caked boots and outerwear in the entryway, dropped off their cuttings in the still room and walked up to the warmth of a fire in their drawing room.

Cullen walked in. 'We brought the mail from the village.' He handed the tray holding several envelopes to Lucien.

Lucien sorted through them.

Cullen and Ella were still with them, biding their time until Ella reached twenty-one so they could marry. Lucien could not imagine life without them. He was as attached to them as he'd been to his crew. Claire loved them like the siblings she'd never had.

'A letter for you from Lady Brookmore.' Lucien handed the envelope to Claire.

She took it excitedly. 'I am so glad to hear from her! She must have received my letter.'

Lord and Lady Brookmore had returned to Brookmore's estate in the Lake District and the nieces he adored. Lucien counted Brookmore and Rebecca among the few aristocrats he truly esteemed.

He glanced over at Claire.

Her lovely face glowed with pleasure as she opened her mail.

Lucien settled into a chair and read his own letter from Sir Richard who was in good health and spending Christmas in Bath.

'This is marvellous!' Claire cried.

She jumped up from her sofa and climbed into Lucien's lap so he could read over her shoulder.

She told him what was in the letter anyway. 'Rebecca writes that she and Garret are expecting a baby, too.'

She pressed a hand over her only slightly rounded belly and gave Lucien a contented smile.

'Listen to this!' She snuggled closer as she read on. 'She thinks she is due in June, too!' She put down the letter and put her arms around his neck.

'Would it not be a lark if we both have girls and if they both look alike?'

He kissed her on the cheek. 'I think it would be like lightning striking twice.'

And he silently said a prayer of thanks for being given what he thought he could never have. A home. A woman to love and to love him back. A family. A place to belong.

He would never take this for granted.

He kissed her again and held her close. 'Who would believe that so much happiness could result for so many when a governess and a lady swap places?'

* * * * *

MILLS & BOON

Coming next month

HIS CONVENIENT HIGHLAND BRIDE
Janice Preston

Lachlan McNeill couldn't quite believe his good fortune when he first saw his bride, Lady Flora McCrieff, walking up the aisle towards him on her father's arm. Her posture was upright and correct and her figure was... delectable. The tight bodice and sleeves of her wedding gown—her figure tightly laced in accordance with fashion—accentuated her full breasts, slender arms and tiny waist above the wide bell of her skirt. She was tiny, dwarfed by her father's solid, powerful frame, and she barely reached Lachlan's shoulder when they stood side by side in front of the minister. True, he had not yet seen his new bride's face—her figure might be all he could wish for, but was there a nasty surprise lurking yet? Maybe her features were somehow disfigured? Or maybe she was a shrew? Why else had her father refused to let them meet before their wedding day? He'd instead insisted on riding over to Lochmore Castle, Lachlan's new home, to agree the marriage settlements.

Their vows exchanged, Lachlan raised Flora's veil, bracing himself for some kind of abomination. His chest loosened with relief as she stared up at him, her green eyes huge and wary under auburn brows, the freckles that speckled her nose and cheeks stark against the pallor of her skin. His finger caught a loose, silken tendril of coppery-red hair and her face flooded pink, her lower lip trembling, drawing his gaze as the scent of orange blossom wreathed his senses.

She is gorgeous.

Heat sizzled through him, sending blood surging to his loins as he found himself drawn into the green depths of her eyes, his senses in disarray. Then he took her hand to place it on his arm and its delicacy, its softness, its fragility sent waves of doubt crashing through him, sluicing him clean of lustful thoughts as he sucked air into his lungs.

He had never imagined he'd be faced with one so young…so dainty…so captivating…and her beauty and her purity brought into sharp focus his own dirty, sordid past. Next to her he felt a clumsy, uncultured oaf.

What could he and this pampered young lady ever have in common? She might accept his fortune, but could she ever truly accept the man behind the façade? He'd faced rejection over his past before and he'd already decided that the less his wife ever learned about that past, the better.

Continue reading
HIS CONVENIENT HIGHLAND BRIDE
Janice Preston

Available next month
www.millsandboon.co.uk

COMING SOON!

We really hope you enjoyed reading this book. If you're looking for more romance, be sure to head to the shops when new books are available on

Thursday 21st March

To see which titles are coming soon, please visit

millsandboon.co.uk/nextmonth